Glory Days

Copyright © 2021 by Rachel Davidson and Nikki Greenhalgh

Paperback ISBN: 978-1-7367641-0-7

First paperback edition March 2021

Book design by Nikki Greenhalgh

www.glorydaystrilogy.com

For Nikki.
—R.D.

For Rachel.
—N.G.

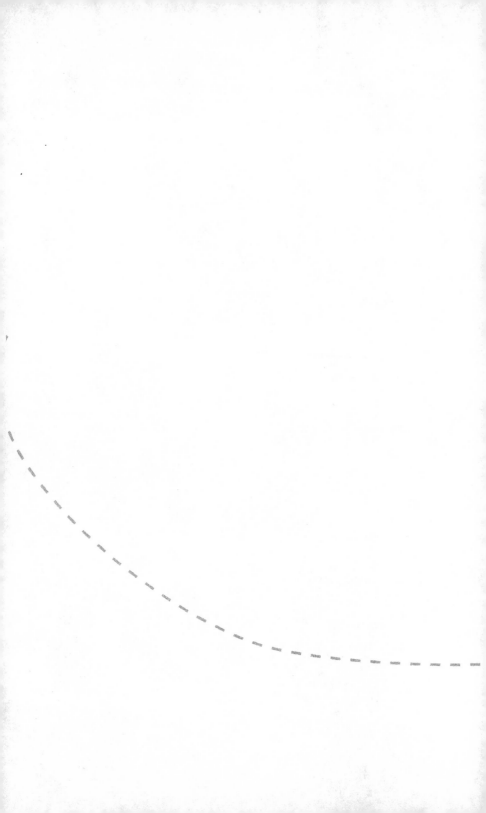

Glory Days

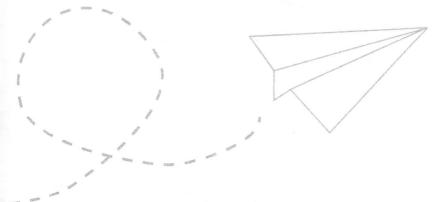

PAISLEY IS SWEATING VODKA. I'm not the only one who notices, what with being the "omniscient narrator" and everything. *Everyone* notices.

It's not just the smell that reeks off her or the flask disguised as a clutch that rolls out from under her gown. It's her mannerisms, her crooked grin dipping in and out of view the more she tries to hide it.

She blows a blonde strand of hair out of her face. It's taken her a while to master this, as for most people it's rather difficult to blow hair that long and that thick out and away. She has these long, stringy curls that took years to grow out. They're a little past her waist now. She keeps threatening to chop it all off to give everyone vertigo, but she never has.

She bends over to pick up her fallen flask. As it reaches her grip, it rolls off her fingertips. Her eyes widen as she makes a grab for it; the 6'3" (half) Filipino freak of nature next to her scrambles with her. Through their panic, he manages to catch it underhanded, looking up to grin first—relieved, stupidly—at the audience before straightening to laugh with Paisley and hand her the flask.

And that's Mason. Honestly, it's a miracle the guy's graduating. Not because he's completely stupid; he's actually got a decent head on him. It's how that head has stayed on him all these years that's confusing. For instance: he almost fell into a creek on the way to school the other day. Please note that this story is taking place in Phoenix. Arizona. A freaking desert.

But no, he's pretty smart when it comes to certain things. People, for instance. He's nearly a mind reader. He'll know exactly what's wrong with you by the way you say, "I'm fine." But does he use these powers for good? No. No, he does not. He doesn't even know he has this ability.

Before handing Paisley back her flask, he ducks around and takes a quick swig. It is *not* subtle. But does he think it is? Probably. No. Most definitely.

Elijah sighs at this. It's not like this kind of thing doesn't happen often—it does. In fact, it happens so often that it's become his natural response to something like this.

The sigh proves he's paying attention. He usually isn't. Without the headphones in his ears or the sketchbook in his hands, he's nearly unrecognizable. *Nearly* being the key word. He's still got that same look on his face, that same light in his blue eyes, that makes it seem like he's always dreaming. Even while watching people shake hands with the principal, it's as if he's dreaming of what comes next.

Or maybe that's just the weed.

There hasn't been a day since his freshman year when he hasn't had a joint between his lips. His response if you ask him about it? "It calms me." Kind of redundant, though, when you consider the fact that the boy naturally exudes calm. He's as warm as the day that surrounds him.

Cassidy, on the other hand, is fidgeting. She's always fidgeting. With the scrunchie on her wrist, with the sleeve of her sweater, with anything she can get her hands on. Now more than usual, as she keeps adjusting and readjusting her long hair as the wind rustles through it. Elijah notices this and rests a light hand on hers in hopes of keeping her still. It works. Kind of.

This day is nothing like she pictured. And yes, she's pictured it many times. It's run through her head, sitting in these bleachers with the sun streaming through the trees. She's imagined Paisley sneaking in a flask (of course) and Elijah sitting right beside her. But this...

There's everything wrong with today. She had to muster up the strength to even get dressed and come to the stadium. Her sun dress felt too tight, like it was constricting her. Like she couldn't breathe. Like she still can't breathe under the heat of the almost-summer sun.

Her leg starts bouncing of its own volition, but with one squeeze of her hand and one brief glance, Elijah settles her down, tells her it's okay. And with one deep breath, she relaxes, lifting her gaze to focus back on the field.

Or, rather, on Mason, who is trying to take the flask out of Paisley's hand yet again. She's doing her best to keep both her composure and her alcohol. But naturally, they're drawing attention to themselves, and naturally, Dani's there in a heartbeat to put an end to it. Without a word, she swiftly takes the flask from Paisley and tucks it inside her robe, straightening and smiling as if nothing happened. She, along with everyone else, knew this would happen, but she wasn't about to let anything ruin the most important day of her life thus far. She's already given her valedictorian speech. All that's left to do is walk.

Both Paisley and Mason are looking back at her, the former with a slightly more threatening expression, but Dani keeps her eyes trained on the principal. She's so close to freedom, she can feel it at her polished red fingertips. Her mom's advice echoes through her head: "Keep your head up high, *mija*. You earned this." And she does just that, making herself appear taller, more confident. Like she was born for this.

Her heart races even faster the more names the principal rattles off. He's reached the D's now. Not too much longer.

The next name called ceases all applause, turns glee into grief.

"William Dickinson, our salutatorian, whose diploma will be accepted by his brother, Jackson." Silence. The wind rustles in through the microphone and out through the speakers, but besides that you could hear a pin drop.

"Jackson?" And still, nothing. He missed his cue. He missed it entirely. Or he isn't there to hear it called. This springs a bout of murmuring throughout the crowd. People are starting to worry. People are beginning to panic. His friends are exchanging nervous glances.

The principal leans into the mic one last time.

"Jack?"

Jack

and the doorbell rings right when I expect it to. Furthermore, it's exactly who I expect it to be.

Cassidy Montag stands with a cross look on her face. In case you're wondering: yes, it *is* a bit awkward for your brother's now ex-girlfriend to see you answer the door in sweats and a Goo Goo Dolls t-shirt.

She drops her hands. "What the fuck, Jack?"

"Nice to see you, too, Cassie." I head upstairs. Knowing that she won't take my departure as an invitation to leave, I ask, "How was graduation?"

"Where were you?"

"Not there."

She follows me up the stairs. "Obviously."

I don't dignify that with a response.

"You don't have anything to say for yourself?" she asks.

"Nope."

"Do you even realize what a big deal this was? I mean, first the funeral and now this?"

I stop at the last few steps and turn. "Get out of my house," I say lowly.

And then: "I was always welcome in Will's house."

"It's not Will's house anymore, is it?" I mean for it to come out as a snap; it doesn't. It's quiet and pitiful and causes Cassidy's face to fall from defensive to apologetic. So I cover it with, "You know what? If you're seriously gonna just sit here and talk about how piss-poor my life choices are, then just go, okay? Seriously."

"Your mom asked me to go through his stuff. Said she's cleaning out his room." Her words are soft. Soft enough for me to finally give in after a minute and sigh. I gesture toward Will's room. She walks past me silently and steps inside.

I follow her after a moment, watch her saunter around. I think I'm just now realizing that she's looking at it the same way I did when I first came home from the hospital. It's not Will's room. It *was* Will's room. It's lived in, but that doesn't mean anyone is currently living in it. It's not a bedroom, it's a museum. A shrine. The laundry on the ground is no longer making it messy, it's giving the place character. It's letting us see a final snapshot of the boy that once was.

I'm, surprisingly, the first one to break the silence. "A lot of this stuff is probably yours, anyway." As I'm staring at the laundry, something nearby catches my eye, something that doesn't quite fit in with the rest. I pick it up with two fingers. "Like these, I'm guessing?"

Cassidy looks over, face growing as cherry red as the panties I'm holding. "Yeah, um— Yeah." She hurries over to shove them into her purse.

I settle myself against the doorframe as she continues to wander around the room.

She stops when she reaches his nightstand, smiles a little when she sees the book lying there.

I crane my neck just the slightest to see what she's got. "What is it?"

"*Great Expectations,*" she says, picking it up. "I gave it to him a few months back."

"And I'm willing to bet he's only a few chapters in."

She straightens. "He read it a few times, actually."

"So he says. You sure he didn't just skim the SparkNotes?"

She rolls her eyes but doesn't disagree.

I, meanwhile, find a stupid rubber ball on his desk, the kind you win from arcades. I toss it up into the air a few times. "I preferred *Gatsby* anyway. If we're talking about 'great' books."

She frowns apathetically at my pun. "We're gonna read that next year, anyway. What's the point of reading ahead?"

"Because everyone says I look so much like a young DiCaprio I just had to see if the rumors were true. And, you know. You can't watch a movie without reading the book first."

Cassidy squints at me, brown eyes searching me as intently as they'd been searching the room. "Yeah, I don't see it."

"Maybe you should take another look."

Her expression changes at this; I can't tell what to. She opens her mouth to respond.

"'Sup, homies."

We both turn toward the door. Enter Mason, the giant labrador puppy. And Will's best friend.

"How the hell did you get in here?" I ask him.

"The door was open, I thought entry was up for grabs. Hey, Cass, what'd you think of graduation? Wish you were up there with us?"

Cassidy continues to flip through the pages of *Great Expectations*. "Don't call me Cass."

Mason's face falls. "Oh. Sorry."

Even I have to snicker at that.

"And if you must know, no, I'm glad I still have another year left. I didn't even want to go to the thing." She looks up, right at me. "But at least I went."

I clench my jaw.

Before any kind of argument can sprout again, Elijah trudges in and taps Mason on the arm. "Why didn't you ring the doorbell?" he asks.

"The door was already open!" Mason protests.

"That doesn't mean you can just walk into someone's house like that."

I raise my hand. "I second that."

"Well, it's what I usually do." Correction: it's what he usually does when he knows Will's around. He turns to me. "Hey, Jack, do you know where Will's baseball cards are?"

As if she were summoned by Mason's dumbassery, Dani enters next, smacking Mason on the arm.

"Hey!"

"No," she says. "Just— No."

Mason, tired of making the same argument, groans loudly. "The door was *open!*"

Dani rolls her eyes. "That's not what I'm talking about, *pendejo*."

"Then I don't see what the problem is!"

Dani jabs a thumb at him. "I swear, he loves baseball cards more than life itself." She moves over to collapse on the bed next to Cassidy.

"I'm just trying to make light of things," Mason argues. "That's what vodka's for."

We turn as Paisley moves into the room.

Mason frowns. "Where is that, by the way?" he asks. "Does Dani still have it?"

Dani answers from the bed. "Yes, but you're not getting it back."

"But—"

"Not your flask, Ocampo," Paisley tells him.

"Not yours anymore, either," quips Dani.

Paisley folds her arms. "So I'm assuming you're gonna give me the fifteen ninety-nine plus alcohol back in cash? Or do you prefer credit?"

Dani hesitates. Then, finally caving: "It's in my car, go get it." She tosses her keys to Paisley, who catches them with both hands. She mouths a quick, "Thank you," before leaving the room.

Meanwhile, Cassidy has moved on to searching Will's desk drawers.

Elijah takes notice around the same time I do. "Find anything?" he asks.

Cassidy shakes her head. "Just school stuff. Papers, notebooks, pencils."

"He never kept anything interesting in there," I tell her. "Believe me, I looked."

Cassidy nods and moves to the closet.

"You looked just before we came?" Mason asks.

I look over at him. "Sure."

He frowns.

I watch as Cassidy struggles to reach a box at the top of the closet. "Now, you want the *really* interesting stuff..." I stand next to her. She looks over as I reach up so casually and take the box from the shelf.

Mason, meanwhile, is lifting up the mattress to see if there's anything underneath. To all of our surprise, he lifts up a wadded bill. "Sweet! Twenty bucks!"

"Mine." It's at this moment that Paisley walks back into the room and takes the money from his hand.

Mason frowns. "Aw."

"You know, I had that," Cassidy says to me as I put the

box on the now askew mattress.

"You're welcome," I mutter.

"Did I ask?"

"Yeah. You did. When you did your little bunny hop trying to reach it."

Paisley heads over to where we're standing. "What's this?"

Cassidy uncovers the lid, tilting her head. "Looks like—"

Mason gasps. "Baseball cards!"

Dani slowly closes her eyes. "Oh, Jesus."

Mason excitedly starts to shuffle through them.

"Mason, no, don't touch—" Elijah tries to protest.

And then Mason grabs the box and dumps its contents onto the floor. Fan-fucking-tastic.

We all fall silent.

Paisley clicks her tongue. "Or just dump the whole fucking box on the floor. You know. Either works."

Mason was right about one thing: there are *lots* of baseball cards in there. But there's something else. Something that stands out from the other contents of the box. A black notebook lies there; PROPERTY OF WILL DICKINSON is etched into the cover.

I bend down to pick it up.

Cassidy catches this. "What's that?" she asks.

I shake my head, turning the book over once. "Nothing. Just... something I got him a long time ago."

Cassidy doesn't accept this answer. "Let me see, what is it?" As she makes a grab for it, I hold it up above my head. Given that she's almost a foot shorter than me, this tactic works perfectly. I know because I have used it on many occasions, many that have almost gotten my ass beat by Will.

Cassidy jumps a little to try and grab it. "Mason," she whines. "Help."

Mason, a good two inches taller than me, shrugs. "Okay." He comes over to take the book from me.

"Mason, no," I say quickly.

He stops. Shrugs again. "Okay."

"Mason, yes," Cassidy counters.

He pauses, confused. "I—" He turns helplessly to Elijah, who does nothing but give a tiny smirk.

"Who do you like better?"

Mason pales.

Dani rolls her eyes. "Guys, stop. *Stop.*"

"Keep going." Paisley's on the edge of her seat. And she's standing.

I give her a look, spreading my arms (arm). *Really?*

"He's Jack's brother." We turn to Dani, who's looking not at me but out the window. "Have some respect."

The rest of the room falls quiet.

I take this as my cue to drop my arm. "Thank you." I nod at Dani and back out of the room.

Cassidy

"that could've gone better." Elijah's eyes are still on the door that Jack left through. It's hard with Jack sometimes because you never really know if he's actually mad or not. He's just... like that. But this was different. This was real.

Paisley purses her lips before taking another swig from the flask.

Mason reaches for it, trying to snatch it from her hand. Paisley, still drinking, turns away, but Mason's nothing if not adamant. He keeps reaching for it, causing Paisley to smack his hand away.

Dani sets her hands on her hips. "Way to be supportive, guys."

"Come on," Mason begs, "one sip? Please?"

Paisley is (somehow) still drinking. I don't know how someone can drink so much alcohol in such a short amount of time. "Uh uh," she says with her mouth around the lip of the flask.

"Paisley!" Mason whines.

Paisley starts backing slowly out of the room, careful not to let the flask leave her lips.

"*Paisley!*" He follows on her tail.

Elijah reaches a hand out. "Mason, you're my—" He sighs. "You're my ride." He follows Mason dejectedly.

Dani stares after the three of them, mouth agape. Then she closes it, shaking her head, glancing over at me. "Are you okay?"

I try to smile. "Fine."

She purses her lips—she doesn't believe me. "Are you going to stay?" she asks.

"Yeah."

"Do you want me to stay?"

She means well. I know she does. But this is between Will and me. "No," I say.

She nods, smiling sadly. "Got it." She leans forward, gives my shoulder a squeeze. "Don't be too late, okay?"

The smile comes easier this time. "Okay."

And with that, she leaves the room. And I'm alone.

I take another few minutes to go through Will's stuff. I was expecting to break down or something when the time came to do this, and until now I've been fine. But I think that was just because I was surrounded by people. Now that I'm alone, my chest is starting to clench up. Tears prick at the backs of my eyes as I finish going through a few more boxes that I took from the closet. I can tell his mom already went through some of it because they're half empty. All that's left are a few first place ribbons intermingled with the participation trophies and some lonely Star Wars action figures from when he was a kid.

I'm suffocating again. Like I was at graduation. I blink back the tears as I shove the box with all its contents back into the closet. And just before I shut the closet door, shut the door on Will, my eye catches something—the hoodie he always wore. His favorite. The one he always said I could have if I wanted it.

I take it off the hanger, bunch it up into a ball, and stuff it in my purse. I do the same with *Great Expectations*, and then I'm out of there.

Maybe for good.

The hall is empty. Quiet. I'm about to walk back down the stairs, but I hesitate because Jack. Jack is still here, and I should apologize. Granted, I don't want to, but I should. So I turn the other way and walk the stretch of hall to Jack's half-open bedroom door.

He's perched cross-legged on his bed, the notebook in his lap, mouth hanging slightly open in concentration. I have to admit, he does look like young Leo. Especially now that his face isn't screwed into a grimace. I just didn't want to give him the satisfaction of being right.

I knock softly on the doorframe. "Hi."

Apparently, he's so deep in concentration that this startles him. He slams the book closed and straightens, trying (and failing) to act casual. "Hi."

I lean against the doorframe, one foot in his room, one foot out. "Doing some light reading?"

The surprise is gone from his face, replaced with a thin mouth and narrowed eyes.

I sigh. I mean, guess I should probably do what I came here to do. "Look, I'm sorry, okay?" I say. "I get that some things are private, and I shouldn't have pushed."

Jack studies me a moment more with those slitted eyes, then silently goes back to reading.

Okay, really? I'm pouring my heart and soul out to you, Jack Dickinson. The least you can do is dignify that with a response. "You gotta understand, though," I start, feeling the need to defend myself. "We dated for a really long time."

He looks up at me incredulously. "He's my *brother*, Cassie. You can get another boyfriend. I'm gonna have to live the rest of my life alone because of what happened."

Yeah, that hits me. Hard. I swallow past the lump in my throat, glance down at my feet. "I just wanna know him like you do," I say softly to the floor. "I want to know all of him."

Jack is silent. I doubt he's even looking at me.

"But I see how it is." I turn around to leave. "I'll get out of your hair."

I've taken only a few steps down the hall when I hear a soft, "It's a bucket list."

I stop, turning back to stand in the doorway once again. "Really?"

He motions me over without looking up from the notebook. An invitation from Jack is rare, and I'm even more surprised when he scoots over to make room for me on his bed. I sit down tentatively, peering over his shoulder at the open book.

He's flipping through the first few pages. It's a numbered list. A long numbered list of all the things he apparently wanted to do, like *walk the Hollywood Walk of Fame* and *visit the Maldives*. Brow furrowed, I point to another item. "Victoria Falls. I didn't know he wanted to go there."

"Yeah, that's the thing about Will," Jack says. "He makes you think he's an open book when really he's only showing you the pages he thinks you want to see."

"I guess so..." I bite my cheek, taking the notebook from Jack's lap. I catch his appalled and annoyed face out of the corner of my eye, but I'm too focused on the task at hand to care. I tap the notebook with my finger, thinking. "You know what we should do?"

"Hm?"

I smile slightly. The idea is forming, and it might just be possible to pull off. "What if we—"

"No."

My mouth snaps shut. "C'mon," I say, "you haven't even heard it yet."

"I don't need to."

God, he's difficult. "Not even if it involves spending an entire summer in Paisley's van?" I try, raising my eyebrows.

"Especially then." He shudders. "That van freaks me out."

I hesitate. It does always smell like vodka and pot. "Yeah, okay. That's fair." I point at the list again. "Don't you think he'd want someone to finish it, though?"

Jack shrugs. "It's his list. It was meant for him to complete."

"But now he can't." I close the notebook, running my finger along Will's name etched into the front cover. "And we can. It's the least we can do to honor his memory."

Jack scowls. "Just because we share blood doesn't mean I'm Will." With that, he snatches the notebook out of my hand and stalks out of the room. His own room.

And I don't know if it's the grief talking or my leftover anger from his skipping out on graduation, but I find myself bristling. Wondering why he can't see that this wouldn't be a way of replacing Will but of remembering him. Wondering how he manages to care so little.

Don't say it, don't say it, don't say it, don't— "You're a horrible brother," I call after him.

"I know," he calls back from just outside the room. "He constantly tells me that." He pauses. "*Told* me that." He runs a harsh hand through his hair. "*Fuck.*"

The longer I look at him, the longer I'm here, the madder I get. So I stand up and storm out of the room, brushing past him on the way to the stairs. "Well, he was right," I mutter.

The last thing I see before ducking down the staircase is Jack going into Will's room and closing the door behind him.

Elijah

are these the people i choose to spend my time with? Yes. Why do I put up with them? Honestly, it beats me.

Now, for instance. Paisley is standing on top of her van.

Let me repeat that—she's *standing* on top of her *van.* It's like a fucked up game of monkey in the middle, with Mason being the one in the middle who has no hope of stealing the flask from Paisley's hand, no matter how high he reaches.

Cassidy walks out the front door then, and I can tell something's wrong. She takes one glance at the Paisley-Mason van debacle, then looks at me. I purse my lips. *I know.* And with a tiny shake of her head, she gets in her car, and she drives away.

I'm more than a little jealous.

"Come on, Paisley!" Mason's yelling. "Please!"

"No!"

"You can't drink and drive!" He's starting to try and climb up the side of the van. "I'll only be helping you!"

I mean, he's got a point, other than the fact that— "Mace, I'm not riding with you if you've been drinking," I say, folding my arms in what Mason calls a "mom gesture."

He pauses to look back at me with big puppy dog eyes, and... yeah, okay, it's adorable. "I'll only have a sip." He looks up at Paisley, who's lifting the flask to her lips again. His eyes widen. "Don't—"

Paisley tips the flask upside down and chugs what I assume to be the last bit of vodka.

He keels over like he's in a Shakespearean play, letting out a cry I can only describe as the sound an injured donkey would make.

Paisley straightens triumphantly, smirks down at Mason.

And she lets out a dramatic sigh before falling over—off the edge of the van, I might add.

"Oh shit," Mason says, scrambling to his feet so he can catch her. Once she's in his arms, he takes a look around at me, at Dani. "Anyone want this?"

Dani sighs, walking over. "I'll take her home. I'm sure she'll survive a night without her precious van."

Paisley moans from Mason's arms, who glances down at her before decidedly letting her go. She slumps down onto the ground, the moan following her descent. I would say she's a mess, but that's just Paisley. She's always a mess.

Dani goes to help her up, holding her by the arm. "What's your address?"

Paisley doesn't look up when she sings, "867-5309 your *mom*."

Dani closes her eyes in a slow blink, and when she opens them she's staring right at me. This happens quite often. We take turns being the camera that we would all look into if our lives were a mockumentary. I can see the absolute doneness in her face, the disappointment. "Why don't you just sleep at my place?" she says to Paisley, who grins.

"Slumber party!"

Dani presses her lips together, starts to drag Paisley to her car, helps her into the backseat. I watch Dani start the car, wishing her unspoken luck.

But, as it turns out, maybe I need to be wishing myself luck. Because I turn, and there's Mason in a full-on bow. "Shall we?" he asks, extending his hand out.

"I—" I sigh. It's not worth it. "Yeah."

Mason starts toward his parked car on the other side of the street, and I follow him, climbing into the passenger seat. He starts the car and pulls out of the neighborhood silently. That's not something I can usually say about him—*silently*. But I guess these aren't usual circumstances.

"So..." Mason finally says once we're out on the main road. "That was... rough."

I lean my head against the window. "Maybe a little," I say, digging into my pocket for a joint and lighting up.

Mason reaches for it as soon as I've taken a hit, and I have to smack his hand away lightly.

"You're driving," I say.

"Right," he responds, nodding. "Forgot about that."

I shake my head, leaning farther back in the seat and tucking my leg up against the door. I've spent enough time in this car to know what the most comfortable position is, and I've spent enough time with Mason to be used to the things he says.

"I'm kidding, I'm kidding!" he says, taking his hands off the wheel for a split second to surrender. "Well, kinda. I'm still a little tipsy. Not Paisley tipsy, though. That girl can drink."

My brow furrows. "You only had one sip." I hold up a finger before he can respond. "And yes, I did catch that."

A tiny smile plays on his lips. He shoots me a brief glance, saying, "I figured you would," before focusing back on the road.

You know, people always assume a lot about Mason. They assume he's a bad driver, even if they've never driven with him before. In reality, he's a better driver than I'll ever be. They assume he's empty up there. Which, yeah, there's a good chance he got dropped on his head when he was a baby, but still. There's something to the way he looks at you, the way he reads you, the way it feels like he knows you, inside and out. And I wouldn't call that empty. I'd call it more than enough.

I finally look away from him, taking another hit off my joint. "Jack's worse than he's letting on, you know."

Mason nods. "Yeah. He was a mess, I could tell. You know he's been sleeping in Will's room?"

I turn to look over my shoulder out the window, even though the house is far behind us. "Has he?"

"Yeah, I could tell. Sheets were all wrinkled. Besides, I saw one of his books on the ground."

"How do you know it wasn't Will's book?"

He laughs a little. "Will only reads when Cassidy tells him to."

I turn back to him. "Read."

His smile wavers.

"We need to get used to that." My voice is soft. Softer than usual. Somber.

And his is even quieter when he mumbles, "Right."

The rest of the drive across town is silent. I killed the mood, and I don't know how to resurrect it. So I just lean back against the headrest and close my eyes, listening to the hum of the engine and the wind rushing by. When we roll over a bump and come to a stop, I know he's pulled into my driveway. But I really, really don't want to move.

"You okay?" Mason asks.

I open my eyes. "Yeah, sorry." I push myself upright and open the door, but before I can step out, Mason takes me gently by the arm.

"Holliday, hold up."

I turn just in time to catch his dopey grin before he kisses me. And, like always, I melt into him. For everything he's not, he is a *fantastic* kisser. I don't know how he does it, how he makes me feel everything at once. But even after the brief moment that our lips are touching, I'm tingling all over.

I bite my lip against a smile, finally getting out of the car. But I find myself looking back at him. I can't help it. He's leaning forward over the console, still grinning up at me. "I'll see you soon, yeah?" I say.

"Yeah. Later, Holliday."

I'm still smiling as I shake my head, closing the door on him and his stupid, adorable face. He backs out of the driveway, and I watch him drive off before going to open the garage. On my way inside, I tap my joint a few times before tossing it into the garbage bin by the door.

Mom is sitting at the kitchen counter. She has designs spread out all around her, a pen tucked behind her ear. Her tongue's sticking out just the slightest. It's not uncommon to see her poring over designs like this; she could sit there for hours and not notice any time has passed.

I walk over and stand behind her, resting my chin on her shoulder. She smiles and tilts her head against mine. "Hey, honey," she says. "How was graduation?"

I take the barstool next to her. "Good. Kind of. Weird."

"Yeah? How's Mason?"

Even though she's literally the only living person who knows about us, I don't get this question very often. "He's good."

"Bet it was nice to see him all dressed up for once."

I laugh. "Shut up."

She gives me this teasing grin, but then her smile falters, and her nose wrinkles. "Have you been smoking?"

"Um..." I avert my gaze. "Yeah."

She sighs. "Lijah..."

"I know, I know."

"You've been smoking more often, haven't you?" She's not mad; she's never mad. She's just disappointed.

"It... helps," I say.

She grabs my chin, makes me look at her. "I know you miss him, okay? But you gotta be careful."

I nod. "I know." I twist away from her grasp, trying to end this lecture before it even begins. "In other news, guess what got posted today?"

Her eyes light up curiously. "What?" I've gotten her attention, which means I'm in the clear.

"Summer assignments."

"Mhm, and why do you seem so excited about that?"

"Because it's AP art."

She smiles. "I see."

"It's freestyle. Graded on creativity, and that's pretty much it. It's to start our college portfolio."

"Let me guess, you're absolutely *bursting* with ideas."

"Not yet. But that's what today's for."

She raises her palms to me. "Then by all means, get to work."

I grin, standing and heading down the hall maybe a bit faster than I need to. I shut my bedroom door behind me before going to close the blinds and draw the curtains over the window. I grab my sketchbook off my desk, my earbuds off my nightstand, and collapse on the bed. I put my earbuds in and crank the volume up to one hundred percent. I've gotten so used to the process that I don't even flinch when the music starts blasting my brain. I set my phone on the bed beside me and hug my sketchbook to my chest, staring up at the stick-on, glow-in-the-dark stars on my ceiling. After a couple minutes, they start to blur together like they usually do when I'm high. I can't separate one star from another in the vast expanse of my ceiling that's slowly morphing into deep space. Can't separate the music from my own thoughts. But, like always, it works.

I have an idea.

≋ ≋ ≋

ELIJAH HOLLIDAY IS AN ADDICT. Of many things, not just pot. Of art, of music, of nature, of people. In some ways, he's addicted to life itself. He's always tried his hardest to absorb things at a hundred and ten percent, to absorb everything at full capacity. He's been drawing ever since he could hold a pencil, always eager to capture every moment, even the small ones. It was only when things started getting bad that he turned to pot. Because for once in his life, there were things he wanted to dull rather than heighten.

It was when his parents got divorced that he started smoking. Throughout eighth grade, during the move from Seattle to Phoenix, he used it to cope. To cope with his own brain. To cope with the fact that he and his mom were starting a new life together, all alone. To cope with having said goodbye to his father and never looking back.

It was when he found his people, the friends he knew would follow him through this new life, that he started smoking less. They became his anchor so that he couldn't let himself fall apart again. They became the lens he could see things through, and he gained back his sense of adoration for the world as a whole.

And it was when one of those friends died, when a few chains on the anchor broke off, that he started to smoke more. And more. And more.

He got suspended during the last week of school for doing just that. He never told anybody; they all just assumed he was grieving. Which, he knew, would have been a normal response. But, like Paisley, his automatic response was to shove that grief back down his throat and numb it until he couldn't feel it anymore. He was numb that day, and he was numb at the

Davidson | Greenhalgh

funeral, numb when he gave his eulogy.

"Not gonna lie, I'm not ready for this. Not at all. I didn't write anything because I'm not ready to be up here. To be... talking about him in the past tense. I don't think I'll ever be ready.

"You know, you don't realize how much weight that has, the past tense. Not until something changes. Not until the difference between 'is' and 'was' is actually the difference between life and death. Between coming to school on Tuesday and lying in a casket...

"Not for long, though, right? Tomorrow... Tomorrow he'll really be gone. Not six feet under gone, but pile of ashes stuffed into a tiny... little...

"Who even thought of cremation, anyway? Who was the first person to say, hey, you know what's a great idea? Burning my dead corpse into dust. *Though it's only fitting that that's what he chose. He hates the thought of being stuck in Phoenix, let alone... let alone... hated...*

"He hated seeing me high. If only he could see me now..."

Paisley

my head hurts so bad. Actually, scratch that. My entire *body* is aching, possibly because my lanky frame has been curled awkwardly into a couch for what seems like the whole night. Or at least part of it.

"You're up."

I look up to see Dani standing over me.

"And it's only..." She checks her phone. "12:42."

I rub my head. "A.m. or p.m.?"

"That would be a.m." She hands me a glass of orange juice.

"*Fuck,*" I groan, taking the glass. I take a sip and stop. "Wait a minute. Where's my van?"

"Will's house. Remember?" She takes a seat in the chair across from me.

I groan again. I do that a lot when it feels like someone's digging a knife between my eyes. "I gotta go get it." I stand. "Will you give me a ride?"

She blinks. "It's almost one."

"Fine. I'll walk." I pour the orange juice into my flask.

"*Paisley,*" she tries again. "It's almost *one.*"

"Yeah, I heard you." I hand Dani the now empty glass before grabbing a wool cardigan from the pile of laundry next to the couch. "I'll give this back to you later," I say, shrugging it on.

"Paisley—"

I'm already out the door.

I must look crazy.

I mean, granted, I always look crazy. But I look crazier

than usual. I mean, I'm walking down the street in my grad dress, a discolored, Mexican cardigan (that I'm now thinking is probably meant to be worn as more of a poncho), and a flask that many may assume to be vodka but is actually orange juice. Even if I don't *look* crazy, I sure as hell *feel* it.

I feel even crazier as I remember how long a walk it is to the Dickinson household. It's about a ten/fifteen minute drive from there to Dani's, which means I'll probably spend about an hour walking. Likely more.

Well, great. Just great. Fan-fucking-tastic. This is exactly how I want to spend my night (well, morning now). Walking. Not sleeping off my vodka but walking it off.

Perfect.

I know. I know it seems completely stupid of me to walk all this way in the dead of night, risking my life for a fucking bus. But it's *my* fucking bus. And I love that thing more than life itself.

So there.

My assumption is, I soon find, correct. It's about an hour walk, but maybe it's only an hour because I keep taking breaks to sit (almost sleep) on various benches. Oh, and because a cop stopped me and asked if I was okay. I said yes. He said, "What's in the flask?" I said, "None of your business," which almost got me arrested. That was fun.

But he let me keep going, which was chill of him.

I arrive at the Dickinson household close to two in the morning. It's dark, it's unfamiliar, it's home.

I've known that family as long as I've known Mason, which means I've known them since elementary school. I became friends with Will through Mason, and with Will came Jack, who is currently sitting on the porch, staring at my van.

"You good, bro?"

Jack's head shoots up. "Oh, uh, yeah. Just... uh... sitting." Even he looks confused at his answer.

"Right." I come up the steps to sit down next to him.

We stare at my ride in silence. A teal Volkswagen from the seventies. I bought it from some stoner grandma off Craigslist and have considered it my best purchase to date. Technically, it's a Volkswagen Bus, but we still use "bus" and "van" interchangeably.

After a minute, Jack says, "I hate your van."

"I know."

"It scares me."

"I know."

He eyes my flask. "Still drinking?"

I silently offer him a sip. He takes it, spitting it out only seconds later.

"What the *hell?*"

I'm so busy laughing my ass off that I almost can't answer. "What, you never had orange juice before?"

He shakes his head with a pinched face. "No, I just wasn't expecting it." He hands me back the flask.

I glance over at the book in his hand. If there's one thing that's always been constant, it's that Jack is constantly reading. He usually sneaks his book with him; whether it's in his backpack or under his shirt or simply hiding it around the house, he always seems to have one.

But this book is a bit different.

I nod to it. "What's that?"

"Oh, uh..." He sort of moves it to his side. "Nothing. It's nothing."

I raise an eyebrow.

"I'm serious!"

I hold out a hand. "Come on, Jack," I try. "You weren't the only one who was close to him."

He seems to at least somewhat agree with this, as he caves and hands me the book.

I begin to silently flip through the pages. Will's handwriting was always unfairly pretty. It's like we learned cursive in third grade (separately, because I didn't move here until fifth), and he hasn't looked back since.

"Show off," I'd always tease.

"I'm not showing off!" he'd insist. "It's just easier!"

Granted, he doesn't always write in cursive. But it isn't uncommon.

(Wasn't. I almost forgot.)

"Wait a minute," I say. "Is this..."

"It's a bucket list," Jack finishes. "Places he wanted to go, things he wanted to do, all compiled into a stupid little notebook."

"Hang on, didn't you get this for him?"

"Thus the basis of its stupidity."

I snicker. "Man, he really planned this out." Each item has a dedicated page or so to it. Costs, location, times, hotels nearby. "I remember a few of these, actually." For example: *Cairo. Pyramids of Giza. Camel ride $20.*

"Yeah, he talked about that one quite a bit."

"Some of these are pretty surprising, though."

"Yeah," he laughs. "That's what I said."

"When?"

"What?"

"When did you say that?"

He pushes his hair back. "I was talking to Cassie about it."

"After we all left?"

He nods, eyes fixed on the page I've landed on. *Yosemite. Entrance fee $35. Hotel a few miles away.*

"What were you guys talking about?" I ask casually.

"Just that," he says. "And this ass-backwards idea she had about completing it."

"Why is that ass-backwards?" I laugh.

He gives me a look. "Because a good chunk of it would be spent in your van."

"Oh, come on." I lean back on my palm and give him a shove. "It's not *that* bad."

"Are you kidding? It's the motorized version of Mason. I only ride in that thing when I have to."

It's my turn to glare. "How *dare you* compare her to such a person."

"It's a 'her'?"

I look at my van. "'Course it's a 'her.' Can't you see it?"

He rests his arms on his knees, looking over. He's studying me intently, but I have a feeling he's focused more on whatever's rambling around in his head than he is on my face.

"I can see the gears spinning," I tell him. "What's up?"

He frowns, taken aback. "Nothing."

I eye him quizzically. "You're thinking about what Cassidy suggested."

"What? No."

"That or you're picturing me naked, which, hate to tell you, but I'm a *raging* lesbian, buddy." He thinks I'm kidding. "But anyway," I continue, "you're debating whether you want to go, which, personally, I think you do."

"Oh, right. Because you know everything."

"I do know everything, actually."

He scoffs.

"Why don't you want to go?"

He shrugs. "I don't know, I guess it'd just be weird pursuing his dreams without him, you know?"

I nod. "Yeah, but you know what'd be worse?"

He frowns, waiting for me to finish.

"Letting his dreams die with him."

He seems to take these words in, straightening as he swallows.

"Well, I'm gonna let you sit on that." I give him a quick pat on the back before standing. "Gimme a call when you figure out what you wanna do, okay?"

He nods.

"Oh, and Jack." I turn back around.

He looks up.

"Thanks for not becoming a recluse."

He frowns. "What do you mean?"

I shrug. "Well, with everything that's been going on, I half expected you to sit at home and wallow. But you're actually talking to us. Which is huge, to say the least."

"Yeah, well. You guys aren't really giving me a chance to."

I smile at this.

Mason

paisley finally drives up to elijah's porch. "Sorry, I overslept."

Cassidy furrows her brow. "It's 2:30."

Paisley waves this away and collapses on the bench next to my spot on the ground.

"See what happens when you drink too much?" I shake my head.

She blinks. "You literally tried to steal my flask, like, eighty-three times yesterday. And I only saw you for a few hours."

"Leave it be, Mace." Elijah's lying sideways in the swing across from Paisley, eyes closed. My gaze lingers on him a moment too long; I almost don't notice Paisley's triumphant smirk. I give her a tiny glare.

Cassidy, meanwhile, is continually looking down the driveway.

Paisley, upon noticing this, says, "He isn't coming." We invited Jack to our little get-together. Let's just say that if he's later than *Paisley,* he isn't coming.

Cassidy looks over. "I wasn't—"

"Saw him last night," says Paisley. "Looked kind of out of it."

Dani frowns from her place in the chair by the door. "How do you know?" she asks.

"Well, it was two in the morning, and he was sitting outside on the front porch."

"Seems pretty out of it to me," I agree.

"I think that might be my fault." Cassidy nervously rubs her hands across her jeans. "I didn't leave him on the best note."

Paisley looks over. "Listen. Whatever you said or did, I

think he would've been out on that porch regardless." She says this confidently enough, but it's obvious she's still a little unsure.

"Anyone who's just lost their big brother is gonna be a little off," Dani notes.

Paisley gestures to her. "Exactly."

"How many big brothers did you lose, Paisley?" I grin. She kicks me.

Cassidy stands at once. "I'm calling him." She pauses. "Does anyone have his number?"

Elijah finally opens his eyes. How do I describe his eyes? They're blue, but when you're looking right at them they seem like they're every color at once. Or maybe that's just me because sometimes I can barely breathe when I see them. They stand out brightly against his dark skin. He has his mother's complexion and what I'm assuming to be his father's eyes. And because of that, he is one of the most gorgeous people I've ever laid my eyes on.

"That's not a good idea," he tells Cassidy, who frowns. "Why?"

Elijah takes another hit off his joint. "If you did upset him, you're probably the last person he wants to talk to."

"But did you apologize?" I ask Cassidy.

She hesitates. "I want to say yes."

"Well, did you or did you not?"

She paws the ground with her foot, mumbling, "I may or may not have called him a horrible brother and left."

I drop my hand. "Oh. Well, in that case..."

Even Paisley is shocked at this. "Dude!"

Cassidy grimaces.

"Call and apologize," I tell her. "That's all you gotta do. Jack's a pretty chill guy."

Paisley scoffs. "Sorry, are we talking about the same Jack? He probably needs time to cool off."

"That's probably what his moment on the porch was for," Elijah mutters, rocking the swing back and forth slowly with the ball of his foot.

"Okay," Cassidy says, still on her feet, "so, uh... what do I do?"

We collectively exchange a nervous glance.

Paisley wavers. "I probably shouldn't be telling you this." She shifts her weight on the bench before subtly rolling her hand.

"He likes your plan."

Cassidy's eyes light up. She looks like a little bird when this happens. "Does he really?"

"Yeah, we were talking about it last night. He didn't say it explicitly, but I could tell."

"Okay," Dani jumps in, "did I miss something? What plan?"

"Oh, I don't know." I shrug. "I was kinda just going along with it."

Elijah smacks me; it's almost delayed because of the weed he's smoking. "She wasn't asking you."

"Cassidy had this plan..." Paisley gestures for Cassidy to explain.

We all turn to her.

"Oh, um. Yeah." She shifts her weight. "Will had this, uh, bucket list. Everything he wanted to do before he died, which obviously didn't get... completed. So I thought, what if we completed it for him?"

I sit up, excited. "Aw, *yo!*"

"So we're talking about a road trip?" Dani reiterates.

"More or less," Paisley says. "Had a few international appearances here and there."

"How international?" Elijah asks.

"Like, Seven Wonders international. Of both worlds, by the way."

Elijah's eyes miraculously widen. He looks, dare I say, excited about this.

"Both worlds..." I say slowly. "Like Mars?"

And his face falls just as fast as it rose. "Mason..." He sighs.

"What?" I ask.

"Modern and ancient worlds, dumbass." Paisley looks up at Dani. "Right?"

"Right," Dani says. "Pyramids of Giza, Taj Mahal, Great Wall. That shit."

"Oh..." I finally get it.

"*Oh...*" Paisley mimics.

I reach up to smack her leg.

"Are we really doing this?" Cassidy asks from her place standing by the stairs. "Is this really happening?"

"As long as Jack's on board," Elijah says, "right?"

Paisley hesitates, idea formulating. "Well..."

"No," Dani says quickly. "*No.*"

Paisley rolls her eyes and sits up. "He's not gonna get his lazy ass in my van unless we put it there ourselves, you know that!"

Dani's not having it. "This is the worst idea you've ever had. And I say that sparingly."

Paisley considers this almost proudly.

"Wait," I say, confused, "what are we doing?"

"We're going to the Taj Mahal, brickhead."

I shake my head at Paisley. "No, I knew that." Kind of. "I mean, what was Paisley's other idea?"

Elijah, ignoring me, adds, "I guess we're not beyond it at this point."

"Beyond what?" I press.

"Kidnapping, Mace," Elijah finally says to me. "We're not beyond kidnapping."

"Um." Dani raises her hand. "I am."

"Well, we knew that," Paisley says. She nods to me. "Even Mason knew that."

"I did know that."

She looks over. "What about you, Cassidy?" she asks. "You've been awful quiet during this discussion of breaking and entering."

A smile slowly spreads across her face. "If it were anyone else, I'd say no."

Paisley grins back.

Dani's muttering defeatedly. "*Ay Dios mio...*"

"If it makes you feel any better, we'll call his mom first," Paisley tells her. "And to send you over the moon, I'll let *you* do the honors."

"You know what?" Dani folds her arms. "I don't know why I even bother at this point."

Paisley's typing on her phone. "Sending you Mama Dickinson's number right now."

"No, no, no, I am *not* calling Laura to ask if we can kidnap her *son*. Besides, Paisley, I already have her number."

"We're not kidnapping him, we're taking him on a bonding experience."

"To help him cope," I add.

"That is the smartest thing you've said all week. Thank

you, Mason." Paisley turns back to Dani with a satisfied smirk.

Dani gestures at her. "Well, what are you waiting for?"

"What do you mean, what am *I* waiting for?" Paisley asks. "You have her number. Do your valedictorian bit and make this sound like a good idea. Which it is. It's a great idea."

"It's a fantastic idea," I agree.

Someone, however, is already a step ahead. "Yeah, hi, Mrs. Dickinson? It's Cassidy."

"Or, you know, she'll do it." Paisley blinks.

"Put it on speaker," Elijah tells Cassidy.

She does.

I lean into the phone. "Hey, Mama D! It's Mason!"

Mama D laughs. "Hi, Mason."

Cassidy jumps right in. "Okay, so I know it's only the first day of summer, and you can totally say no—"

"No, you can't," Paisley says quickly.

"Wait, say no to what?" Mrs. Dickinson asks. "What's going on?"

I bounce where I'm sitting. "We're going on a—"

Elijah puts a hand over my mouth. I pretend not to notice how warm he is.

Cassidy continues. "We were wondering if you'd be okay if Jack went on a road trip with us."

"Um, okay," Mrs. Dickinson says. "Where to?"

Cassidy exchanges a nervous glance with Paisley.

"Uh..." Paisley rolls a hand for Cassidy to keep going.

Cassidy turns her focus nervously back to the phone. "Um, well..." She looks helplessly at Dani.

"Don't ask me," Dani mouths.

And so Cassidy, with all her help, blurts, "We don't really know yet."

Everyone on the porch groans.

"Jack has the list."

"List?" Mrs. Dickinson repeats. "What list?"

Cassidy, stressing, tries to explain. "The... The list of places we're gonna go."

"What?" mouths Paisley.

"I don't know!" Cassidy mouths back.

"List of places you're gonna go..." Mrs. Dickinson says slowly. "Did he write this list?"

"Uh... yeah." Cassidy winces. "I mean, no. No, he didn't write it. It's—"

"Will wrote it," Paisley cuts in. "It's Will's list."

There is a long, *long* pause on the other end. "Oh."

Paisley nods at Cassidy, gesturing for her to continue.

Cassidy runs a hand through her hair, eyes closed. "Yeah," she says, calmer. "It's Will's list. A list of places he wanted to go. And I feel like— I feel like we need to do that. For him. We just— We have to."

Silence.

Then: "I didn't... know. I mean, I knew he wanted to travel, he had a very... a very free spirit. But... I didn't realize that there was a physical list. Where did you find it?"

"In his closet," Cassidy answers softly. "Jack found it."

Mrs. Dickinson sighs. "Of course he did. Jack knows that room better than Will does, I swear." A bout of silence follows this. A long one, at that. One that gets all of us exchanging anxious glances.

Paisley's the one to break it. "Soooo?"

Another sigh. "Oh, I just don't know. I want him to be able to go on this trip, I want Jack to be able to let him go." My heart sinks at this. Because that's what we're doing, right? With this trip, I mean. We're letting him go. And as difficult as it is for me, I can't imagine how much of a toll this is taking on Jack. Suddenly, I'm starting to get cold feet about this whole thing.

"I really would be more comfortable if I knew where all of you were planning on going," Mrs. Dickinson is saying.

Cassidy hesitates before saying quietly into the phone, "I remember a few of the places. In the U.S., at least. A few in Arizona, a few scattered. New York's the farthest, I think, but it would make most sense to end up in California." Right. Even though Will's been to New York on college tours, there are still lots of things he never checked off.

I don't feel great about leaving out the international destinations, but I think we all know it's the only way we can convince Mama D. She's already iffy as is. "California?" she repeats hesitantly. "I don't know..."

"We wouldn't go everywhere," Cassidy's quick to say. "Obviously. We don't even have to go to California."

"Okay, well—"

"*Ow!*" Cassidy shoots a shocked glare at Paisley, who had kicked her upon hearing that we wouldn't have to go to California. "*I'm trying!*" she mouths to her angrily. Then, back into the phone, massaging her calf: "Even if we just check off the ones in Arizona. And maybe the surrounding states."

Paisley's had about enough of this. She leans forward toward Cassidy and sticks her hand out. "Give me the phone."

Cassidy frowns and tries to tuck it into her chest, but Paisley's too quick, yanking it out of her hand and tossing her hair back over her shoulder. "Hey, yeah, hi. Um... we've gotta go to California."

Mrs. Dickinson sighs. "Hi, Paisley." She's learned to deal with Paisley throughout the years just as we all have. It's nothing new. It's always a bit strange.

"We don't know much about this bucket list" —she swats away Cassidy, who has tried to make a grab for the phone— "but of the places we do remember, I can tell you that we'll be making appearances in Arizona, Colorado, and Utah." She sits back against the porch railing and shrugs, crossing her ankles. "He was a national parks junkie, so I'm mainly basing it off of that."

Mrs. Dickinson gives a thankfully amused laugh. "That still doesn't exactly answer my question."

"I know it doesn't. And we're gonna get that answer for you once we get your son."

"Oh, do you want me to go grab him?" she offers. "He's just up in his room, I can—"

"*No!*"

An awkward pause hangs in the air.

Paisley presses her lips shamefully together and clears her throat. "I, uh, I *meant* that I think it would be quite fun to surprise him with this."

She hesitates. "So he has no idea you're planning this?"

"Ah..." Paisley sucks in her teeth. "Well..." Her eyes scan the four of us, looking for some sort of out. Surprisingly, her gaze lands on Dani. I don't think I've ever seen her outright ask for Dani's help before. But hey, desperate times call for desperate measures, I guess. Even at the cost of Paisley's pride.

Dani takes the phone, much to Cassidy's dismay. "Hey, Laura." Yup. They're on a first name basis. It's okay, though. Because I'm on a "Mama D" basis.

"Am I just being passed around?" Mama D asks with a light laugh.

"Yeah." Dani smiles, picking nervously at her nails. "Uh... sorry about that. I just figured... you know."

"I do know."

Dani glances over. "I think what Paisley is *trying* to say is that—"

"You're going to kidnap my son?"

Dani hesitates. "Well..."

"No, no." Mama D sighs. "Sometimes he needs the push." True. Very true. I've actually pushed him into the pool numerous times. And Will. Him, too. I might have a problem with that.

Dani stifles her laugh. "So does this mean you're on board?"

"No."

Shit.

"But I'll consider it."

Un-shit.

"Can you maybe... consider it quickly?" Paisley asks. "Quicklier? More... quickly?"

Dani gives her a look. "Paisley, Jesus."

Paisley puts her palms up. "I'm just saying, if we're gonna pull this off, we've gotta get an early start. Early start being as soon as possible."

Dani's eyes narrow, but she says nothing. I think even she knows that Paisley makes a good point.

Mrs. Dickinson groans. "Fine. Fine, okay," she caves. "I want to talk to you guys, though. Before I make any decisions."

"Yeah, of course," Dani jumps back in. "Do you want to meet over coffee?"

"Coffee's good." Then, again: "Coffee's good. Bring Cassidy, too." Cassidy lights up at this. Must make up for having her phone stolen.

"Want to say... twenty minutes or so?" Mrs. Dickinson asks. "The Starbucks up by the dry cleaner's?"

"Yeah." Dani eyes Cassidy, who nods. "Yeah, that works. We'll see you soon."

Paisley furrows her brow. "So, like, is this a girls trip or a *girls* trip?"

"I, uh..." Dani shifts. "I don't think you're invited, Paisley."

She sits back, unperturbed. "Cool."

42

"See you there, Mrs. Dickinson," Cassidy calls.

"Yup. Bye, girls." She hangs up.

Cassidy finally finds an opportunity to grab her phone.

"Wow." I look over at Elijah, who had spoken in a slight daze. "She didn't even address us."

"Well." Dani stands and looks to Cassidy. "We should probably go. We'll keep you guys updated?"

"Yeah, yeah." Elijah continues to rock the swing with his foot. "We'll just hear it through the grapevine, I guess." He takes a drag on his joint.

Dani just purses her lips and goes. Cassidy follows closely behind.

Paisley puts her hands on her legs before standing. "Sounds good to me." And as she's walking away, she mutters, "More or less."

My phone wakes me early the next morning. It apparently wakes Elijah, too.

"Mason," he mumbles tiredly, smacking me lazily on the arm. "Phone."

I whine a little but grab it, disoriented from the morning. "Yeah?"

"Hey, sorry," comes the other end, "did I wake you up?"

I rub my hand over my face. God, I didn't even check the caller ID. I'm only half sure of who's speaking. "Yeah, you're good." I stretch my arm out, let it drape across Elijah's shoulders. "What's up?"

"She's not good," Elijah mumbles, burying his face in my side.

"I just wanted to let you know Mrs. Dickinson texted."

Cassidy. It's Cassidy who's calling. She's calling about the trip. Yup, I'm awake now.

"Oh, really? What'd she say?"

Elijah perks up a little, enough to scoot closer to me so he can hear the conversation in its entirety.

"Yeah, I'm actually kind of surprised," Cassidy tells me (us). "I mean, we were at Starbucks for, like, an hour, and she didn't seem too convinced. But she's on board now."

This puts a smile on my face. "So, when are we leaving?"

"Wednesday."

I blink. "Oh, wow, that's... really soon."

"I know," she says. "Which is why I wanted to tell you guys as soon as possible so we can all start packing."

I nod along to what she's saying. "And Jack still doesn't know?"

She sucks in a breath. "Nope. Paisley's set on the idea of surprising him."

I consider this. "I mean... I'm kind of okay with that." Really okay with it, actually. I think it's gonna be funny as shit.

"Yeah, well. We'll see how it goes over."

"Hey, don't worry about it," I tell her. "I'll handle him."

"Oh." She sounds a little surprised by this. "I guess I kind of assumed Paisley would be doing the... uh... kidnapping."

I shrug. "I just figured it'd be a friendlier fight if it were me. If he's not budging, we'll bring her in."

Elijah raises his eyebrows when I glance down at him. After I wave away my comment, he sighs indifferently and sinks deeper into me, running his palm up my chest. I rub up and down his arm while Cassidy talks through the phone.

"I'm..." She lets out a little laugh. "I'm looking forward to it."

I snort. "Have you told anyone else yet?"

"Working on it."

"Gotcha."

"And on that note, I should probably go. I'll see you Wednesday, I guess?"

I smile. "Yup, see you then."

"See you soon." She hesitates only a moment longer before hanging up.

As soon as we're done, I put my phone back on the nightstand and roll over to put my arms farther around Elijah.

"Mmmm." He sighs against me. "You know, I only heard, like, half of that."

"That's okay," I say into his shoulder.

He's happy again, letting his previous state of drowsiness take over and lull him to sleep—

The doorbell rings.

Elijah groans into my side.

44

"I can go get it," I say, rubbing his back.

He rolls away from me regretfully. "Yeah, it's probably just my mom. She must've forgotten her keys again."

"Okay." I start to leave his room.

"Wait, wait, wait," he slurs sleepily, lifting his head just the slightest. "Put a shirt on."

"Oh. Right." I take my hoodie off the ground and pull it back over my head before heading out.

His mom's house always has a good energy to it. It's hard to describe, but when you've got two artists living under one roof, you can feel it. In the walls, the paint stains on the carpet, the papers scattered on the kitchen counter. There's a faint smell of candles drifting through the halls.

Elijah's mom is very forgetful sometimes. It's not surprising she left her keys; if she has a brain anything like her son's, I'd imagine it'd be easy for things to get lost up there.

I swing the door open to let her in. To my pleasant surprise, it isn't his mom. It's Cassidy.

"Um..." She frowns, looks over her shoulder before looking back up at me. "Hi."

"Hey." I smile. I hear a faint *thud* followed by hastened footsteps coming from Elijah's room.

Cassidy cocks her head a little. "What are you..." It's not until she says this that I realize why this whole situation might be a problem. Because she doesn't know I'm dating Elijah. Hell, she doesn't even know I'm gay. How am I supposed to explain this?

I freeze. "I'm..." Nope. Nothing. My brain is loading slower than Internet Explorer. I can't see Cassidy anymore. I can just see an error message.

"I was just gonna tell Lijah the news, but I guess... Uh..." *He probably already knows.*

"Right, um..." I scratch the back of my neck. "Well, he's—"

Elijah scrambles down the hall, skids behind me to a stop. "Hey, Cassidy." He's out of breath. "Hey. Hi. Mason slept over."

"I—" My eyes widen as I turn to face him.

But she doesn't seem at all fazed. "Oh. Okay."

She's fine with it? She's fine that I slept over? That I *slept over?*

"Well, I'm guessing you already know what I came to tell you?" Cassidy continues like nothing happened.

45

Elijah nods quickly. "Yep. The trip is a-go. Really great. I'm really excited."

She's back to being confused. "Okay..."

"What?"

She shakes her head. "No, you're just acting kind of weird."

"Weird? Nope. Not me."

She hesitates. "Are you high?"

Elijah almost relaxes at the insinuation. "Yeah. That's it. Didn't wanna tell you because—"

"Because it's nine in the morning?" she asks with a little raise of her eyebrows.

"Exactly."

She sighs. "Well, I'll leave you guys to... whatever you're up to."

I eye Elijah, who swallows. "Mhm," he hums tightly. "Yeah. Thanks for stopping by."

"I'll see you bright and early on Wednesday."

He groans. "That sounds about right." Honestly, I'm kind of an early riser, anyway. Maybe it's because I've been conditioned by early morning practices for basketball and even earlier morning trips to games. Maybe it's just because I tend to like mornings better than evenings. I don't know.

I give Elijah a little nudge. "It's gonna be fun," I assure him.

"Yes. It is." Cassidy smiles. "See you." She bounces down the porch steps, all but floats back across the street to her house. It's obvious she's happy, and I won't lie, it's a little contagious.

Elijah rests his forehead against the door when he closes it. "Why does she have to live so *close?*"

I shrug, settling next to him with my back to the door. "I think the bigger question is how she didn't suspect anything."

"Well." He turns to look up at me. "She sleeps over all the time. She's used to it."

"Oh." I consider this. "Okay."

"And besides, she thinks you're straight," Elijah continues. "Like, really, *really* straight."

Yeah, okay, that's completely fair.

He sighs and winds his arms around my waist. "I wanna go back to bed."

I smile down at him. "Okay." After he doesn't move, I say, "So go back to bed."

"No." He takes my hand, tugging me back toward his room. "You're coming with me."

I grin and let him lead me away from the door.

Jack

i've only gotten up for pizza rolls. I know how that sounds. But honestly, that's kind of the only thing getting me moving throughout the day.

And yeah, I know how hypocritical that seems, especially given what Paisley said last night about being glad I wasn't becoming a recluse. But right now? It's worth being hypocritical so long as I can stay in bed.

So call me a hermit and shove a pizza roll up my ass because I'm not going *anywhere*.

I'm trying to forget. I'm trying to keep myself... I don't know. Happy, I guess. I've found I can't do anything that causes me to lose focus for too long because if I zone out I start thinking again, and if I start thinking again I'll start feeling again.

And believe me when I say I don't want to feel anything right now.

I've drowned myself in books, anything I can get my hands on. My room is littered with them—from the bookshelf out in the hall, from the one in my room, hell, even those from the library that I should have returned years ago.

But somehow it's still not enough. Because every so often I'll let go of my vision, I'll let my eyes brush the edges of the words without really reading them, and I start thinking about Will, and suddenly, he's all I can think about. All I can feel.

I hate it. I hate it all so much.

A knock comes at my door around three.

"Hey, honey, can I get you anything?"

I shake my head without looking over at my mom. "Fine," I say shortly.

She lingers in the doorframe; I can feel her eyes on me

for the longest time.

"I'm making dinner," she says softly. "If you want to come down later? Get something to eat besides pizza rolls?" She's trying. She's trying so hard, and I know I should be more appreciative of that. But I just want to be alone, which I'm not sure if she really understands. She has Dad to lean on. I had Will.

"Maybe."

She lingers in the doorway. "Jack?"

"Hm?"

"Just... I love you."

I hesitate. "I know."

"So much."

I look up with a small attempt at a smile. "Love you, too, Mom."

Another second bouncing between my room and the hall, and she's gone.

I roll over on my bed and stare up at the ceiling.

I don't know. Maybe it was seeing them all again. All of Will's friends, I mean. And seeing his poor girlfriend, how heartbroken she was. Her words keep ringing in my head: *"At least I was there."* I *was* there, Cassie. I was there at the memorial service, I was there at the funeral (or, at least, as much as I could handle), I was there when...

I suck in a breath, suddenly very aware that my hands are shaking. I roll back over and try to pick my book back up. It falls out of my tremoring grasp and flops onto the floor.

"*Shit,*" I mutter, leaning down to reach for it. As I do, my hand brushes another book that lay dormant on the ground.

I hesitate before picking up the notebook—*the* notebook—and sitting back up on my bed. I push my hair back and open the book once more, though I've already skimmed these pages what seems like a thousand times.

Bungee jump. Navajo Bridge.

Navajo Bridge. That's not far from here, actually. Coconino County, if I'm right. This isn't the first time I've had this thought, but it's the first time it processes. We could go do this. We could easily go check this off his bucket list.

But what kind of a brother would that make me, doing all these things without him?

"You're a horrible brother."

That's also been in my head. Am I really that horrible for not wanting to infringe on his dreams? These were meant for him and him alone. What kind of brother would I be to do something like this without him?

And that's when Paisley's voice comes into my head: *"Yeah, but you know what would be worse? Letting his dreams die with him."* She, for once, makes perfect sense. But there's still something holding me back. Why can't I figure out what that is?

I spend the rest of the night like this, ducking in and out of my own emotions; head underwater, trying to see how long I can go without air. Because air hurts sometimes. When you finally cave and come up for a breath, your lungs feel like they're on fire. And suddenly, it's like you'd rather be drowning than have your own body working against you.

At least, that's how I'm feeling right now. But maybe I've been reading too much.

I don't come down for dinner. I haven't had a full meal since... well, you know. I prefer it that way, strangely enough. Just some light snacking throughout the day. Some pizza rolls. Lots of pizza rolls.

Man, I'm a mess.

My bedroom faces west, so come sunset the light's pouring in through my window. I find myself so absorbed in my book that I barely notice when it goes away until my eyes are straining from reading in the dark.

I notice even less that my eyes are sagging, and my brain is mushy; with each turn of a page my limbs feel less like my own.

I guess I must have drifted off at some point, if only for a few minutes, because the next thing I know I hear a loud *thud*, and my head feels like it's hit a rock.

I scramble to a sitting position... right next to my bed. I've fallen off my bed. Awesome. How the hell does that even *happen?*

I grumble a few choice words to the floor beneath me and get to my feet.

The starry night's kind eyes meet mine as I face the window. Cool nights mean cool breezes, which are rare in Arizona. So I open my window and breathe it in.

I should go back to sleep. I know that. But I go through this same routine every night. I lie in my bed; I toss and I turn until my head is at the foot of the mattress. I try to get comfortable, but the nagging at the back of my mind grows into a rock in my chest, and I can't sleep.

Because there's no one in Will's bed. Will's bed is empty.

And I don't know what about that is so terrifying to me. Better yet, I don't know what about going in there helps me get at least a little bit of sleep.

Somehow, though, it does. Tonight I finally don't question the inner workings of my mind. I just go into Will's room and collapse on his comforter.

I'm back asleep within minutes.

At least, I think. I think I've been dozing in and out by my best knowledge. I'll wake up on another end of the bed, roll back over, and close my eyes.

I'll tell you one thing: Will's bed is *much* more comfortable than mine. The past seventeen years of my life have been built on a selfish lie. The only flaw I can seem to find is that if you roll over just right, you can spot the blood stain on the carpet. It wasn't from anything bad, just a seizure, which I guess is pretty scary if you aren't used to them. But I've been dealing with them for quite some time, as Will was diagnosed with epilepsy when he was fairly young.

The point is, rest comes easy. All is finally peaceful. All is finally—

"Hey, homie!"

When I tell you I *scream.*

I fall off the bed for the second time that night, hitting the floor harder than before.

I groan, slowly looking up. Mason's standing over me, concerned.

He tilts his head. "You okay?"

"Fine," I grumble, standing, rubbing my head. "What the hell are you *doing here?*" I hiss. "It's two in the morning!"

"Uh, actually, it's four in the morning."

I stare back, deadpan. "My mistake." I brush past him to find the glass of water I'd gotten the night before to get a drink. I turn back to repeat my question, but he's gone. Just like that.

I sigh. "You've gotta be fucking kidding me." I trudge

out into the hallway. "Mason?" I whisper yell. *"Mason!"*

"In here!"

I roll my eyes and head into my bedroom, where Mason is raiding my closet.

My jaw comes unhinged as I watch him go. He stops only to ask, "Hey, where do you keep your suitcase?"

"My— Mason, *what* are you doing? How did you even get in here?"

"Your mom let me in."

I blink. "And the real reason?"

He gasps. "Oh! I remember where they are!" He bounces out my bedroom door like I'm not even there.

This is already exhausting. Part of me's tempted to believe that this is some sort of fever dream. But even my own wildest dreams know that this is just crazy enough to actually be happening.

I follow him downstairs, which is pointless because just as I reach the last step he flies back up, leaving me to turn around and follow him back up to my bedroom.

"Will you slow down for, like, two seconds, Mace?"

He continues to ignore me, unzipping the suitcase and shoving stuff inside. When I finally look over his shoulder, he's stopped, confused at his own work.

"Now what?"

He frowns. "I think I did it wrong."

That's an understatement. I have every pair of underwear that I own and a single sock. For some reason, Mason thought it necessary to try and fit my globe in there. Twelve books lay scattered over the top, making it impossible to close.

"I don't know whether to be more concerned about where you think I'm going that I'd need no pants and two copies of *Les Misérables* or the fact that you broke into my house at four in the morning."

"Do you use a toothbrush?"

I stop. "*Yes*, Mason. I use a toothbrush."

"Oh. Well, I'm gonna need to make room."

"Oh, but don't take the unopened wax candle out. How did that even get in here?" I pick it up out of the suitcase. Mom must've shoved it into my closet to make room downstairs.

Once again, I make the mistake of taking my eyes off

Mason, and once again, he's gone.

I toss the candle onto my bed and try to find Mason yet again. He comes back with an armful of things from my bathroom and dumps them onto my comforter. "Okay, uh, shampoo, conditioner—"

"That's my mom's."

"That's your mom's." He sets the bottle aside. "Comb, deodorant, toothbrush—"

"That's, uh." I take the toothbrush. "That's Will's."

He goes quiet. "Oh. Sorry."

I go to put the toothbrush back in the bathroom. I come back and see him organizing things into different piles. That's honestly a shocking sight.

"Okay, I think I'm done. Let's go!" He throws my suitcase over his shoulder. Yes, folks, you read that right. He threw my *suitcase* over his *shoulder* like a sack of fucking *potatoes*.

"Mason, where the hell are you going with that?"

He thumps down the stairs.

I follow him out the front door, protesting all the while. "Mason, wh—"

"You might want to put a shirt on, homie."

"Why—" I stop outside Paisley's van. She's sitting on the edge of the bus, letting her legs dangle from outside the front door. Everyone inside is staring out at me through the windows. I meet Cassidy's eyes first. She's quick to look away.

It all comes together as soon as I see Mason loading my suitcase in through the hatchback.

"Oh my God."

"Get in the van," orders Paisley.

"Nope."

"Jack. In. Now."

"*No*."

She stands. I start to back away.

"Paisley—"

"Jack—"

"*Paisley*—"

"*Jack*—"

"*Mason!*"

We both look over to find Mason trying to climb in through one of the windows, despite the protesting Elijah.

Paisley and I elect to ignore whatever's going on *there*.
"Get in the van."

"*No,*" I say firmly. "No. There is *no way* that you or... or *any one of you* is getting me in that van."

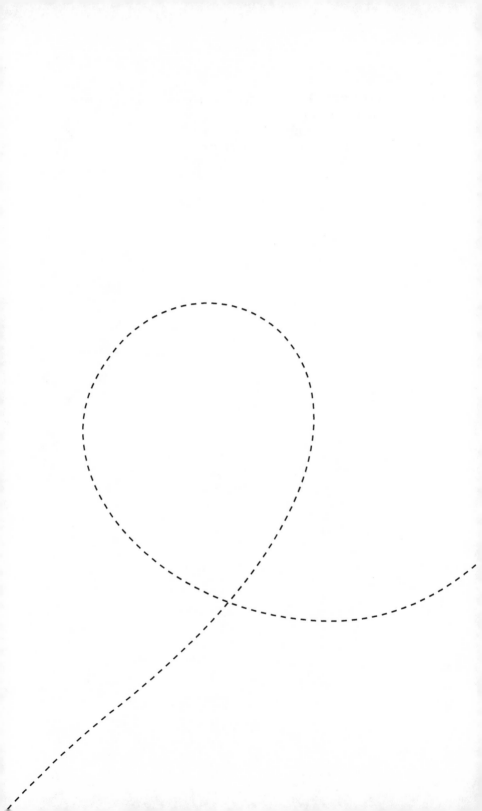

North America

Dani

jack is still pouting. We've been on the road for over an hour, and he hasn't said a word to any of us. All he's done is stare out the window, slouched against the side of the van. Cassidy's been dozing off and on, but it doesn't take more than a bump in the road to wake her again. Elijah's had headphones in the whole time, and he's stayed quiet. So has Paisley, which is unusual, to say the least. She seemed pretty proud of herself when she was able to grab Jack around the waist and drag him to the bus (after punching him in the gut, that is), but since then she's been pretty focused on driving.

For the record, I didn't condone any of this. You can't force a grieving person to do something he doesn't want to do, especially when it entails getting into a car after said person's brother just died in a car crash. But this is a democracy, and my vote barely counts. Actually, it never counts. The only thing I can do is come along for the ride and hope they don't get themselves killed.

Which is entirely possible, seeing as the first thing we've planned on doing is bungee jumping.

I've been periodically checking on the others over my shoulder, and by the millionth time of doing so, I've had enough. "Are you gonna say anything?" I ask, directing it at Jack.

He doesn't respond. He just slumps farther down in his seat, staring broodingly out the window. Mason was so kind as to give him his purple Lakers hoodie, which he seems to be trying to hide in.

I sigh. It's really not worth it.

Mason reaches into the duffel at his feet and pulls out a bag of pizza rolls. "We got pizza rolls," he says, jiggling it. And as untraditional as this attempt to cheer him up may be, I catch Jack lift his head up the tiniest bit. And I guess I have to give Mason some credit for that.

"No, no, no," I tell both of them because someone has to. "No pizza rolls at five in the morning."

"Oh, fuck off," Paisley finally speaks up, "there's no rule against it."

"Any time is pizza roll time," Mason says.

Cassidy lifts her head. "I am getting kinda hungry, though. Could we stop for breakfast?"

"We can make the pizza rolls if you're hungry!" Mason grins, jostling the bag again.

"Real breakfast, Mace," Cassidy says, stretching her arms out in front of her with a yawn. "Real food. Eggs. I want eggs."

"Besides," I say, "do you have a microwave to put them in?"

Mason's face falls. "Oh."

Yeah, that's what I thought.

"This day just keeps getting better and better, doesn't it," Jack mutters, arms folded.

"He speaks!" I exclaim.

He scowls, turning back to the window.

"Yeah," Paisley says, glancing at the rearview mirror, "we gotta get some food in that kid."

Elijah perks up, taking one earbud out; I didn't realize he'd been listening. "I saw a sign for a diner off the next exit."

The van swerves suddenly, and I'm thrown against the divider between the front seats and the back. "*Paisley!*" I shout, along with the others.

"What?" she says, defensive. "I wouldn't have made the exit otherwise!"

I'm pretty damn certain she would have. Looking back over my shoulder, Elijah is straightening himself up from where he fell over. Jack's arms are around Cassidy, who had fallen into him. She glances up at him. "Um... you can let me go now," she says.

"Jesus, sorry." Jack lets go, and she topples onto the floor, unprepared for it. He smirks before going back to sulking.

Cassidy pushes herself to her feet, groaning as she returns to her seat.

I roll my eyes. "Nice going, Paisley."

She scowls, turning away from my accusatory glare. Which, naturally, causes her to lose focus and swerve again. I curse under my breath. But at least I'm not on the floor again like Cassidy or, God forbid, in Mason's arms.

"I got you, buddy!" Mason says, grinning at Elijah.

"Really?" Elijah wrenches around to get out of his grasp, and Mason lets go, frowning.

This trip is already a disaster. I can only imagine how much worse it'll get.

The diner is quite honestly adorable. Elijah couldn't have picked a more retro, '50s-style restaurant, and I'm all for it. We got here right when it opened, and we claimed the only circular booth in the place.

Jack has yet to talk to any of us. The only words he's uttered since we got off the interstate have been to order his food from the waiter. And until we get him to talk and maybe—just maybe—give us Will's notebook, we can't really go any farther.

Mason is not-so-subtly eyeing Jack's untouched plate of bacon and eggs. "Say nothing if I can have your breakfast."

Jack only blinks.

Taking this as an invitation, Mason reaches for his plate, but Jack yanks it away from him. He then passive aggressively stabs his eggs with his fork.

I sigh. Enough is enough. "Can I talk to you, Jack?" I ask, setting my fork and napkin down. "Alone?"

"Oooh," Mason sings like a goddamn third grader. "Someone's in trouble."

"Shut up," Elijah mutters.

Jack lets out an incredulous little laugh. "You're seriously gonna act mad at *me* when *you guys* were the ones who forcibly removed me from my home? You know, in some places, they call that kidnapping."

Mason's brow furrows. "Isn't it called that he—"

Paisley smacks him before he can finish.

"Jack," I say sharply, shooting him a pointed look.

He stares me down for a moment before rolling his eyes and looking at Cassidy for her to move so he can get out. She does, and I make sure Jack is behind me before heading toward the bathrooms. He leans against the wall outside the men's room, arms folded. After a second, he spreads his arms, exasperated. "Well? You going to say anything after you dragged me away from the breakfast that Mason's probably eating?"

I close my eyes for a second. How do I say this nicely? "Look," I start, "I know you don't want to be here. I don't want to be here either. You don't think I'd rather be anywhere else than stuck on the road in a van all summer?"

He's silent, eyes on the ground.

"I *know* you miss him. I miss him, too. And I know you're not your brother. It's not your list." I glance over at the others. "But their hearts are in the right place. You have to admit that."

He looks up. "Then why did you come?"

"What?"

"If you're so miserable, then why'd you come?"

I roll my eyes. "Because I have to keep you guys in check. Obviously."

He almost smiles, tilting his chin up. "What's the real reason?" he challenges.

My face falls; I swallow. "Because he wouldn't shut up about traveling," I say softly. "And if he doesn't get to live out the life he wanted, then the best we can do is try to live it for him." And still, there's this voice in the back of my head saying, *That's not the whole truth, is it?*

Jack wavers. After a second, he reaches into his pocket and pulls out the black notebook from Will's closet. He runs his thumb over it, studying it somberly. I can practically hear the conversation he's having with himself.

I try one last time, even quieter: "Of all people, you should know it's what he would have wanted."

He looks back up, a newfound determination on his face. "If we're gonna do this, we're gonna do it my way."

"I think that's pretty reasonable." I spread my hands. "Go ahead. Take the lead, Jack."

A smile almost breaks through on his face as he shakes his head and heads back to the booth.

It's a start.

⧗ ⧗ ⧗

DANIELA ROCHA IS A GENIUS. She is a genius because things seem to naturally click for her. She is a genius because she has never let her doubt consume her, not once. She is a genius because that's what she pushes herself to be. She is, in many ways, just like Julie Andrews in this sense: practically perfect in every way. But she has a few major flaws.

For one, she tends to take life too seriously. Or, as Paisley likes to say, she has a stick up her ass. This is most clearly evident in the way she settles conflict like her mother does, with a firm hand and a blunt tongue. It's evident in how overprotective she is of her little brother and her friends, how she's constantly weighing the consequences of breaking this rule or that rule more heavily than she weighs the possible rewards. Sometimes it seems like she's already lived once, maybe twice over, and she's trying not to make the same bad decisions this time around. It's easy to forget she's only eighteen.

For another, there have been many instances where she's pushed herself too hard. When she's tried to tackle too many things at once. When she's underestimated her breaking point and gone past it just to prove to herself that she could, to prove that she is more than her bloodline, more than her ancestors. Because Dani is the first in her family to go to college. When she keeps pushing and doesn't stop pushing, it's because she wants so desperately to make history. She wants to clean the slate and show the world that the child of two undocumented immigrants can and will graduate from a top-tier university. She doesn't know the definition of "stop" or "relax" or even "take a break." Because she thinks that if she stops, if she slows down for just a moment, she's not going to make it.

And she never lets herself cry in public. Even when it's best for her, even when it's best for the people around her to know that they're not the only ones breaking down. She didn't cry when she had to bury her childhood dog under the tree in her backyard. She didn't cry when she got waitlisted (at first). She didn't even cry when she was informed that her best friend had died in a car crash.

At least, not until she got home. That's when the dam of emotion she'd erected came crashing down all at once, and her pillow was left to absorb all the tears she'd been holding back, all the pain she had refused to let herself feel until right then. Behind closed doors, she was broken. But to the rest of the world, she was strong. Brave. Untouchable, even by the worst kind of grief.

Her eulogy reflected that strength. It exemplified that bravery to her friends as they wrote their own eulogies. It remained untouched by her true emotion, her own pain, using her grief only as the ink to write what she thought fit some sort of assignment. The eulogy shown to the public was written from the responsibility she felt she had as a friend, nothing more, and nobody expected any different. Because of this, she delivered it in much the same way she delivered her valedictorian speech.

It didn't feel like her valedictorian speech when she was writing it, though. Perhaps it would have hurt more if she had truly poured her heart out. Maybe that's why she kept it so formal. Maybe that's why she kept her real eulogy tucked safely away in her desk drawer.

"The first words Will ever said to me were, 'Can I sit here?' The most unassuming of introductions, if I'm being honest. I was just another freshman in his AP World History class. I was just another girl with an open seat next to her. He could have sat anywhere in that room, but he sat next to me. Of course, I couldn't have known what that seemingly unremarkable incident would blossom into. I couldn't have known that the boy who decided to sit next to me in class would become my best friend. I couldn't have known that he would quickly become the person

I trusted most, the person I'd come to first with news, be it good or bad.

"Will and I were very different people. On the surface, we had the same goals, the same drive to go far, the same hope for the future. We were both perfectly fine spending every Wednesday for a year in the library poring over our chemistry textbooks. I would come to his baseball games, he would come to my volleyball games. He was there when I finally received my acceptance email from Stanford, and I was there when he was accepted to NYU.

"There were always things I envied about him, though. The things that made us so different. See, Will always drew people in. I usually scared them off. I envied his charisma, his charm, that way he could always connect with others the way I never could. At times, it seemed as though I had to work twice as hard as him to reach the same goal.

"The point that I'm trying to make is that he loved people. He always—always—put others before himself. I honestly don't know how he managed to remain so selfless across the years. When he loved something, he loved it with everything he had. It was the same with people, too. If he cared about you, you knew he would do anything and everything for you. I remember I once called him a people pleaser, and without so much as looking up, he simply said, 'And that's a bad thing?'

"He's gone now, but that doesn't mean his spirit is gone. We can't control when Death will greet us. But we can control Life after Death's unwanted visit. We can control how someone is remembered and what they are remembered for.

"I want Will to be remembered for the right reasons. I want him to be remembered for the sheer amount of love he held in his heart. I don't want to focus on what he's unable to do now but what he did when he was alive. I want him to be remembered for all that he did to help me, to help everyone in his life. To help all of you, I'm sure. I want him to be remembered for all that he didn't have to do but chose to do anyway. I want him to be remembered for every smile, every laugh, every hug, every seed of good he planted wherever he went. And under his watch, I hope that together we can watch those seeds flourish. I hope that he can look down from above and see goodness sprouting even in the darkest of places. I hope that he can look down and be proud of what he's left behind."

Cassidy

"okay, i got a map so we can draw everything out," Paisley says.

"That's the kid's menu," Dani points out. "Anyone could have grabbed that."

"Yeah, but no one did." Paisley flattens the menu out on the table. "I think it'd be best to start out by mapping the U.S. and then we'll go to our international destinations." *If* we go to our international destinations. "Because it's too early to plan *everything*."

It hasn't really hit me that we're actually doing this. I've been running on the high of coming up with the idea, and I haven't even thought about the practicality of it. Or the extent.

Jack is the one who voices my thoughts. "Question: how long is this going to take?"

Without looking up, Paisley says, "Answer: don't worry about it."

Jack purses his lips. "I gotta call my mom..."

"I already told you she's on board with this," Mason says.

Jack stares at him. "I... thought you were kidding."

"Why would I be kidding?"

"Because..." He deflates. "Never mind."

Paisley taps a crayon against the menu. "We're starting at Navajo Bridge, yeah?"

"Again," Elijah cuts in, raising a hand, "I strongly object."

"Again, you're strongly a pussy." She looks up, ignoring Elijah's glare. "What's next?"

Dani takes the notebook from Paisley. "From there, we can hit up Horseshoe Bend and Antelope Canyon, can't we?"

"I don't know, someone look it up."

Dani scoffs.

"What? This map doesn't have exact locations. Just northern Arizona's two amenities." Paisley sighs. "It's a kid's map, Dani."

Dani sets her jaw. "I'm aware it's a kid's map," she says sharply. "I'm also aware of middle school geography."

Paisley glances around the table. "Okay, who here has never heard of either Horseshoe Bend or Antelope Canyon? I don't care which."

I raise my hand, and so do Jack, Mason, and Elijah.

"I haven't heard of either," Mason says, grinning. As if that's something to be proud of.

"Not surprising," Elijah mumbles.

Dani squints at all of us in turn. "You live in Arizona."

"Yeah," Jack mutters, "but we can't pull Antelope Canyon out of our asses."

I start to laugh but stifle it as Dani's head whips toward me. "Okay, you know what?" she says. "How about I take care of the map then?"

Paisley's eyes widen, and she defensively pulls the menu closer to her. "Don't touch my map."

Dani gestures to it emphatically. "It's not even a real map!"

In return, Paisley waves it in her face. "Looks real to me."

See, I would say something to get them to stop, but this happens all the time. I'm pretty sure we're all used to it by now.

"Look," Dani says, setting her hands on the table, "if you guys are serious about this, we're going to need a real map."

"There's a 'real map' on the wall, want me to go take it?"

"No, that's not—"

Mason, however, is one step ahead. He marches straight up to our waiter and says, "Hi, can we use that?"

The waiter glances at the map, considers it for a minute, then shrugs. "Sure. We need a new one anyway."

"You've gotta be kidding me," Dani mutters under her breath.

"Well." Paisley blinks. "That's one way to do it."

Elijah's mouth hangs open as Mason takes the map down before heading back over to the booth. "You really just..."

Ignoring him, Mason spreads the map across the table, picking up a crayon and wielding it like a sword. "What's our first stop?"

I quickly take out my phone and open Google, typing *Navajo Bridge* into the search bar. "Navajo Bridge is only a couple hours away," I tell him.

"Okay, uh..." He circles Phoenix on the map with his crayon and then hesitates. "And Navajo Bridge..."

"It's in Marble Canyon."

He looks for it and circles that, too.

I change the locations in my search bar. "From there to Horseshoe Bend is thirty-seven minutes, so Dani's right, we should go there next." I set my phone on the table and turn it toward Mason, who glances at it and then circles the location on the map. Another quick search. "And from there it's a straight shot to Antelope Canyon."

"Where's that?"

I show Mason my phone again, and again, he draws a circle on the map.

Dani suddenly clears her throat. "Jack, what do you think?"

"Uh..." Jack takes the notebook back, flipping through it. "Pikes Peak is next, how are we gonna get there? Should we just go straight from Antelope Canyon?"

Elijah perks up. "Pikes Peak?"

"No," Dani's quick to say, "you aren't getting any weed."

"That's not what I—" Elijah sighs. "Yeah, okay."

I still have Google pulled up on my phone. (Thank God for Google.) "Antelope Canyon to Pikes Peak is about a ten hour drive."

"Great, that's about a full day on the road." Dani doesn't seem too happy about that.

Neither does Jack, to be honest. Then again, I don't think he's too happy to be here in the first place.

"I'll drive," Paisley says.

"No, you'll sleep," Dani tells her.

"I'll drive!" Mason says.

"*No,*" we all yell at once.

"I'll drive." There's an air of finality in the way Dani says this.

Paisley considers it. "Okay. Fine. And if we're both tired?"

"*Me,*" Mason tries again.

"Elijah or Cassidy," Paisley decides. I guess I'm fine with that verdict. "Then Jack—"

"Why am I under—"

"And *then*," Paisley continues, "if all else fails, and everyone else is maimed or otherwise fatally injured, Mason will drive."

Mason grins, dimples showing.

Elijah shakes his head. "That's not a compliment."

Already tuning out of the current conversation, I take the book from Jack, who frowns. I'm starting to get a little excited. "If we do this right, we can fly out of LAX and do a straight shot to Asia."

"Where is all this money coming from?" Jack asks.

"Um..." I press my lips together. "Not important."

He raises an eyebrow. "What?"

"Don't worry about it," I say, casting my eyes down.

"Don't wo... *What?*"

I fall silent, flipping through the pages.

Paisley interjects with: "You know what? I take it back. I'd drive with a broken arm over Mason—"

Jack cuts Paisley off, staring at me. "Why aren't you answering me?"

I see the others awkwardly lower their heads out of the corner of my eye.

"Who's gonna tell him?" Paisley mutters.

"Tell me what?"

"Tell him what?" Mason asks.

Elijah rolls his eyes. "That we're using Will's college funds, dumba— Oh shit."

Silence.

All the color drains from Jack's face. "What?" he asks lowly.

I swallow. I was hoping this wouldn't come up for a while. "Your mom offered."

He sucks in a breath, clenched fists as white as his face. "I need to get some air." He turns to me, jumpy and panicked. "*Move.*"

I quickly scoot over and follow Dani out of the booth. As soon as Jack's up on his feet, he's rushing out the door. I share a look with Dani, who gestures for me to go after him.

"I, uh..." I glance out the window. "I don't think he wants me."

"Maybe not," Dani says, "but he needs someone."

She's right. Of course she's right. But if my time with Jack Dickinson has taught me anything, it's that I am the least qualified person to comfort him. I'm like the oil to his fire. I can only make things worse if I go out there. In one last attempt to get out of this, I say (more like whine), "Can't you work your magic and do what you did before?"

Dani folds her arms. "*Go.* Fix this."

"You heard her," Paisley says through a mouthful of burger.

I stare at Dani, pleading with my eyes, but she doesn't budge. I sigh. I guess this is happening.

I head out the door and find Jack sitting on the curb over by the road. "You okay?" I ask him apprehensively.

He doesn't look up. "Go back inside."

"I'm..." I exhale. "I'm sorry we didn't tell you sooner."

He hesitates, shifting a little on the curb. And then, quietly: "I'm sorry your eggs are getting colder as we speak."

I glance down at my feet. Did I not say this was a bad idea?

"Just go back inside, Cassie," he says gently. "I'll be fine."

Bad idea or not, I can't back down now. "You clearly won't," I say, sitting down on the curb a few feet away from him. I catch him rolling his eyes, but I don't falter. "You know I have to stay here till you talk to me, right?"

"You don't *have* to do anything."

"Yeah. I do." I turn toward him. "Talk to me, Jack. Tell me what you're thinking."

He still doesn't look at me. "I'm thinking I want you to leave me be."

I bite my cheek. "Fine." I don't move. I don't speak. I just sit there. If he's gonna be stubborn, the least I can do is return the favor.

I listen to him breathe for a long, long time. And then, finally, he says, "Why didn't you guys just tell me?"

"Because we knew you wouldn't take it well." I gesture to the curb we're sitting on as exhibit A.

He considers this, grinding his shoe into the asphalt.

"He's not gonna use it, Jack," I say softly. "Why not put it to good use?"

He lets out a breath and rakes both hands through his hair. "But it's not our money to use, Cassie."

"That's one way to think about it." I nod. "Then again,

isn't this up to us now? Aren't we all just trying to figure out what Will would have wanted?"

He swallows. "You know, I can't figure you out."

"Why's that?"

"One minute you know nothing." He finally looks at me, eyes cloudy. Unreadable. "The next it's like you know everything."

"It's because I *don't* know anything. I'm only trying to figure out who he was." I'm only trying to latch onto him and hang on because if I let go I might fall apart.

"Well," Jack says, pushing himself to his feet, "you sure know how to get my ass off the curb." He offers me his hand, and I take it, standing.

I can't help but smile. I've done my job. I actually did it.

"Don't get too cocky," he warns. "I'm just getting hungry."

I shrug. "Still a win."

I catch the ghost of a smile tug at his lips before he turns to head back inside. I follow him to the table, and then it's back to business as usual.

Jack

"fuck!" Elijah's face is green. He is nauseous, pale, and sweating. I don't think I've ever seen him this scared in my life. Hell, I don't think I've ever seen him with such vivid emotion in my life.

Dani, of course, is trying to calm him down. "You okay, Lijah?"

Elijah shakes his head from on top of the railing. "I can't do it. I can't do it, I can't do it, I *can't—*"

"Sure you can!" Mason is probably the most excited out of all of us. Or maybe he isn't. But he sure is acting like it.

Ladies and gentlemen, it is at this moment that something historical happens. Something monumental. Something that may only occur once throughout this entire trip.

Elijah raises his voice.

And with this newfound volume and power, he screams, *"No, I can't!"*

Mason somehow doesn't seem the least bit fazed. "Come on, Lijah. You know you want to."

Elijah's nostrils flare. "I'm gonna be sick..." he mutters.

The worker helping us is trying to reassure him. "It's okay if you want to come—"

Paisley points at him. *"No."*

The worker doesn't like this answer. "Ma'am, with all due respect, if he doesn't want to—"

And that is when Mason pushes Elijah off the railing.

"AAAAAAAAAAAAAAAAAAAAAH!" Elijah's voice fades with his growing descent.

Paisley leans over the railing to observe. "Well, that's one way to get him to man the hell up."

Dani is in shock. *"Mason!"* she scolds.

"What?" he protests. "It's not like he was gonna go!"

The worker is more flustered than Dani (if that's even possible). "Excuse me, sir!"

"I wouldn't," Paisley warns. "He'll push you off, too."

The red flooding up to his face hides the vast amount of freckles. "You guys signed a waiver."

She responds with an unimpressed raise of her brow. "And?"

He sucks in a breath. "Just... You can't sue us." He goes to pull Elijah back up.

Once Elijah's on solid ground again, Mason leans in, waiting for some sort of reaction. "So...?"

Elijah is *fuming*. Or he would be, if he weren't shaking so badly. "You... fucking... *dick*."

"Yeah," Mason agrees, "but you did it!"

Elijah only stares as Mason gets geared up and ready to jump. Within seconds he's gone, shouting with glee all the way down.

Paisley nudges Elijah, silently handing him her flask. He snatches it gratefully and begins to chug.

The worker takes notice. "Ma'am, I think I have to take that."

Paisley looks up. "Why? You want some?"

He opens and closes his mouth.

Mason, meanwhile, is being helped up and over the bridge by a second worker who cares significantly less than the first one, who shall henceforth be known as "Guy With Freckles." He begins to help Paisley into place as Guy With Freckles decides, "Okay. You know what? I think I'm gonna have to ask you guys to leave."

Paisley, already strapped in, glances over at Mason. She shrugs at him. "Well, you heard the guy."

Guy With Freckles' eyes widen as he realizes what she's planning. "Wait, ma'am, *don't—*"

Paisley sprints off the bridge, hoisting herself over the railing and diving down.

He rushes over to the edge, watching her plummet downward. Then, mostly to himself: "How did she manage to break all of our protocols in the span of a minute?"

Honestly? That's just Paisley. She's always been like this,

for as long as I can remember.

I haven't said more than a few words this whole time. I've just been... watching, I guess. Watching the clouds move across the sky, watching the Colorado River beneath our very feet pass by. It's this beautiful, murky turquoise that contrasts so greatly with the orange rock around it. There's another bridge right next to this one; I've decided to look the other direction, as I've found that the jarring metal sort of ruins the view.

I don't think Cassidy is enjoying it nearly as much as I am, though.

Her stance is relaxed enough, but her face is almost pinched, and her foot's tapping against the metal rail.

"You look scared shitless."

She blinks me in, almost jumps at my words. "What? No. I'm fine." Her words are quick and sharp. She's definitely *not* fine.

I sigh, push myself off the railing, and wander over to the other side, where she's standing so nervously. I rest my back against the metal behind me, look over at Cassidy, who's facing the view over the bridge.

"Well," I say, "compared to Elijah, yeah. I guess you're fine."

We both look over at Elijah, who's sitting in the middle of the bridge, trauma sunk into his eyes.

"I... don't think he's gonna be sleeping tonight," I guess.

Cassidy laughs just the tiniest bit. But she's still tapping her foot. She's still nervous.

I tilt my head at her. "What are you looking at right now?"

"Just... the view."

"Yeah, but what specifically? If you're as scared as you seem to be, you must have focused in on something to calm you down." The wind is subtle but present enough to comb itself through her loose curls. "So what is it?"

Cassidy hesitates. "See that cloud over there?"

I turn around and squint to where she's pointing. "I think so."

"Yeah. It looks like a dick."

I emit a small burst of laughter. Because she's not wrong. "Oh my God, it does."

After a minute, she sighs disappointedly and rests her

elbows on the bridge railing. "It's gone."

"Damn," I say, "so it seems."

She glances past me anxiously to see Dani climbing up onto the railing.

I bump her shoulder. "You're next."

She swallows. "Great."

"Come on," I try. "You're not looking forward to this even a little?"

"No, I am." Her hands are still shaking. "I am."

"Okay, stop that," I say with an air of laughter, covering her hands to keep them from shaking. "Now you're making me nervous."

She freezes. Her face shifts to match her expression, which is tense—more so than before. She quickly yanks her hands away. "I'm fine."

I put my hands into an annoyed surrender. "Just trying to help."

She straightens. "I don't need help." And she heads for the railing to jump without another word.

Cassidy has to be bipolar. We were talking about dick clouds not two seconds ago. And now she's mad at me? Is she this way with anyone else? Is she this way with Will? I should ask him.

And I swear to God, I pull my phone out. My phone is in my hand, and I'm about to call Will to ask him about his psychotic girlfriend. But I can't ask him. I can't call him. I can't call my brother.

I put my phone in my pocket and grip the railing. I debate calling him anyway, listening to the voicemail, but the first time I did that, it just put me into more of a panic.

Panic. I'm panicking right now. Or, at least, I'm about to if I don't get a hold of myself quickly.

I glance over. Cassidy has not yet gotten into the harness. She's still discussing something with the worker.

"Okay," he's saying, "now, before we start—"

I head over and step out in front of her. "Nope. Sorry. My turn."

Cassidy frowns, borderline appalled. "Jack, what are you—"

"I'm going." I look at the worker. Not Guy With Freckles.

"She's scared shitless."

Not Guy With Freckles shrugs. "Okay." He begins to put me into the harness.

Cassidy folds her arms. "Asshole," she mutters.

"What?" I put a hand to my ear. "What was that?"

She juts her chin up, a newfound anger rushing through her now steady hands as she cups them around her mouth. "*Assssshoooole.*"

I put a hand over my heart. "Oh," I say. "That hurts me. It really does." I turn wistfully to the railing. "However will I go on now?"

"How about you throw yourself off the bridge?" she suggests. "I think that'll do."

My eyes are sad as they slide back to her. "I think you're right." I climb up and onto the railing, facing her.

Her expression remains apathetic. "You've gotta be joking."

"Cassie," I start. The others have turned to watch. My eyes stay on Cassidy as I finish, "I hope you'll always remember me."

She rolls her eyes. "Go to hell."

Guy With Freckles runs back in, flustered as all hell from dealing with Paisley and Mason. "Sir, you can't do tha—"

But I'm already falling.

And holy *God,* am I glad for it.

It ignites my chest, seeps into my palms, my arms, the straps wound around my ankles—

I'm flying.

I'm fucking flying.

I never want this feeling to end. I never want to live my life without this type of adrenaline rush ever again. If I could feel like this every day, believe me: I would. I don't see how something like this could ever—*ever*—grow old.

The jump comes to a jarring halt, and I'm suspended in midair.

I'm dangling upside down over the water. My hand reaches out to touch the translucent river from three stories up; my feet make a feeble attempt to keep their balance standing on the sky.

I want to capture this moment. I want to be able to keep this feeling, be able to describe it to myself every night.

But I can't.

There's no way I can describe what I'm feeling right now, not in words that will make sense anywhere but in this moment, this suspension.

Fuck, what I wouldn't give for the water to become the sky on command. What I wouldn't offer to have the clouds at my feet.

Maybe this wasn't such a bad idea after all.

Elijah

i am livid. All I wanted to do was get off the bridge that my boyfriend so lovingly decided to shove me off, but I couldn't even do that because after Cassidy jumped, Jack and Dani wanted to go again. (Paisley and Mason wanted to go again, too, but the worker wouldn't let them. I can't imagine why.) I don't know what kind of psychopaths would enjoy free-falling over a canyon so much that they'd want to do it not once but twice. Except I do know. Because those psychopaths are my friends.

Now, however, as I *finally* step off the bridge and onto solid ground, I can start to breathe again. My legs stopped shaking a while ago, but my hands are still trembling a bit. You know how exposure therapy is supposed to help people get over their fears? Well, I call bullshit. I don't think I can even go near a bridge for another ten years, maybe more. And it's all thanks to Mason.

The walk back to the interpretive center isn't very long, but it feels that way because Dani and Jack won't stop recounting their jumps together, and I'm reliving it again. My stomach flipping in midair, the water rushing up at me faster than my eyes could follow—

I thought I was gonna die.

I'm thankful when the parking lot comes into view. The jump must've done something to my bladder because I really have to use the bathroom. I let the others know and head toward the building.

I don't leave when I'm done, though; I stand in front of the mirror, elbows resting on the counter, splashing water on my face. That helps a bit, along with taking deep breaths. Except that all goes out the window when I straighten to see Mason in the mirror. I flinch. "Mason, what the fuck?" Did he really follow me in here?

He doesn't say anything. He just comes up behind me and wraps his arms around my waist.

See, normally, I'm a slut for these types of things. I love affection. But now—

"Mason," I hiss, trying to pry his arms off me. His grip is strong, though. Weirdly strong. "Stop, you can't—"

He nuzzles against my neck, kissing me softly, gently.

"Mason!"

"I'm sorry," he mumbles into my neck.

I'm trying to wriggle out of his grasp, but it's *hard*. He's got me wrapped up in his arms, and I can't budge. "Are you really?" I ask.

His arms tighten around me, and he nods against the crook of my neck.

I give in. There's no escape. "Somehow I don't believe you."

He lifts his head. "Are you really mad at me?"

"Um, yeah, I'm mad at you. You shoved me off a *bridge*, for fuck's sake."

"Yeah, because I wanted you to feel what I felt."

"You hadn't even gone yet!" I whirl around, managing to catch him by surprise and break out of his hold, shoving against his chest.

He recovers, stepping just a bit closer. "Yeah, but I've been bungee jumping before."

"When? When have you been bungee jumping?"

"Like, eighth grade. I thought you knew that."

My brow furrows. "When you went to Rio?"

"Yeah, it was," he says, smiling. I want to poke his dimples, but I can't. I'm mad at him. "See? I did tell you!"

"Rio's crossed off on the list," I say. "That was you? You took him on that trip?"

"Well," he says, "it was a class trip."

"Did you... know about the list?"

He shakes his head. "Nah. He always talked about things on his bucket list like anyone would. But never an actual list."

I'm trying to put the pieces together in my head. "Then why isn't bungee jumping crossed off?"

"Because he never jumped. He was too scared."

There it is. The thing that makes it all fall into place. I let out a long breath. "Oh."

"I just didn't want you to make the same mistake he did," he says. And then, after a beat: "I'm sorry, Holliday."

I don't look at him. I can't look at him. If I look at him, I'm gonna fall for him all over again, and I'll be screwed. "I get it," I say to my feet. "I do."

"So... you forgive me?" I hear the hope in his voice. The excitement. Even the guilt.

I swallow. I look up, look him right in the eye, and say, "No." I look away as soon as possible. And I walk out.

Mason won't stop splashing me. Every time I try to paddle away from him downriver, he catches up to me and flicks water at me with his own paddle.

"Talk to me," he whines.

"No," I say. "Go bother someone else."

And he does. He paddles his kayak closer to the others and splashes Paisley. Bad idea. Paisley fights back, splashing him harder, more violently. Mason's drenched in an instant. Paisley laughs evilly and paddles away.

His next victim is Dani, but she shuts that down before he can even try: "Don't even think about it."

Mason frowns, going to flick water at Cassidy instead. She squeals, mouth open, probably because of how cold the water is. (I can attest.) She laughs, recovering. "Dude!" She quickly tries to paddle away from him.

With a grin now, Mason splashes Jack. Jack whirls around, already lifting his paddle to retort, but he ends up splashing Cassidy instead.

"Oh, really?" she says, hair drenched. "Really?"

"I was aiming for Mason!" Jack protests, but the smile on his face says otherwise.

"Sure you were." Cassidy splashes him back aggressively, and Jack does the same—they're just in a full-on splash war now.

I see my opportunity, and I take it. I paddle as quietly as I can down the river to Mason, dipping my hand in the water and swinging it up as hard as I can to splash him.

Except I may have caught him a tiny bit by surprise because he jolts at the spray of water and loses his balance, falling off his kayak and into the river.

I start to fear for my life when he turns around to say, "You're dead, Holliday."

Death by splashing. Not the worst way to go.

He can't swim very fast, but then again, I can't paddle very fast. My arms are starting to get sore from paddling, but I keep going nonetheless. He's already pushed me off a bridge; there's no limit to what he's capable of. Which is why I'm still going, trying to reach the shore where at least I might be safe from being pulled off my kayak and into the water. I can hear him swimming up behind me, can hear him following me all the way to the shore, where I scramble to get out of my kayak. Except I don't scramble fast enough, apparently, because I've barely made it into the bushes before his arms come around my waist, and we both fall to the ground.

My breathing is heavy as I roll over onto my back, him on top of me. His hair, an even darker black than usual, is dripping onto my face. "You suck," I pant.

He's grinning. And let me just say: he has no *right* being this hot. "Can I kiss you?"

"I feel like you're gonna kiss me even if I say no." Because that's what he does. I say no, and he still wraps me up in his arms. I say no, and he still pushes me off a fucking bridge.

"Nah," is all he says.

I raise my eyebrows. "Bet."

He cocks his head, flinging water droplets onto me in the process. "You gonna say no to me, Holliday?"

I bite back a smile; I can't help it. "I'm gonna say no to you."

He brushes his thumb softly against my chin. "I wish you wouldn't." His eyes drift down to my lips for a moment, then back up to my eyes. And when he starts to climb off me, I just can't bear it.

"Wait," I say. I grab the front of his shirt and yank him back down, pressing my lips to his.

I can't stay mad at him. I just can't. Not when his touch makes me shiver. Not when he makes me melt into the ground, throwing my arms around his neck, bringing him even closer.

Not when he makes it clear, almost certain, that I don't need oxygen when I can just breathe it from his lungs.

Sometimes he gets a little too excited, though. Now is one of those times.

I have to grab his hand as it starts to pull my shirt up from under my life jacket. "Hey, hey, hey," I mumble against his lips. "Public, we're in public."

To compensate, he just kisses me harder, pushing me farther into the dirt at my back. And to be completely honest, I don't give a shit about the dirt or the water or the fact that we're making out behind a bush. Because right here, right now, I wouldn't give up kissing my dumbass boyfriend for the world.

"Well, I guess you guys don't need any help after all."

Though it looks like I might have to.

Mason jumps, glancing up. "Uh..."

Paisley doesn't look mad, at least. She's just standing there, eyebrows raised, stunned eyes darting between Mason and me.

"This isn't... what it..." Mason's trying so hard. I can hear the cogs turning in his brain as both Paisley and I wait to see what kind of excuse he can come up with this time.

Paisley folds her arms, and I think that makes Mason all the more nervous.

"We were..." His forehead creases. "There was a leech?"

Oh my *God*. I don't know what I was expecting, but it wasn't *that*. Though, to be fair, he has come up with worse excuses in the past.

"In his mouth?" Paisley asks, unimpressed.

Mason nods.

She purses her lips. "So you decided to try and get it out..."

"Yeah," Mason says with a bit more confidence, "with CDR."

Paisley's face reflects the disappointment I'm feeling. "CPR?"

"Yeah, that."

I lean my head back on the ground. "Mason..." I say. "No."

"I..." He looks down at me. "Oh, he's still in a... um, state of shock from being leeched."

"Right," Paisley says.

"So I've gotta... uh..." He leans down to kiss me again.

You know, I guess I probably should have seen this coming. "Stop." I shove against his chest. *"Stop."* I manage to push him away, only to see Paisley observing, arms still folded.

"Yeah, Paisley," Mason says. "I think we need some medical assistance."

"Yup. You're right." She pulls her phone out of the Ziploc bag she'd put it into for safekeeping. She presses three times, obviously dialing.

Mason swallows.

She glances up, finger hovering over what I assume to be the call button.

God, this is getting out of hand. "Paisley," I say, "don't—"

"I'm gay," Mason blurts.

Oookay. So this is happening.

"What a shock," Paisley deadpans, sealing her phone back in the bag.

I turn to Mason, eyes wide, then back to Paisley. And I just don't know how to handle this. Shifting my gaze back to Mason, I mutter, "This is not how I thought this would happen."

I thought maybe we'd sit everyone down, and Mason would come out, and we'd break the news that we're dating. I didn't think we'd get caught making out behind a bush by *Paisley*.

"Did you find them?" I hear Dani call from the river.

Paisley looks us over, then calls back over her shoulder, "No, not yet." She gestures for us to hurry up.

"You gonna get up?" I ask Mason, who's still on top of me.

He breathes out, relieved. "Yeah." He stands up, offering his hand to me.

I take it, letting him pull me to my feet and brushing the dirt off my ass.

"Where could they have gone?" Dani's voice again.

Paisley glances back at us. "Uh... Oh! Found 'em!" Then, through her teeth: "Hurry *up*."

She starts walking, and Mason and I follow. Except after he's taken a few steps, he stops. "Hey," he says, "you're not gonna tell anyone about this, are you?"

My heart sinks. Just a little bit. I know he's not ready to come out, I know he's not ready to tell people about us. But sometimes it hurts. Sometimes it feels like he's ashamed to even be with me.

Paisley shoots Mason a look over her shoulder. "No."

Mason's shoulders relax, and he keeps walking.

It takes me a minute, but I do, too. And because I can't help it, because of my stupid, fragile heart, I mutter, "Thank *God* for that."

❧ ❧ ❧

MASON OCAMPO IS SEVERELY UNDERESTIMATED. Since the first grade, he's always looked at life a little differently than other people. He's seen it for its people and how their emotions affect the world rather than their actions.

He has never cared much about knowing the most or being the best. He's only ever cared about existing. In many ways, he is the opposite of Dani Rocha.

Mason doesn't care what others think of his mind, or that he may come across as stupid to the untrained eye. He cares how others see his heart, and this is perhaps the worst flaw someone can have. You can train your mind to become smarter, but you can't tell your heart who to love.

There was a period of time in the early years of high school where Mason was trying to figure himself out. Nobody knew about this, not even his best friend since first grade. (Well, not at first.) People thought he was dating so many girls because he was a ladies man. He certainly did look the part, after all. But after a while, he quickly realized that it wasn't the type of girls he was seeing that was the issue.

He loves Elijah Holliday. From the moment he laid eyes on him he just thought Elijah was so beautiful, so gentle, so deep. He is in many ways the calm to Mason's storm. Sure, he has a bit of a mean streak at times, but Mason has always—*always*—been able to overlook that.

Mason has tried many times to convince himself that coming out isn't that big of a deal, that his parents won't think he's been lying to them for the past seven months, that the boys in the locker room won't suddenly avoid him, even with the prior knowledge that he *has* a boyfriend.

Up until a few weeks ago, there were three people on the whole planet that knew Mason's secret. Now there are two.

"My home life has always centered around work. For as long as I can remember, my parents' careers have always sort of prevented me from having a normal family. I love my family, don't get me wrong. And they love that the Dickinsons, that Will, adopted me into their home when they couldn't give me one.

"I remember when I was really little, and my dad was on a trip, and my mom had her hands full with my older brother, my half brother, who got arrested—but it's okay, he's doing fine now. I know he doesn't like me talking about it, sorry, Thomas—and she realized that one of Dad's employees lived close by, and she had two kids of her own. And I was suddenly there a lot.

"Sometimes Will would just invite me over, and his parents wouldn't even realize that I'd been sleeping in their basement until the next morning. That was kind of my second bedroom when it wasn't being occupied by Paisley.

"So thank you, Mr. and Mrs. Dickinson, for giving me a home away from home. You too, Jack. You and Will really made my childhood feel like childhood.

"But childhood's gone, and so is he. And I guess we have to let him go. Which is really hard for me because I've known him almost my whole life. Well, I've known him long enough that I can't imagine my life without him. It's gonna be really weird to do that from now on."

Paisley

so mason and elijah are dating. I'm not sure how I didn't see it before. They're always together, they're always sneaking off somewhere, and Mason is constantly following Elijah around like a lost puppy. I guess I just thought that was how they acted around each other. I guess I was wrong.

Sure, it's kind of weird realizing that maybe you didn't know your best friends as well as you thought you did. But hey, they sure seemed happy together, and who am I to shit on their joy?

It's just gonna take some processing. Two out of three amigos are in a relationship. With each other. It's a lot. But I'm cool with it. I think.

We've left Horseshoe Bend and are on our way to Antelope Canyon. We are *soaked*. Or, at least, Mason is. The rest of us are a little wet, but not sopping. None of us actually fell *in* the water.

We're in a similar if not identical setup as the drive to Horseshoe Bend. I'm driving; Dani's sitting shotgun; Mason, Elijah, Cassidy, and Jack are sitting behind us.

It's a rather relaxing drive. Well, except for Dani seemingly mad at me for existing.

"Paisley," she finally says, "you look exhausted."

"Thanks."

"You're sure you don't want me to drive?"

"Dude, it's, like, fifteen minutes. I'm fine."

"I'm just saying, you're going to have to let someone else behind the wheel eventually."

No. I don't. It's my bus, and so far I've only had one accident with it. (Two.)

"Meh. Not *really.*"

"*Yes,* really." She sets her hands on the dashboard. "Okay. We're going to establish some rules."

I scoff. "Okay. Rule number one: get that stick out of your ass and toss it out the window."

She rolls her eyes but otherwise ignores me. "If you've been up for longer than sixteen hours, you don't get to drive."

"The Red Bull in the trunk says otherwise."

"The Red Bull in the trunk doesn't get a say in this."

"Yeah, tell that to the Red Bull, I don't think it's gonna be too happy to hear you talking shit."

Dani sighs. "Do you agree to the terms or not?"

I flick the turn signal. "Not yet, I don't. You've only listed one term." I know, a dangerous remark, but if she doesn't shut up, I don't have a chance to agree to anything.

"Okay, fine. Do you agree to the *term?*"

I hesitate. I know she's right. Deep down, I know it's only fair that we each get some sleep. Neither of us are going to be happy with the situation we're in if the only thing keeping us awake is spite.

But more than that, I know that I shouldn't be this obstinate about her driving my van. About anyone driving her, really. (Yes, my van is a "her." Most vessels are. We've been over this.) But it's Dani, right? What's the worst that could happen?

So finally, *finally,* I say, "Okay. Fine. Sixteen hours max." This seems to relax her. So I add in, "But what if I mix the Red Bull with the vodka? I'm basically a sleepless being by then."

"I'd be more worried about your heart stopping at that point."

"Heart only stops when you add a shot or two of espresso. Which I've done before, actually." Not really. I just want to see the look on her face.

She eyes me carefully. "You're kidding, right?"

I give her a sly side smile. My eyes move back to the road, and I continue driving.

Antelope Canyon is *gorgeous.*

I'm not sure what I was expecting. I guess it probably

would have been smart to look it up. But at the same time, I'm glad I didn't. Because now I'm left to stare in awe at the rock around me, shades of rippling red and orange glowing up the walls.

It doesn't look *real*. It baffles me that this is natural, that this came out of the earth's gentle hand. But then again, nothing man-made could aspire to be this surreal, hold this much natural beauty.

Mason, meanwhile, instead of appreciating the canyon's wonder, is running around, periodically trying to climb the walls. The guide is none too happy with him. "Sir— *Sir—*"

Elijah just watches him with dismay. Previously, I always thought that he looked at him like that because, well, it's Elijah and Mason. Their personalities contrast more often than not. But now I'm starting to realize that it's because this is who he's chosen to put up with. This is who he's chosen to date. And now I feel even worse for Elijah every time he sighs at Mason.

Jack, on the other hand, is staring up in awe. There's an ache in my chest at this because the longer I look, the more I realize that in this moment he looks *exactly* like Will. His jaw, nose, even his eyes are similar if not the same. There are, of course, a few key differences. Jack is taller, Will has a broader smile and a slightly deeper voice. But when Jack is looking up at the canyon wall, when he seems small in comparison to the world around him, it's almost like Will has come back for a fleeting moment to paint his expression onto his little brother's face.

Cassidy is in a similar position. She actually seems to be enjoying herself; I haven't seen her this relaxed in a while. It's almost as if the vibrant colors have lifted a weight off her shoulders.

Dani, however, is quite the opposite. She's tense as ever, more nervous than usual, looking as though the canyon might collapse in on her at any given moment.

"What are you doing?"

Dani looks over her shoulder at my question. "What do you mean, what am I doing? I'm walking."

"You look like you're critiquing the fucking rock." Seriously: all she needs is a clipboard and a pencil skirt to replace her shorts. "Just enjoy it, Jesus."

She scoffs. "I am. It's beautiful, for God's sake."

Wow.

"Okay," I say finally. "Lean against that wall."

Dani stops. "Why?"

"What? Don't trust me?"

"Not in the least."

I smile at the sky, almost proud of myself. "All right," I say, bringing my gaze back down. "You said you were enjoying this, right?"

She eyes me quizzically. She's always been confused by me; never like this, though. "Yeah."

"Prove it," I say simply. "Just lean against the wall and look up."

She looks over at the guide. He's leading the group farther and farther away. She glances back at me for another second before finally leaning against the wall behind her and looking up.

I place my weight against the wall opposite her, doing the same lean but watching Dani rather than the sky above as she lets out a relieved sigh. Her shoulders visibly relax at the wall's gentle touch.

I hesitate before releasing my next words. "If we're gonna do this" —I gesture to the canyon, gesture to us, gesture to the group that has already disappeared— "you're gonna have to not be 'Dani Rocha: Stanford-bound valedictorian, out for Paisley Joplin's blood.'"

She kind of laughs at this, looking back down at me. "I am pretty stuck-up, aren't I?"

Yes. "You could be worse."

"Eh." She looks back up at the sky. "Honestly?" She sighs again. "I'm scared. I don't know what comes next. After high school, after... *this.*"

I exhale. "Well," I begin, "you'll go to a good school, marry a guy from Harvard who's even more uptight than you are. You'll work for... I don't know... fucking... Google or some shit, have two kids, Brittany and Noah. Your husband will have his wits and his daddy's money, and you'll turn out just fine."

She looks uneasy at this.

"Or maybe you won't," I finish. "But at least you have options. I think personally it'd be a lot more terrifying if you didn't get a say in any of it."

"What, like you?"

I'm silent at this. But yeah. Like me. Like the chick who's currently living out of her van because her conservative mother doesn't believe she's a lesbian.

(Dani isn't aware of this. None of them are. There was only one person who knew.)

After a moment, Dani scrunches her face up. "Brittany?" she repeats. "Really? Who do you think I am, a white suburban mom named Karen?"

"Well," I say with a smile, "it was your husband's dead mother. So you caved."

She laughs and pushes herself off the wall. "If my husband's dead mother were named Brittany, I never would've married him." I grin as she walks off to find the tour group.

I don't. Why? I don't know. I'm just not feeling it. Will this bite me in the ass later? Yeah. Probably.

Oh well.

I move my focus around the canyon, trying so desperately to see it through Will's eyes. I knew him well. I will confidently say that. But some of these places on the bucket list—I have to admit, they confused me. Like this one. Why would he want to come here, of all places? This place is obviously stunning, the way the light glides off it so perfectly, turns the rock into liquid, the viewer into an insignificant sea creature bumbling in the midst of its vast ocean.

But what made *Will* want to come here? And why would he put off seeing it for so long?

Dani

i've been to colorado before, back when I was really young. I remember the mountains being a lot bigger, but maybe that's just because I used to be a lot smaller. That's not to say they're not still gorgeous; they are. What I wouldn't give to strap on a pair of hiking boots and spend a day climbing up the one looming in front of me now.

Then again, that'd be practically impossible, given the altitude. Not to mention my lack of training. And my current state.

I drove all the way here from Antelope Canyon, through the night, not stopping once. Needless to say, I'm a bit tired. It did give the others a chance to sleep, though. I glance back over my shoulder to see Mason, Jack, Cassidy, and Elijah all passed out, sitting up. Paisley is slouched down in the seat beside me. And despite this being quite possibly the most peace and quiet I'll manage to get on this trip, it's time for them to wake up.

I lay on the horn.

Paisley jolts up. "*Fuck!*"

"Oh, sorry," I say gently. "Didn't mean to do that." Yes, I did.

Paisley glares at me, sitting up and leaning back against the seat.

"We're here," I say, turning around to see the others blinking the sleep out of their eyes.

Mason leans over and rests his arms on the divider, craning his neck to see out the front window. I catch the look of wonder on his face, the white-tipped peaks reflected in his brown eyes. "No, we're not," he says. "The mountain's all the way up there."

I have to laugh at that. "Mason, I pulled over. We still have to pay to drive up."

"Oh," Paisley says, arching her back to stretch it out. "Then it's my turn." She looks over at me. "Move."

I'm not about to fight her on this one. It is her bus, after all, and I've already been up for nearly sixteen hours. I'm not one to violate my own rules. I climb out of the van and go around to the passenger side while Paisley slides into the driver's seat.

I pull the door closed just as Paisley starts cooing to the steering wheel, "Hi, you stupid slut. You miss me?"

I try not to judge other people's relationships, but frankly, the one Paisley has with her van is a bit unsettling.

Paisley puts it in drive, pulls out of the spot, and drives up to the tollgate. It's fifteen dollars for each of us, and then we're on our way. We have a long drive ahead of us, but there's no question it's going to be worth it.

And, of course, not two minutes into said drive, Mason asks, "Are we there yet?"

I close my eyes slowly before turning around to look at him. "You *can't* be serious. It's a fucking mountain, Mason."

"I'm kidding, I'm kidding!" I'm almost satisfied until a beat later, he says, "Not really. How much longer? I need to pee."

Elijah doesn't take his eyes off the scenery to say, "You didn't think to mention that before we started driving up the mountain?"

"I thought there would be rest stops!"

"That *was* our rest stop!" I tell him, exasperated, though it occurs to me that I don't actually know if there are more rest stops.

"Just pee in that bottle," Jack says, gesturing to a discarded plastic water bottle on the floor.

Cassidy's eyes widen. "*Jack!*"

"What?"

"Hey," Paisley snaps, "no pissing in my van!"

I huff, turning back around to look out the window. "Can we just, you know, appreciate the view for a minute?" I mean, it's just so *green*. We don't get that in Arizona. Well, we do. Just not to this extent. The road is lined with trees, forming a slight opening for the mountain range to peek through. The morning sun bathes the landscape in soft light, and I just want to capture it. So I take out my camera and snap a couple photos.

The silence that my remark has kindled doesn't last nearly as long as I want it to.

The thing that breaks it is the faint sound of what I'm desperately hoping isn't pee landing in a bottle.

"*Mason!*" Elijah yells.

Cassidy throws her hands up, turning away from Mason and toward Jack. "You *had* to suggest it!"

Jack doesn't seem fazed. "Would you rather he complain about it the entire drive up?"

"I'd prefer anything to *that*," Cassidy says, nose wrinkling.

"Uh..." Mason holds up the bottle, now filled about a fourth of the way with his urine. "What do I do with this?"

"Chuck it out the window," Elijah says absently.

"Hey, no." Paisley glances in the rearview mirror. "*No!* It'll get on the walls and ruin the paint!"

I turn to her. "*That's* what you're worried about?"

"I don't care what you do with it, just get it out of here," Cassidy says, still trying not to look at it.

"Come on, Cassie," Jack says, smirking, "it's not so bad. See, if you look closely, it really isn't all that yellow. I mean, it's basically water at this point."

Cassidy gags. "I'm gonna be sick."

"Not in the bus," Paisley calls over her shoulder. "*Not in the bus.*"

"I can't control where the vomit goes, Paisley."

"Bullshit, I've vomited lots of times."

"Not surprising," I mutter.

Paisley shoots me a glare. "*My point being* there is a magical, minute amount of time between 'I feel sick' and '*bleh*' that you use running to the most convenient place to put the puke." She turns over her shoulder to look at Cassidy. "Use it wisely." Then she focuses back on the road.

"Do you have a bag at least?" Jack asks Paisley. "Because I feel like she's gonna use that magical time to aim at me."

Cassidy narrows her eyes at him. "I might if you don't *shut up.*"

His eyes widen in mock terror. "Paisley? Bag. Now."

Cassidy smacks him on the arm.

Mason, who's been holding the bottle up this whole time, says, "I still don't know what to do with th—"

Elijah turns, grabs the bottle by the lid, and throws it out the open window.

"You little *shit!*" Paisley shouts.

Elijah isn't bothered. He just turns back to the window, leg tucked up against the wall.

Paisley goes on for a little while, eyes darting from the road to the mirror and back, yelling at Elijah about her bus as he rests his chin on his hand, bored. Frankly, they're both idiots. I mean, we're supposed to be enjoying the drive up a fourteener, not bickering about *pee* of all things.

"There is *piss* on the side of my *bus!*"

Elijah rolls his eyes. "Oh, come on, it didn't touch the bus."

His response only fuels Paisley's fire as she keeps shouting about paint and "her wife" (her van) and the money it'd take to fix it. "You know what? You should just go out and clean the piss yourself, you fucking piss thrower, you—"

Mason

"whoa," **is about the only thing** I can come up with. I've seen mountains before. I've even hiked a couple. But each one, I've found, holds its own respective beauty.

We've all stepped out of the van to take a look.

See, I've never understood the "purple mountain majesty" line we so casually throw around here in the U.S. But the mountains are purple. They're a stunning shade of it, one I've only seen at daybreak.

The rocks are a faded coral; the view is coated with a vast amount of fog unless you angle yourself just right.

Everyone seems to have forgotten their vendetta long enough to stop and look around.

"Elijah," Paisley breathes, "you're still dead to me."

Never mind.

Elijah sighs at her sentiment. "I know."

They both walk off to enjoy the scenery. I don't blame them. There's just so much to see.

Though we hit the tree line a while back, a few pines are still visible if I look down the mountain. I'm close to going and taking a closer look, but then I spot Elijah sitting on a rock. He's not too far from the edge, which both shocks and delights me.

Though I guess it's generous to call it an edge. Either way, you could easily slip and slide down the mountain a good few feet before catching yourself. There's a chance that I speak from experience.

I come up behind him. "What are you doing?"

He jumps. "Gah—" He realizes it's only me and relaxes. "Oh. Hi."

I sit down next to him. Though he doesn't actually answer my question, I can still see what he's doing. He's drawing in his sketchbook, pencil whispering lines gently over the pages, sketching recklessly yet delicately on one page and writing little notes to himself on the other.

I love watching him draw.

I put my chin on his shoulder to get a better look. After a hesitant moment, he tilts his head slightly to the side so that it knocks briefly into mine before going back to its previous position hunched over his art.

Guess he's not mad at me anymore.

My eyes follow his hand movements, darting back and forth between writing, scribbling, and methodical drawing. The more I watch, the more I settle into a subconscious daze.

I sigh contentedly and wind my arms around his waist.

He ceases working at once. "Mason, public."

"Oh. Right." I slip away and sit back. It's easy to forget sometimes, and it's never not annoying.

The more he sketches, the more I see it start to come together.

"Is that Will?" I ask him.

He nods. The deeper into his art he sinks, the less vocal he becomes.

I smile. It's Will's neck and face, but his head is split open, and instead of the top part there lies what looks to be the sun, poking out from the broken pieces.

"It looks *really* cool."

Elijah stops drawing long enough to give me a weird look. "I literally just started sketching, like, yesterday."

"I know," I tell him. "But it's still a lot more than I can do."

He considers this and goes back to drawing. And I go back to watching. I swear to God, I could do this all day.

"I'm gonna be *sick—*"

My head darts up to find the source of the yell, pulling me away from Elijah's work. It was Cassidy, running toward the Summit House.

I see Paisley talking to Jack not too far from where Cassidy was a moment ago. "Your turn," she's saying.

He seems taken aback, even from this far away. "What?"

"I have to deal with my piss-ridden van. Elijah couldn't

give two flying fucks." True. He's still sketching like nothing's happened. "Mason has already dealt with my vomit more than enough times." Also true. Don't want to talk about it. "And Dani is nowhere to be found." Dani repeatedly told us that she was going down a little farther to take pictures of the scenery.

Paisley pokes Jack in the chest. "*Your* turn."

Jack emits a loud groan before caving and following Cassidy into the Summit House.

Elijah still hasn't looked up. "This isn't gonna end well."

I bite back a smile. "Nope." No, it will not.

Cassidy

i didn't think i'd be spending my time on top of Pikes Peak upchucking into a toilet at the back of the gift shop, but hey. I guess this trip is just full of surprises. The only other time I've felt like this was when I was out of school for a week in seventh grade because of the flu. And even then, my head didn't pound so much.

I grimace at the acidic taste in my mouth and sit on the floor, wiping the tears out of my eyes. My stomach is still rolling, but I feel a little better after emptying it.

Just as I close my eyes, fingers to my temples, there comes a knock at the door. "You okay in there?"

Shit. Of course it's Jack. Why does it have to be him? Who was the genius who decided, out of everyone out there on the peak, that *Jack* should be the one to come check on me? Honestly, he's the last person I want to see me like this.

"*No*," I tell him, voice hoarse. I mean, does it sound like I'm okay?

I hear him muttering incoherently through the door. And then: "Do you need anything?"

I'm about to respond, tell him to leave me be, but my stomach does a backflip just then, and I'm back up and over the toilet bowl, retching.

Jack groans. "Why me?" he says, probably to himself. I'm wondering the same thing. He raises his voice to say, "Cassie—"

But I cut him off with, "Go away, Jack."

"I'm coming in."

I sit up, lifting my head from the toilet. "No, no—"

But he's already opening the door. He steps in, grimacing a little at the smell, and hands me a bottle of water.

Given the events that occurred not too long ago on the drive up here, I regard the bottle warily.

Jack rolls his eyes. "It isn't Mason's piss, if that's what you're worried about."

I'm not worried about it, per se. I'm just a little scarred. But hey, I'll take anything to help me not feel like shit, so I take it from him, shifting to lean against the bathroom wall beside the toilet. "Thanks."

"Small sips," he tells me, crouching down. "Or, actually, I'm not sure. I'm using my knowledge of hungover Paisley to deal with you."

I snort halfheartedly. "So this is what that feels like?"

"It feels a little worse than this, trust me."

I sigh. "I'll take your word for it." I take a tentative sip from the bottle.

Jack studies me a moment. "Headache?"

I nod, feeling my head pound again in response.

"I think I saw some Advil in the gift shop. Want me to get some?"

Okay, what is this? Why is he being so nice to me? I eye him carefully, but he seems pretty genuine. So I bite my cheek and look down at the bottle in my hands, letting out a tiny, "Yeah."

He nods, stands, and heads out of the bathroom, leaving the door wide open. His voice drifts back to me, spouting something about altitude sickness.

"Oh," I hear Paisley say. "And here I was worried she was hungover."

"Nah, that's your bit."

I lean my head against the wall. So that's what this is. Altitude sickness. I guess that makes sense. It sucks, that's for sure. And one Google search tells me these symptoms could last a couple days, and that just makes me groan. I've stuffed my phone back into my pocket and am rubbing my temples again when Jack returns with a thing of Advil.

"Hey," he says, crouching down once again, "we're gonna go."

Go? Go as in leave the mountain? As much as I want to just lie down and take a nap, I know we need to make the most out of this. And that means not driving all the way up here only to drive back down not ten minutes later. "But we just got here," I say.

"Yeah, well." Jack shrugs. "Talked to an employee outside, said the best thing to do was not to go any higher. Figure the opposite of that is going back down."

God, way to make me feel guilty. I glance out the door where I know Paisley must be waiting for us. "But I don't wanna cut your guys' time sh—" I don't get to finish because my stomach has suddenly decided it doesn't want to cooperate. I roll back around to grab the toilet and once again heave my guts out.

And I'm not expecting it, but after a second, I feel Jack holding my hair up out of my face.

Breathing heavily, I lean away from the toilet, wiping my mouth on my arm. Jack drops my hair, and I breathe out, hand on my stomach. "Yeah, okay."

Jack brushes his hands off like they're dirty. "Paisley's rounding up the others. You know where the van is when you're ready to go." He stands and heads out the door.

It takes me a minute, but eventually, I stand, too.

I guess I'm glad it was Jack who came to my rescue—he seemed like he knew what he was doing. Though I'm pretty sure any one of them would have held my hair back for me.

And that's what hits me as I flush the toilet and make my way out of the building: if I had come here with Will, if I had gotten the chance to, he would've been the one holding my hair back. He would've been the one comforting me, getting me water and Advil from the gift shop. He would've been *there*.

He should be here. But he's not.

And he'll never get to be here.

Jack

the drive back down the mountain is a lot shorter than the drive up. I remember reading something when I was younger that this usually seems to be the case because when you drive up, you're taking in a shit ton of new scenery. The drive back, you've seen it all, so your mind just kind of skips over it.

Dani turns around to face the rest of us. "It's an eleven and a half hour drive to Zion from here."

Cassidy, whose head is currently in Elijah's lap for lack of space for her to fully lie down, is none too happy about this. "*No...*" she moans.

I have to admit, I'm feeling pretty bad for her. Even though I'm still pissy about being the one chosen to hold her hair back while she hurled her guts into the toilet. "Really got the short end of the straw, didn't you?" I say, more so to my book than to her.

Cassidy lets out another groan before kicking me. Elijah got her head; I got her feet.

I keep reading.

"What happened to not-asshole Jack?"

Not sure. Maybe it was something about the bathroom floor or the fact that she's been complaining about her stomach the entire ride down. "That's really the best you could come up with? Even with her head in a toilet, Paisley could have ended me."

"Years of training before I was able to do that," Paisley says to the disappearing parking lot. "*Years.*"

"Well, I'm sorry that my head is pounding so hard I can barely think," Cassidy snaps.

"Maybe more drinking water, less freaking out over some guy's piss, and you wouldn't be in this situation."

"Hey!" Mason protests.

Cassidy sits up in a huff, yanks my book out of my hand, and begins to smack me with it.

Suddenly, the entire bus is in an uproar: Dani telling us to stop being children, Paisley telling us that we're "distracting the driver," Mason telling us to break it up, me trying to block Cassidy's attacks, and Elijah, my new favorite, just sighing.

"Nope," he says, putting his arms around her and forcing her back down. "No."

Cassidy pouts and folds her arms as I take my book back. I scoot away from her and continue reading.

It's a fairly silent drive from there. The only voice is the one on Paisley's phone telling her to turn right every once in a while. And even that shuts off once we hit the interstate.

"What's even at Zion National Park?" Mason speaks up after a good hour or two.

We all look at each other, not because we have been once again graced by Mason's stupidity, but because none of us know the answer. To be fair, I'd only kind of heard about it before reading it in Will's journal.

Dani, however, rolls her eyes. "God, Mason," she chastises. "It's a nature preserve in a cliff dwelling."

"Oh," he says. "Okay."

"We can drive through the canyon, but I'm pretty sure Will would have wanted the full hiking experience."

At this, my gaze naturally slides over to Cassidy, whose eyes have become huge.

"So who's gonna stay behind with *that?*" I ask, nodding to her.

"I can," offers Elijah.

"*Thank* you." Cassidy glances up and flips me off.

I just sigh at her finger. "Right back at you." And I'm looking back down at my book.

It is a *relief* once we get to our first hotel.

We have been driving virtually nonstop since Arizona. Do you know what that can do to your stomach?

Well, Cassidy does. She's curled into Elijah, who looks

none too happy about his current position as her crutch.

"Okay," Dani says once we're in the lobby, "so I think we should split up the rooms by gender."

Mason and Elijah exchange a glance.

"What is this, grade school?" Paisley laughs at Dani. "I don't want to share a room with you."

"All the more reason."

Paisley stares over at me like I'm a camera and she's in a mockumentary.

Dani shoulders her purse. "I'll go check us in."

"*I'll go check us in,*" Paisley mocks.

Dani stops to give her a look. "Really?"

Paisley sighs. "And the stick is back in." She follows Dani.

I swear to God those two are married.

We gather our keys and head up to our respective rooms: Dani, Cassie, and Paisley in one room; Elijah, Mason, and me in the other.

I call first shower (even though it's probably a better idea if Mason, the one who fell into a river the day before, showered first).

The complimentary shampoo and body wash are bound to the wall in large dispensers. I find myself disappointed that they aren't in the tiny travel bottles.

My heart sinks as I realize the reason behind my dismay.

"Why are you always taking those?"

Will smiles down at me, all twelve years of him. "Because, Jack. You can go home, and you'll smell like vacation. Well, those of us who actually shower will."

My breath hitches at the memory, and I adjust the shower water to make it warmer. My hands come to rake through my hair like they usually do when I'm nervous. Or stressed. Or, as Paisley has previously noted, pissy.

I'm done washing fairly quickly. I step out and wrap a towel around my waist; I wipe away the condensation, stare into the mirror.

To make it perfectly clear, I do *not* look like Will Dickinson. Or, at least, I didn't used to. But now it seems that he's taken up residence in my face, warping the bones in my structure to fit his, moving away the normalcy in my eyes to fill the grief in his.

People always say that we look alike. I never saw it until after he was gone.

My elbows hit the counter as my head comes into my hands with a heavy sigh.

Bonk!

My head shoots up at the noise, and I swing the bathroom door open with a frown. Elijah is on the bed, eyes slightly wider than normal, carefully studying my book in his hands.

"Uh," I drag. "What..." My voice trails off as Mason comes up off the floor, poking his head out from behind the other mattress.

I hesitate. "You good, Mason?"

He nods energetically. Elijah refuses to meet my eye.

"Okay..." I shut the door. That was weird. Even for them.

Thankfully, it's enough to pull me out of my thoughts and into my sweatpants.

I step out after brushing my teeth. Elijah now has his sketchbook; Mason is now pulling his toiletries out of his bag. I'm honestly shocked he remembered them.

"Bathroom's open," I tell him, walking over to the window. On my way, I stop in front of Elijah's bed. "Enjoy my book?"

He doesn't look up. "Mhm," he says tightly. "Yeah. Really good."

"Great." I take the book off the bed and keep moving. "Enjoy your shower?"

"Oh yeah." I sit up on the window sill and open my book, continuing where I left off.

I get the feeling it's going to be a long night.

Elijah

Cassidy is not the worst person to be stuck in a van with. She's quiet. She lets me sketch. Even though I know she'd rather be hiking (believe me, I would, too), the peace and quiet is a little refreshing after being on the road with the others the entire morning.

I'm surprised I'm not more tired. I don't even know when I went to sleep last night; all I know is that it was way too late. But I have this problem where if I'm in the zone, it's hard to get out of it. Even to do something as vital as sleep. I know my exhaustion will hit me eventually, but for now I've got Surfaces on shuffle, my feet are propped up on the seat back, my sketchbook is balancing on my thighs. I'm content. At this point, after having spent most of the night on them, I'm just touching up my various pages of pencil sketches, all different versions of the same thing, trying to decide if I like the concept enough to use it for my project. I like it, but would Will? I'm not really sure.

"Elijah..."

I glance up to see Cassidy sitting up, leaning over my shoulder to see what's on the page. "What?" I ask.

She shakes her head. "No, it's just... Wow."

My eyes skate over the sketch one more time. It's my most recent one, the most detailed of them all. I'm still not sure about the whole sun thing. That's just how he always felt to me—he felt like the sun. And maybe that's just because a lot of the time I feel... separate from everyone else, from the earth, like any second gravity would just let go of me, and Will was the only thing that could ground me. He centered me. He kept me in orbit. And now... Well, you know.

"Do you think I should change anything?" I ask Cassidy.

"No, I think it's perfect."

Perfect. God. "It's far from perfect," I tell her. "It's just a sketch."

"Still." She rests her chin on her hands, eyes latched onto the sketch. "You got him so perfectly. It feels like him."

I study her. The curled strand of hair falling in her face. The gleam in her eye. The something else that's so obviously buried inside. "How are you doing?" I ask, setting my book down.

She sits back, trance between her and the sketch broken. "Oh, a lot better, actually. My head doesn't hurt so—"

"That's not what I'm talking about."

Her mouth closes; her eyes fall to the floor. "Oh." And then, with a strained smile, she looks back up at me. "You know how I'm doing, Lijah. Do you really have to ask?"

I twist so I can lie fully horizontal across the seat. "No. I don't. But I'm trying to be a good person, on the off chance you want to talk about it."

"I don't."

"I figured."

I don't blame her. She hasn't really brought up the accident, at least with me, since the day it happened. Since she showed up on my porch, shaking and teary-eyed. She didn't actually talk about it then, either. I just held her until her sobs softened to whimpers, until she was all out of tears.

It was a good distraction for me, too. Because that's my poison: distractions. I've always found that keeping things bottled up and fighting emotion with pot is a lot easier than facing your problems head on.

Speaking of. I dig one of my last pocket joints out, along with my lighter. I offer it to Cassidy before I take a hit, knowing full well she won't take it. And then I inhale, close my eyes, and exhale.

"Should you be smoking in here?"

"Paisley doesn't mind." I look at her. "But I won't. You know, if it makes you uncomfortable."

"No, no, it's okay," she says, leaning back again. "I just wish I were out there with the others." Her eyes dart back to me. "No offense."

"None taken." I take another drag, tap my finger against the side of the joint. "You know," I say slowly, "if I didn't fear for my life, I would say we should drive up the canyon and go exploring."

She raises her eyebrows. "I don't feel like puking for once."

"But you know if Paisley found out..."

"Yeah. Yeah, you're right." She clasps her hands, looks down, presses her lips together.

"But..." I trail off, glancing at the front of the bus. "Paisley *is* the one who left the keys in the ignition."

"That's very true."

"I mean, she was basically *asking* for us to drive it."

"Yeah." Cassidy bites back a grin. "Why else would she leave the keys?"

"I have no fucking clue." I sit up. I look at her. And as soon as our eyes lock, we're both rushing to the front of the bus. I quickly ash my joint, sticking it in a discarded empty bottle for the time being, and head around to the driver's side.

I've never been behind the wheel of Paisley's bus. I've never had the privilege—nay, the honor. But right now I feel a giddy excitement at the thought of driving it. Not to mention driving it without Paisley in the backseat. Would she kill me if she knew I drove it? Probably. If she knew I drove it *high?* Definitely.

I turn to Cassidy, who's putting on her seatbelt and grinning. That's the thing about her. She's a lot more fun than people usually give her credit for. I would say I only spend so much time with her because we live across the street from each other, but that's not true. There are nights when she'll text me, and we'll hop in her Mini and just drive. And honestly? Those nights have been some of my favorites.

It's been a while since we've done anything like that, though. Neither of us have wanted to since Will died.

So this is nice. To say the least.

"This probably isn't the best idea," she tells me, but she's still grinning.

I run my hand over the wheel, grin back at her, before putting the van in drive. "I know." And with that, I pull out of the parking lot.

Paisley

i didn't expect zion to be this stunning.

And yeah, that seems to be a recurring theme throughout this trip. For me, at least. I should learn to expect the unexpected.

However, nothing can prepare me for how stubborn Dani Rocha can be when it comes to skincare.

"Dani," I try to tell her a little over two-thirds of the way through our hike, "you really should put some of this on." I hold up a bottle of SPF 50 that I've already put on.

But alas, just like all the other times I've suggested this, she simply shakes her head. "I'm good. I don't really burn all that much."

I only find myself able to stare. "We're spending the whole day out in the sun, dude. Might want to think about it."

"I'm telling you," she insists, "I rarely get sunburned. Even when I'm out all day. It's a genetic thing." Remind me again how she got into *Stanford?*

"Rarely's not never."

She shrugs and sits down on a nearby boulder, uncapping her water bottle and taking a long sip.

I give up. "Don't say I didn't warn you." I hand the sunscreen to Jack, who's only slightly tanner than I am. He slathers some on and hands it to Mason who, after he's done, tries to offer it to Dani one more time.

After a minute, he catches up to me. "Here," he says, handing me the sunblock.

"She didn't put any on?" But I already know the answer. He shakes his head.

I sigh, taking the bottle. "She better pray we have aloe in the van." We do. I just want her to overhear and start to panic.

I look up and holy God.

It's like Antelope Canyon all over again. We're so small compared to the rest of the place. I'm so insignificant compared to the walls towering over us, in contrast to the trees jutting up and into the small crack that leads to the sky.

There's water flowing consistently throughout the hike, but with each new area, with each turn around the bend, the water becomes a different color. Sometimes it's murky and beige, other times it's crystal clear. There have even been some instances of a shimmering turquoise.

At one point, I see Jack off ahead of the rest of us, standing on a rock, taking it all in. Or, he would be, if he didn't look borderline miserable.

"You look like shit."

"Thank you," he replies, annoyed.

"No, really," I tell him, stepping up on the rock with him. "You do. Did you sleep last night?"

He takes a minute before answering. "That's why we were at the hotel, right?"

I give him an annoyed scowl.

He finally rolls his eyes. "No. I didn't." Called it. What did I say?

I drop my hands. "So why did you come hiking with us, you dumb fuck?"

"Because, I mean... We're doing this for Will, right? And besides, you would have been on my ass about it if I wussed out."

"No," I say earnestly. "I wouldn't have."

He sighs at this, waving away my concerns. "I'll sleep later."

"Wasn't my question."

I have an idea of why he came with us. I'm almost tempted to vocalize it. But I know that would be a terrible idea. I shouldn't tell him the real reason he came with us, or at least a large chunk of the real reason. It'll just explode into a huge fight, and we definitely can't have th—

"You just wanted to get away from Cassidy."

Wow. Can't keep my big mouth shut for five minutes. Way to go, Paisley.

He takes a good while to respond. The sudden size increase in his averted eyes tells me I've got him. "No..." he insists quietly.

"It's really comical." All right, so I'm blabbering now.

I'm taking this bit, and I'm running with it. "She's like this tiny chihuahua, and you're scared to death of her."

Now he's getting defensive. "I'm not scare—"

"It's like when Mason first met Elijah," I laugh. "And now look at them." *And now look at them.* They're dating. Mason was a blubbering idiot around Elijah when they first met. That was probably because he was attracted to him.

Oh my God.

Nope. Uh-uh. No, no, no. *No.*

We're gonna save this for a later date. Because *no.*

Unless...

No.

Jack yet again rolls his eyes at my accusation. "You don't know what you're talking about."

"Guys." Dani jogs up to us, a little breathless. "You left me alone with Mason."

I don't tear my eyes away from Jack as I say, "Mason, knock it off."

I hear a tiny, "Okay." I want to picture his foot halfway through a crack in the rock that could send him plummeting with one wrong step. But I don't dare look to confirm this.

Dani gives a relaxed huff. "What did I miss?"

And because I'm an asshole, I say, "Apparently, Jack hasn't been sleeping."

Jack's eyes widen accusingly. "Paisley, what the fuck?"

Dani looks over, gaze concerned, sigh disappointed. "Jack..."

"Dani, you fucking hypocrite," he argues, "you wouldn't even put on sunscreen."

"He's got a point," I agree.

She shifts her weight. "Yeah, well, sleep is important."

"So is not getting skin cancer," I tell her, "but here we are."

"You're not going to let me forget that, are you?"

"I won't have to in a little bit. You know..." I poke her skin. "You're already starting to look a little pink."

"Yeah," Mason agrees, jogging over to join the discussion, "she's getting a little tan, too."

Dani blinks. Slowly. "Mason. I'm Mexican."

"Oh. Right." He walks off.

"Mason— God, is this what Elijah always has to deal with?"

I bite back my laughter. "Oh, you have no idea."

She mutters a quick, "*Pobrecito*," before following him.

Jack folds his arms, watching them go. "She has a long day ahead of her."

"Yeah." I grin. "I'm gonna make it longer."

He only sighs.

We arrive in another area of the hike, now trekking up the canyon even deeper into the rock. I've never felt so comfortable with feeling trapped. The rock feels like a warm blanket around us.

Mason is also enjoying himself, both because of the scenery and because he's jumping over various rocks, playing some game of *every safe place to step is lava* with himself.

"*Mason!*" Dani is trying so hard to keep up with him. I almost feel bad for her.

Almost.

"Hey, Mason," I say, "I'll give you a dollar if you jump into that pond."

He doesn't hesitate to shrug his shirt off.

Dani's eyes widen. "No, that's not— You know what, it's not worth it."

Okay. Challenge accepted. "I'll make it five if you skinny dip."

Mason strongly considers it.

Dani's nostrils flare. "Mason, I swear to God if you take your clothes off—"

"Dani," he protests, "it's five bucks!"

Jack is at least trying to be helpful. "Honestly, you've just got to offer him more money to keep his clothes on." Damn him, he figured it out.

Dani shakes her head and reaches into her wallet. "Here's a twenty. You want it?"

Mason's eyes widen. The way he's looking at it, it's as though he's never seen that much money in his life.

"Keep your goddamn underwear on."

Mason makes a grab for the money. Dani steps away.

"Put your shirt on first," she orders.

I'm just sitting back now, thoroughly entertained.

"You're mean," Jack tells me.

"I'm bored," I counter. "You got any better ideas?"

Mason puts his shirt back on and looks at Dani, who sighs. "Fine," she grumbles. "Here." She hands him the money. He gladly takes it and jogs off.

We follow him out of the area, back out into the open. We hike higher and higher up the canyon. And not two minutes later, Mason stops.

He turns uneasily back to the group. "Uh... Dani?"

"Hm?"

"I..." He purses his lips. And then, ever so quietly: "I lost the money."

She's *fuming.* "You have *got* to be kidding me."

It's obvious he feels really bad. "Here." He pulls out his own wallet and hands her a twenty.

Dani opens and closes her mouth. Disappointedly. Defeatedly. And then she takes it with two fingers. "*Thanks,*" she grits.

"Don't forget interest, Mason," I remind him.

"Oh. Right." He pulls out a five and hands it to her.

Dani just stares. I half expect her not to take it, but hey, profit is profit. Even she's got to know that. She takes the money, shaking her head all the while.

"See?" I say to Jack. "You can't make this shit up."

He considers this with a defeated raise of his brow.

The rest of the hike is gorgeous. No more mishaps, less frequent yelling at Mason, and less of Dani yelling at either one of us. Whoever looked at the place and said, "Huh. Might make a good nature preserve," I have to give them credit.

Zion is truly beautiful. But you know what else is beautiful? My bus.

I let out a sigh of relief as we arrive at the parking lot. But I draw it quickly back in as I realize that this lot is missing a very, *very* important detail.

"Um," I say tightly, "where's the van?"

Dani's nearly as panicked as I am. "We *did* park here, did we not?"

"I'm sure as shit we did," I tell her with the sudden realization that my van was not alone. "What did those fuckers do with my bus?"

Mason tries his best to calm me down. "How do you know it was them?"

I click my tongue. "Well, unless someone broke in and kidnapped them—" I stop. There she is. There's my bus, in all her teal glory. She's flying through the parking lot, Elijah and Cassidy in her front two seats.

Elijah, who's driving, is grinning like an idiot. Said grin falls off his face the second he sees me.

Jack just stands back with a grin of his own. While Elijah and Cassidy's faces say, *Shit*, his says, *This should be fun*.

Elijah parks and steps outside with Cassidy. "Paisley," he tries, "I can—"

I open my mouth. I open my mouth to let loose hell on them, I open my mouth to scream, to yell, to scare them into never stepping foot in my bus again.

But Dani gets to it sooner.

"Really, guys?" she snaps. "*Really?*"

Their eyes grow huge.

"You can't just run off like that, okay? When we tell you to stay put, it means *stay put*. It doesn't mean taking a joyride while the rest of us are hiking. Do you know what would have happened if you'd crashed?"

Jack turns to mutter to me, "It's like they didn't even care they were going twenty in a fifteen."

I elbow him with a small snicker.

Dani whirls around to face him. "Oh, you think this is *funny?*"

Jack bites back a smile. "No, ma'am, I do not."

"Serious." I nod. "Very serious."

Dani looks at me. "You're not the *least* bit upset?"

"Oh, I'm pissed off my rocker, but I think you're handling this quite nicely, so by all means" —I spread my hands— "carry on."

Dani turns back to the culprits. "What do I keep saying?" she goes on. "If we're going to survive this summer, we need to be *careful*. We need to be responsible. We need to—"

"—*not* put scratches on my van?" I walk slowly up to my bus, my pride and joy, my reason for living, and run my hand slowly over the new dings in her paint. It's not super obvious, but it's enough to piss me the hell off. I turn back to them. "*Dudes!*"

Dani waves it away. "That's not important."

"Says you, you're not paying for this bitch."

"What's important," she continues, "is that we're here

for *Will,* not ourselves. You can't just do whatever the hell you—"

"Who says it wasn't for Will?" Cassidy asks softly. Then, seeing all eyes on her, she straightens. "Don't you think I wanted to go with you guys? See what he wanted to see? See it through his eyes?"

All of our gazes meet the pavement. She has a point. And now I almost feel bad for Dani yelling at her. Or, I would, if she hadn't hijacked my van.

Dani closes her mouth and sighs. "Just don't run off again, okay? I worry about you guys." She starts toward the van. "I don't want anything happening. To any of you."

I follow her, stopping in front of Cassidy and Elijah. I'm taller than both of them, so it's not hard to look down on them. "Your driving privileges just got bumped below Jack," I tell them before stalking off.

As I'm heading inside, I hear Elijah sigh. "You know what? It was worth it." And he follows Cassidy inside.

Cassidy

for the most part, I think Elijah and I got off pretty easy. I was expecting Paisley to chew us out, sure, but even Dani's rant about safety wasn't half as bad as I expected. I mean, I was prepared for lectures the whole two-and-a-half-hour drive to our hotel.

I wasn't prepared to hear Will's name so much.

"You know," Dani says, head resting against the seat, smiling, "the more I think about it, the more sense it makes that he'd want to go see David. In AP World, he was always so... captivated by Renaissance art."

He was? I don't remember him ever mentioning it.

"Wait," Mason says, brow furrowing, "who's David?"

Elijah reaches over to smack him on the arm. "Michelangelo's David?" he says incredulously. "The most famous sculpture in the world?"

"Oh." Mason rubs his arm. "Well, when you put it like, 'He wants to see David,' it can be confusing."

"Not really," Paisley calls over her shoulder. I know she's more than ecstatic to be driving again.

"You know," Elijah muses, "I'm kind of surprised there isn't *more* hiking on there."

"I'm not, are you kidding?" Mason laughs. "Any time we had to run the mile in middle school he'd complain. Worse than Paisley, actually."

"Bullshit. I hold that crown, and I'll be damned if I lose it to Will."

Elijah frowns. "I thought he liked running."

"Well, that's what he *said*," Mason explains. "He really only started doing it for fun because of Dani."

Everyone turns to Dani, who puts her hands up in

surrender. "Sorry," she says.

"Dammit, Rocha," Paisley sighs. "You turned him."

The way they're talking about him... It's like all of this should be obvious. I didn't know he loved to hike. I didn't know he hated running. We never really talked about either.

"Yeah, but still." Mason leans back. "You'd think he'd have more 'Navajo Bridges' on there."

Dani raises her eyebrows. "Are you kidding me? He was *terrified* of heights. Maybe as badly as Elijah."

Elijah's face falls. Mine does, too. More so than it already has as I watch all of this go down.

He was afraid of heights?

"That's the point!" Mason gestures emphatically to Dani. "He was always trying to push himself to the next challenge. His bucket list is filled with the things that he couldn't do, of course they'd be on there!" He sits up, resting his hands on his knees. "I'm willing to bet there's something in there about the ocean."

He was afraid of the ocean?

Jack, who hasn't said much this whole time, finally speaks up from the passenger seat. "There is."

Mason spreads his hands and leans back once again. "There you go."

How do they know all of this? When did Will mention it? Why wouldn't he mention it to me? I love the ocean; I grew up in Florida, for God's sake. Shouldn't that have come up?

Dani turns to Jack curiously. "Let me guess, the Maldives?"

Jack turns farther around in his seat, surprised. "Yeah, actually. How'd you know?"

Dani smiles softly; her face says she's somewhere else, a different time. "He's been talking about it since freshman year. Ever since he saw a photo of the bioluminescence."

Jack hesitates. "I remember that phase. Vaguely, but I do remember he wouldn't shut up about it one night at dinner."

Four years. He's been interested in it for four years. How did I manage to miss that?

"You know what else he wouldn't shut up about?" Elijah says after a minute.

"Oh God," Jack says, "that list could go on a while."

Elijah smiles. "The Hanging Gardens of Babylon."

Everyone—and I mean *everyone*—chimes in with, "*Ohhhh.*"

Like it's this big moment of realization, of remembering something so blatantly obvious that they can't imagine how they didn't think of it first.

Except me. I didn't think of it at all.

"I'm pretty sure he would've built a time machine just to go back and see them," Elijah continues.

"Oh yeah." Paisley nods. "That and to shake hands with Michel-fucking-angelo."

Elijah sighs and turns his gaze out the window. "If only."

Mason gives him a small pat on the back.

Dani tucks her legs up underneath her, adjusting herself. "Well, Michelangelo and Columbus." She pauses. "Wait, no, he wanted to *punch* Columbus."

"Yeah," Paisley says, "I was going to say, he would *not* shake hands with Columbus."

Mason laughs. "If he did, it would turn into some sort of judo flip."

This is the first I'm hearing of his apparent vendetta against Columbus. Why is this the first I'm hearing of it? How did Will and I date for almost an entire *year*, and not once did I hear him talk about David or hiking or the Maldives or the Hanging Gardens or decking *Columbus* of all people? I mean, if he loved to travel, if he wanted to do it so badly, if he loved history so much, why didn't I know? God, what did we even talk about? There's an empty, throbbing ache that enters my chest as I realize I have no idea. Nothing comes to mind. Nothing important, anyway. Nothing that wasn't superficial. That's all we were—superficial.

That whole time... did I even know who I was dating?

Mason's words cut into my thoughts. "He was really passionate about historic sailors. And vikings. He loved vikings."

Jack groans. "Oh God, don't even *talk* to me about Will and vikings. Jesus, he was obsessed with them in, like, what, third grade? Fourth?"

"Fifth."

"Fifth, right."

Right. Of course.

I want them to stop talking. I want to numb this stupid feeling in my chest. I want to turn back the clock and sit on my bed with Will, and I want *him* to talk, and I want him to never stop talking.

"And we are officially in Nevada." Paisley's announcement spurs a bout of cheers from the others.

She grins over her shoulder at Mason. "You know what that means."

Mason frowns, and then his eyes light up. "Vegas!"

"Eyes on the road!" Dani yells.

"Oh shit." Paisley whips back around to steady the wheel. "All right, so my plan for tackling Vegas follows as su—"

"No," Dani says firmly.

Paisley scoffs. "You didn't even hear my plan."

"I don't need to. It's not happening."

"Okay, but we're staying the night in Vegas at a hotel, right? So why can't we just take a look around?"

Dani folds her arms; her calm, relaxed demeanor has been replaced with her usual disappointed glare. "Because we're going to sleep, and we're leaving in the morning for the Hoover Dam."

Paisley huffs. "God, Will, put the fucking Hoover Dam on there but not *Vegas*." With that, she flicks the turn signal and changes lanes, shaking her head.

🍬 🍬 🍬

PAISLEY JOPLIN IS A MESS. Always has been, probably always will be. She has never, in her eighteen years of living, made anyone proud of her. Not her parents, not her friends, not her teachers or counselors or extended relatives.

The only thing constant about her is the alcohol she drinks and the curls in her hair. Her unpredictable nature also remains a consistent theme throughout her life. Because if she were boring, no one would want her around, no one would be left waiting on the edge of their seat wondering, "By *God*, what will she do next?" The only one who could truly predict her next move was the one she lost.

Maybe that's why she hurled a half empty bottle at her beloved van, causing the dent that she swears up and down came from a car wash and not her own grief. Maybe that's what caused her to skip the last few days before graduation and strongly consider not accepting her own diploma. The only thing that put her on that stage that day was the simple notion that if she could graduate, she could rub it in everyone's face. It wasn't so much a, "Fuck you, I didn't drop out," as much as a, "Yes, even *I* graduated. You aren't special."

Because if no one was special, that meant she wasn't either. It meant that her fucked up head was just another young girl walking down the street.

"Oh, right. My turn. Fucking... Oops, sorry. I forgot I'm not allowed to use that word up here. Let's see, ah... Hold on, I've just gotta... get my speaking cues together. It's been a long night. A long *night, ladies and gentlemen, boys and*

girls, friends and enemies.

"Oh, and Dani, who's shaking her head at me from the front row because she knows I'm drunk. Yeah. That's right. I'm drunk. I drank before I came here, I drank while all these other fuckers were giving their speeches. Can you believe how little everyone knew him? Out of all the people that came up here, there were only, like, three that I'm like, 'Oh, you actually knew that son of a bitch.'

"Hey, hey, hey! Hands off! Don't drag me out of here, drag his uncle! I caught that fucker trying to pocket his dead nephew's class ring!

"Hey, Mom. You're not gonna do a fucking thing to stop this, are you? Why the hell are you even here? You didn't know him! You didn't give two shits about him! None of you did!"

Paisley

if i had a bucket list like Will Dickinson, here's what it would look like:

1) Go to Vegas.
2) Go to Vegas.
3) Finish bucket list.

Or, you know, something along those lines. I mean, sure. That sounds extremely cliché, especially considering my... ah... *personality.*

But we're already here, so might as well knock something off, right?

I try to share this sentiment with Dani yet again, but she still doesn't get my logic. Which is not surprising.

"I don't understand why we can't just stop there for an hour or two," I argue.

Dani, who is currently in the midst of checking us into our rooms, speaks over her shoulder. "Because you and Vegas are a horrible combination."

"Not if you're there to keep me in check, right? Isn't that what you're always saying?"

Let me make this perfectly clear: I want more than anything for Dani Rocha to *not* go to Vegas with me. I want her to not go to Vegas with me more than I actually want to go to Vegas. Does this sound like an asshole-ish thing to say? Probably. But hey, she'd be about as happy there as I'd be staying at the hotel.

She continues to ignore me and carries on her discussion with the receptionist.

Elijah, meanwhile, has his forehead against the wall.

His arms are dangling at his sides; he's hunched over enough so that I feel inclined to ask if he's okay. I have no idea *what* took it out of him (maybe it was taking a joyride in my bus, I don't know), but he's been like this for at least an hour. "I'm too tired for Vegas," he mumbles sleepily.

I can only stare. "You're joking. Tell me you're joking."

He can barely shrug. "Sleep deprivation is real, Paisley," he says to the wall.

I roll my eyes. "Okay, Jack, what about— Where's Jack?" I take a look around; he's nowhere to be found. "Never mind."

"Vegas?" Mason perks up. "I wanna go to—"

"Well, I know you do. But nobody else does because they're a bunch of *prissy-ass—*"

"I'm going to stop you right there," Dani interrupts as I begin to raise my voice. "Rooms 233 and 234. Here are the keys." She holds them out in front of me.

I stare her down for a good while. After a minute—one filled with the frustration I hope she feels—I take my respective key and trudge off.

Mason follows closely behind. Good thing, too. Gives me someone to rant to.

"I can't believe they don't want to go to Vegas. I mean, technically, we're already *in* Vegas!"

As I say this, Jack walks through the door with the rest of the bags. Which is one.

"Hey, dick face!" I call.

He turns toward me.

"Wanna go to Vegas?"

He frowns. "We're already in Vegas."

I give him a look. "You know what I mean."

He considers it. He really does. For a minute, I think I've got him. But alas, the moment passes, and he shakes his head. "Nah, I'll pass. Sorry." He starts off.

"Pussy."

"Bitch."

I turn to Mason. "Guess it's just us. Which sounds *super* fun." With Mason you either get a playmate or a babysitting job. There is absolutely no in between.

He spreads a grin, meaning I might be stuck with the second option. I slowly close my eyes.

"I'll go."

We turn to see who had spoken. And to my surprise, it was Cassidy. She's sitting on one of the lobby couches, watching us.

It takes me a minute to realize she's, in fact, not kidding.

"Wait, seriously?"

"Yeah. Should be fun, right?"

Mason grins. "Yeahhh, Cassidy!"

I'm still not thoroughly convinced. "You're *sure?*"

She stands, rubbing her hands on her jeans. "Mhm."

I squint at her. She's 5'2". Even if she weren't short, I would still say she was little. She tends to have a very nervous demeanor, which is why I've been hesitant about her driving my van. Well, that and because it's my van.

Cassidy Montag is *not* someone who would want to go to Vegas.

I pull Mason aside, turning my back toward the girl in question. "This sounds like a bad idea," I mutter.

"Why is it a bad idea?" he asks. "It's just Cassidy."

"I know it's just Cassidy. That's kind of the problem that it's 'just Cassidy.' She's like a... fucking... baby bird, all... innocent and—"

"She'll be fine," Mason insists. "We'll keep an eye on her."

"I'm worried she won't keep an eye on herself."

Mason frowns as he considers this.

"You know I can hear you, right?"

Shit.

"Uh..." Mason tries. "No, you can't."

I turn back toward her.

"You can't stop me from coming," she tells us. "I'm coming."

And damn, maybe I'm just tall, but she seems so tiny in this moment. And that's what I'm worried about. "And you're—"

"Yes, I'm sure."

I still think this is a bad idea. Which is ironic because according to Dani, I'm the CEO of bad ideas. But nonetheless, I find myself saying, "All right then. Let's hit the road." I hesitate. "Before Dani gets back."

Cassidy frowns. "Now?"

"Yeah, now," I almost laugh. "What, did you think we were going tomorrow?"

"No," she's quick to refute, "I just... Yeah, okay. Let's go."

Mason's already bouncing out the door.

I start to call after him. "Ma— You know what? Not even worth it."

We head toward my van.

"I'm not a baby bird, you know."

I glance down at her. It's really ironic that she says this. *Really* ironic. Because her feathers are ruffling at the folds of her arms. She has a bounce to her step as she attempts to keep up with me.

"Oh, don't get your panties in a twist," I tell her. "It was a compliment." She has an enviable aura about her. I tend to scare people off; she only brings people closer.

"Sure didn't sound like it," she mumbles.

"Believe me, it was." I shrug. "But hey, take it how you like. If you want to stay bitter about it, be my guest. Not gonna get you anywhere, though."

She pouts. She fucking *pouts*. Are you fucking kidding me? This is who agreed to go to Vegas with me? "Do you... Do you still have that flask on you?"

"I always have that flask on me." I take it out and hand it to her.

She takes her swig with a grimace.

"What?" I frown. "Did I put orange juice in there again? I did that to Jack a little while back. Completely forgot it was in there. Well, as far as he knows."

She shakes her head. "No, it's just... been a while since I last drank."

Bull. *Shit*. I narrow my eyes at her. "You've never drunk before, have you?"

She pauses a *really* long time. "What makes you say that?"

"Literally everything about your face right now."

Cassidy takes another swig to cover it up. But I'm still not convinced.

"Are you sure this is a good plan?" I ask again.

"Of course it is," she tells me. "It's the best plan."

I sigh. "Hand me the flask."

She hugs it to her chest. "No."

I stop dead in my tracks. She stops with me as I say, "Okay. Rule number one: when Paisley needs a drink, *Paisley needs a drink.*" I hold out my hand.

She gloomily gives it back. "Can I have more, though?"

I glance over mid-swig before nodding. "Yeah," I say, handing it back. "If you don't cause me to drink it all."

I catch her taking one more drink as I unlock my van.

Jack

"where the fuck did they go?" Dani is *livid*. I can't tell if she's angry, or nervous, or both.

But it's getting annoying.

"For the last *time,* I don't *know.*"

Elijah mumbles something. It's hard to make out because (a.) he's mumbling, and (b.) he's currently lying face down on the bed. Which means the only thing that can hear him is the mattress.

"Oh my God," I mutter. "*What?*"

Elijah tilts his head up, but only for a second. His eyes are almost sunken in. "They're in Vegas. Obviously." His head falls back down. Yeah, I didn't sleep well last night. But Elijah didn't sleep at *all.* In the hours I spent staring at the ceiling, I could hear the scratches on his sketchpad.

Dani is not impressed. "Thanks. You're such a big help." She drops her hands and turns back to me. "They could be anywhere in the city."

I rake a hand through my roots. "I know, I'm... I'll figure out something."

Elijah once again props his chin up. "I have Mason's location." And he's back down just as fast.

Dani's stress/anger/whatever the hell she's feeling quickly dissolves into a frown.

I can only stare. "*Why?*"

Elijah finally—*finally*—sits up. "Because he's an idiot, and I knew there'd come a time when I'd need to track him down."

Dani and I share a murmur of agreement.

Elijah takes out his phone. "Now is that time."

Dani blinks. "You really didn't think to *lead* with this?"

Elijah ignores her and continues to type on his phone. I sigh impatiently. "You know, this is a great plan and all until they get separated."

We all stop at my words. The three of us exchange one horrified glance before racing out the door.

"Looks like Mason's on Paradise Road," Elijah says from his spot in the middle, "right by Las Vegas Boulevard."

Dani relays this to the cab driver, who follows her orders down another road.

"God, they're probably already lost." She shakes her head, mumbling, "Why don't they ever listen to me?"

"Well," I point out, "with Paisley, the only way you're gonna ever get through to her is with reverse psychology. Mason, well, he's Mason. As for Cassie... Yeah, I've got nothing. I honestly never would have pegged her as the type to run off to Vegas."

"Yeah," Dani says. "I thought she, at least, would have some common sense. Mason and Paisley... I mean, I'm pretty sure the only thing we can do at this point is keep them on a leash."

Elijah scoffs. "Even then they'd find a way."

I nod. He has a point.

Dani leans her head against the seat in front of her, Elijah-style, and groans. "I'm supposed to be preparing for Stanford, not chasing a couple of idiots through Vegas." I didn't even think about that. She's already got to be stressed out of her mind, and now she has us to worry about. Out of all of us, she's always done the best under pressure. But maybe that's just because we always put that pressure on her.

"Well," I try, "now you can put 'adept in dealing with children' on all your resumes."

To my surprise, she laughs, forehead still pressed comfortably against the seat back. Dani doesn't laugh often, but when she does, it has the power to bring just a bit of light to any situation. Even this one.

At least, that's how Will always put it.

It's strange that out of the three of us, one breaking down and the other already broken, I'm the one who hasn't cracked yet. Why is that? Shouldn't I be stressing more than I am?

Shouldn't I be worried about Mason, who's dumb as a brick and has virtually no impulse control? Or Paisley, who isn't stupid like Mason but will make the same decisions nonetheless because she thinks it's fun?

Or Cassie, who doesn't pull shit like this? What happened to her? She doesn't do this sort of thing, not since I've known her. Is she okay?

Are any of them?

Cassidy

"**wooooooo!**" Mason shouts, pushing his way through a cluster of people.

Mason and Paisley, I've found, are really good at navigating crowds, even when drunk. Paisley more so than Mason, even though she's a whole lot drunker than he is.

And me. I'm drunk. I never thought I would say those words. I don't drink. This is not me. I don't drink, and I especially don't drink in *Vegas* of all places. But right now, Vegas is my lifeline. Vodka is my lifeline. The light, airy feeling in my bones, the hordes of people on the sidewalk around me, the *lights*. It's exactly what I need to take my mind off everything else.

I can't help but grin at our surroundings. "Vegas is prettier than I thought," I say.

"WOOOO!" There's Mason again.

Paisley leans closer to me. "*What?*"

I giggle. Everything is funny right now. Everything. "I said—"

"*WOOOOOOO!*"

"Not you," Paisley says, swatting at Mason. "I was talking to Cassiby." She pauses in the middle of the sidewalk, causing Mason and me to stop, too. "Cassiyadyia. Cass—" She points at me. "Her."

I shove another giggle back down, shouting, "Vegas is pretty!"

She pumps her fist in the air. "Hell yeah!"

"*YEAH!*"

"Mason, so help me *God*, I will *hit* you over the head with— *Oh my God, there's a dog!*"

I gasp, look around, try to follow her gaze. "Dog?"

"Right over there, there's a little—"

But Mason is already running over to it, a little scraggly chihuahua-looking thing. I follow him and ask the owner if we can pet it. Paisley comes over, too, and the three of us kneel down to pet the dog until the owner moves along.

I'm so happy. I think this is the happiest I've been in a long time.

"We should do something!" Paisley yells, words starting to slur together.

"Like what?" I yell back.

Mason gasps. "Like *that!*"

"*Like that!*" Paisley echoes, taking off. Mason takes off after her, and I do, too, pushing my way through a crowd of people. And then...

They're gone. I stop, turning in a circle, looking all around. I don't see them anywhere. Someone bumps into me, and I stumble. Looming in front of me is the biggest casino I've seen in my life and probably the most likely place that Mason and Paisley would want to explore. So that's where I go, if only to get away from the crowds.

The casino is bright and loud. I'm expecting someone to ask for my ID, but no one does. Good thing, too, because I don't have a fake one like Paisley and probably Mason. After taking a glance around, nobody looks familiar. I still don't see the others.

Desperation sinks in as I realize Paisley was right: I am a baby bird.

And the best thing this baby bird can think to do is sit and wait at the bar for someone to come get her.

I probably look sad. I probably look crazy. I probably look like a sad, crazy, down-on-her-luck teenager trying to find solace in alcohol. I probably—

"You look lonely."

Yeah. I probably look lonely.

I turn and come face-to-face with a stranger. The first thing I notice are his striking green eyes. He's about Paisley's height, with a decent build and a mess of brown hair. And I have no idea how to respond to him.

"Let me buy you a drink," he says.

I bite my cheek. On one hand, I really want another drink. (Alcohol may taste disgusting, but the feeling of being drunk, I'm quickly learning, is worth it.) On the other, I don't know who this guy is. "I'm good," I say, "thanks."

"Come on, sweetheart," he drawls, leaning against the bar. "You look like you need a little pick-me-up."

Which is exactly my predicament. Nonetheless, I tell him, "Really, I'm fine."

"All right, how about this." He straightens, moves a bit closer to me. "I'll buy you a drink, we can just... set it on the table. It'll be yours for the taking."

I pause. I consider it. I mean, it's not an unreasonable proposal. In fact, it's pretty damn reasonable. "Okay," I say after a minute.

He smiles, flagging down the bartender and ordering something I've never heard of. He's not half bad-looking. He kind of looks like a younger version of my sophomore year English teacher. In all honesty, he looks harmless. Kind.

"Thanks, I guess," I tell him.

"No problem." He slides the drink toward me.

I don't drink it. I just run my finger around the rim of the glass, contemplating whether or not I should.

He pulls out the barstool beside me and takes a seat, facing me. "You here with anyone?"

I nod. "Yeah. My friends."

"What kind of friends would leave you alone like this?"

"They didn't. I sort of lost them."

"Shame." He scoots the barstool even closer. "Some friends, huh?"

It's not their fault, really. Compared to Mason, I'm impossible to spot in a crowd. Even if they had tried looking for me, I doubt they would've found me.

I stare down at the glass, still tracing the rim.

"How about I keep you company until they get back?" he offers.

"I don't think that's..."

He shrugs. "Up to you. But you're probably a lot safer if you stay with me."

I consider this, looking him over again. He seems genuine. And would I really rather be alone in a Vegas casino? "I guess you're right," I say.

He smiles, but it's quick to fade. He casts his eyes down,

tapping his fingers on the counter. "You know, my ex was in the same situation as you the last time I was here."

I perk up at that. "Really?"

He nods sadly. "She, ah, ended up on a bus to Denver. Never saw her again. I just hope she's okay."

Jesus. "Oh my God, I'm so sorry."

"It's okay." He shoots me a look, eyes sad. "It would just break my heart to see the same sort of thing happen to you."

He's right—I'm better off here with him than alone where anything could happen to me. I glance back down at the drink in my hand, and I don't give it another thought. I take a sip. This time I fight the urge to grimace.

"There's a good girl," he coos, setting his hand on my back. "You got time to kill, yeah? Might as well spend it right."

I do have time to kill. And the longer I sit here, the more that horrible feeling in my chest starts to creep back in. The vodka helped fight it off, but now that I actually have time to think, I'm reminded of all the things I'm trying to forget. So I pick up the drink, and I down the whole thing.

The guy chuckles. "At the rate you're going, I'm gonna be broke by the end of the night."

"Oh, sorry," I say as he waves down the bartender again.

He meets my eye with a crooked smile. "Anything for someone as beautiful as you."

My cheeks flush at the same time the ache flares up. I take a sip from the new glass, the same kind of drink as before. "I haven't been called beautiful since my boyfriend died."

"Wow," he says, "I'm so sorry."

I stare down at my glass again before going in for another drink. And another. And before I know it, it's all gone, and the guy is putting another one in front of me. And I start to drink that one, too. "It happened about a month ago," I say quietly. "Car crash."

"That's horrible."

I'm fighting against myself at this point. Combating my pain with alcohol, one sip after another.

"So…" The guy shifts closer to me, a light hand on my arm. "Have you found anyone else?"

"Kind of."

He nods, taking this in. "You've been hit pretty hard." He

hesitates. "Listen. I have a room here. How about you come up for a bit to get away from all..." He gestures around the room. "This."

"Um..." I push my empty glass away from me. "I don't think that's a good idea."

"Just for a little bit. Just until those friends of yours come back."

I glance at the casino entrance. "They shouldn't be too long. I think I should just stay here where they can find me."

"Come on, baby," he murmurs, thumb brushing softly over my arm. "I'll make you forget all about your boyfriend." He tugs me to my feet.

I waver. Another pang in my chest, but it's softer now. Weaker. Muffled.

I don't know where Paisley and Mason are. I don't even know if they're in here. Who knows how long it could take for them to find me?

And besides, he's already leading me to the elevators, away from the bar. "Well, okay," I say, to which he smiles.

He's pressed the button, and we're waiting for the door to open when I feel a hand on my other arm.

"Hey, sorry, I think this is mine."

"Jack?" I squint up at him.

Jack looks past me at the guy. "I'll get her out of your hair, thanks, man."

The guy lets go of my arm, regarding Jack curiously. "You the friend or the new boyfriend?"

"None of your business," Jack says coolly. And then, looking down at me, he mutters, "I've been looking everywhere for you."

Has he? Does he really care that much?

No. No, he doesn't. They just told him to come find me, so that's what he did. It doesn't mean anything.

Well, it does, actually. It means he thinks I'm a helpless little baby bird, too. They all do.

I yank my arm away from him. "I can take care of myself."

Jack is kind of scary when he gets mad. Now is no different. "You call hooking up with strange thirty-year-old men 'taking care of yourself'?"

I roll my eyes, folding my arms. "We weren't gonna *hook up*."

143

His eyes widen frantically. "He was leading you to his hotel room!"

"That doesn't mean we were gonna—"

The guy steps in before I can finish. "I was just trying to keep her safe, bud." He takes my arm again, more forcefully this time. "You were the one who left her in the first—"

Jack punches him.

It happens so fast. One minute he's standing there beside me, the next his fist is flying.

"*Jack!*" I yell.

I've seen him get violent before. It's just... It's been a while. And it always takes me off guard, seeing that look in his eyes.

"Hey, hey, *hey!*" There's a security guard in the mix now, grabbing Jack by the arms and pulling him away from the guy.

The guy steps forward shakily, eyes wide, blood trickling from his nose. "I— I don't know what happened. He just attacked me."

Jack struggles against the guard holding him back. "She's underage, did she tell you that?"

The guy's face pales.

"Wait," the guard says, releasing Jack, "what's going on?"

"She was lost," the guy is quick to say. "I was trying to help her find her friends."

"Oh, come on," Jack says. "That's bullshit."

"What's bullshit is some kid coming in and beating the shit out of me! Are you even allowed to be in here?"

The guard looks between Jack and the guy, eyes narrowing. "How old are you, son?"

"I—"

It's too much. All of it, it's too much. I grab Jack's arm, cling onto him like my life depends on it. "Jack, I wanna get out of here." I *need* to get out of here.

I see his jaw clenching as he glances from me to the guy to the security guard. "It doesn't matter," he says to the guard. "We're leaving."

Thank God.

"Young man—"

I don't get to hear what the guard has to say because Jack has put his arm around my shoulders, guiding me out of the casino, back out into the night.

Once we're outside, I let out a breath. "Thank—"

"What the *hell* were you thinking?" Jack snaps.

I wince. I don't like it when he yells at me. I really don't like it.

I cast my eyes down so I don't have to see the anger written on his face. "I guess I wasn't."

"Yeah, no *shit!* You just wander into a casino? Alone? In *Vegas?*"

"I couldn't find Paisley and Mason," I mumble. "I didn't know what else to do."

"You didn't know what else to do but get fucking drunk with some guy? You can't just wander off like that, Cassie, you scared the shit out of me!"

This pressure builds behind my eyes. First myself and now Jack. Everyone is disappointed in me. I can't stop the tears from rolling down my cheeks, and I don't try to.

Jack exhales, calmer now. "How much did you drink?" he asks softly.

I sniff, meeting his eye again. He doesn't look mad anymore. "I don't know, a few glasses. Some of Paisley's vodka."

He slowly closes his eyes. "Okay." He backs up a bit. "Walk in a straight line toward me."

My forehead scrunches up. "What?"

"Just trust me."

I wipe my eyes with my sleeve and then walk toward him.

I think I'm doing a good job until I start to lose my balance and stumble. And Jack is right there, grabbing my arms to steady me.

I look up at him. "That's not good."

"No, it's not." He turns his head toward the casino. "You really don't know where Paisley and Mason went?" he asks, looking back at me.

I shake my head. "We were in a crowd, and when I got through they were gone."

He looks me over. He looks me over for a good, long second. And then he does something I never—*never*—thought would happen, not in a million years.

He hugs me.

I don't know what happens then. Something breaks

145

open inside me, I guess, and I just lose it. All the emotions I've been stuffing down push their way back up in the form of an unrelenting stream of tears. I'm shaking, eyes squeezed shut against the outpour.

Jack sits down, bringing me with him, arms still wrapped around me. Here we are, sitting on the sidewalk on the Las Vegas Strip, and I'm sobbing. Head pressed against his chest, probably (definitely) ruining his shirt with my tears. He doesn't say anything, though. He doesn't say anything for a long time. We just sit there, and he just lets me cry.

After a little while, I feel better. Well, not so much better as dry. I'm all dried up, all out of tears. I let out a slow, shaky breath and sit back up. My voice is quiet when I say, "I didn't even know him."

"Good thing, too," Jack says. "That guy was an asshole."

My brow furrows. What is he— Oh. "No," I say. "Not him. Will."

His mouth opens. Closes. And then: "Oh."

"We dated for so long. I never even knew he liked any of the things you guys were talking about."

"And you still haven't figured out why?" Jack shakes his head. "He looked at you the same way he looked at vikings, the same way he looked at the Hanging Gardens of Babylon. He was fascinated by you, Cassie. He wanted to know every bit of you."

Somehow, that only makes me feel worse. Like the whole time we were dating it had to be about me. Always. Because shouldn't I have tried to get to know every bit of him, too?

"It shouldn't have been like that," I say. "I mean, I was his girlfriend, but Mason knew him better than I did."

"Well, Mason's known our family since he was in first grade. Same with Paisley. Almost."

I choose to ignore that. "Dani knew him better than I did. Hell, even Elijah knew him better than I did."

He doesn't say anything to that. He just wraps an arm around me, starts rubbing up and down my arms.

I close my eyes. "What kind of girlfriend am I if I don't even know who he was?"

This is it. This is what I want to forget so badly. This is what the alcohol tried so hard to erase but failed.

Jack keeps rubbing my arms. And then, after a minute,

he says, "He hated beans."

I open my eyes, looking over. "What?"

"Whenever my mom would make chili, he'd pick around them. He's been that way since he was four."

I don't know why that makes me feel better, but it does. The ache doesn't hurt so bad. I don't feel so guilty.

"And the color blue," Jack continues. "Well, certain shades. He loved turquoise. But that was it."

I almost laugh. "Then why'd he want to go to the Maldives so bad?"

"He said it looked like magic. He wanted to know if it felt like it, too."

For a brief moment, I can imagine Will saying that. I can imagine him telling *me* that. I can imagine falling asleep next to him and dreaming about feeling that magic.

And then I can't.

"I wish he would've told me," I mumble.

"Must've slipped his mind," he says softly, absently.

I sigh, resting my head on his shoulder. "Tell me more."

He takes a moment to think. "He never wanted to go to Vegas."

I smile just a little. "I could have guessed that."

"Yeah. He always hated the idea of it. Any time Dad mentioned going to Vegas for his twenty-first birthday, he would always shut it down. That and Atlantic City."

"He never really was much of a partier." Neither was I, I guess, until now. "That much I remember."

I feel him nodding.

I lift my head to look at him. "Thank you."

He smiles. "Yeah."

There's something about him. Something about the way he's smiling, the way he's looking at me, the way he was able to make me laugh when I thought I couldn't. Something that makes him feel... safe. That's what it is, I feel safe. I feel good. *He* feels good. He does care after all. He came and found me. And he's here. He's still here. And he's looking at me, and his hair is falling in his eye, and all I want to do is brush it out of the way. So I do. I feel myself leaning in naturally, feel myself closing my eyes, feel—

"Hey, homies!"

I swear, my heart leaps out of my chest. I quickly lean away from Jack as he yells, "Jesus!"

Elijah comes up behind Mason, more tired than I've ever seen him before. "What did I say?" he scolds. "*Don't* scare them."

"But—"

Jack and I stand at the same time, and I get lightheaded and have to grab his arm to steady myself.

"Did you find Paisley?" he asks, stepping away from me.

Elijah's face falls even farther. "I was hoping you found her."

Jack slowly closes his eyes. "Cassie, do you remember the last place you saw her?"

I think back to before the casino, before everything started getting weird. "Yeah, uh..." I point down the sidewalk. "Over there. That's where I lost her."

"Is that where you lost her, Mace?" Elijah asks.

"Nah," Mason says. "We went in together, but I lost her as soon as I saw the craps table."

Elijah blinks. "So... she lost you?"

"Well..."

Elijah sighs. "Let's go."

Mason

i don't think i've had a single coherent thought since we entered the Strip.

Hell, I don't think I've had one of those since we rolled into Nevada.

Elijah notices this better than anyone, which isn't surprising. "*Mason*," he hisses. "Be careful."

I'm running around the casino, darting back and forth between different areas, different games. I mean, we're here, right? When in Rome...

Wait, what was the last part of that saying?

Anyway.

I try to convince Elijah that I'm fine. That I'm always careful. "I'm always—" I trip over myself and fall flat on my face.

Elijah, surprisingly enough, helps me to my feet. "What did I say? Stay close."

He's right. I need to stay close. If we're going to find Paisley—

Holy *fuck,* what is that?

"*Mason!*" Elijah runs after me.

Halfway to whatever has caught my eye, I forget what I'm looking for. Whoops.

Maybe it was that over there? It looks like a blackjack table. But, like, a really *cool* blackjack table. I should take a look. When in Rome...

Seriously, what is the other half of that? I should ask Elijah. He knows everything.

I turn to ask him but accidentally fall into him instead. It's a miracle he catches me; even more so that I manage to catch myself before I knock him over. I look up (down) at him. He's tired. That much is obvious. But deeper still, beyond the blue and into the tiny bit of green that lies mixed within, he's concerned for me. "You have really pretty eyes," I tell him.

He smacks me upside the head.

I dart off again, partly to explore a bit more and partly to piss him off.

"Mason—"

I bump into someone else, but this time it isn't Elijah. I look down to apologize. It takes both of us a minute to recognize each other.

I light up. "Dani!"

"What the he—" She looks up at me, almost shocked. "Mason?"

I lift her by the waist and carry her off.

"Hey, hey, *hey!*" she protests, feet kicking in the air, hands working to pry my arms off.

I spot Cassidy and Jack, who turn to me with wide eyes. "Found her!" I say, setting Dani down.

"Dani, did you find Paisley?" Cassidy asks, question hinting a slur in her voice.

Jack sighs at this.

Dani opens her mouth before quickly closing it. "I saw her come in here," she tells mostly Jack. "But I can't find her for the life of me."

Jack doesn't meet her eye; his gaze is fixed over her shoulder.

She furrows her brow. "What?"

Jack points silently past her.

She turns. She freezes, face pale and equally exhausted. "Oh, dear God."

Dani

"she isn't," I say. I mean, she can't be. Even for Paisley, this is just too much.

Mason laughs. "Haha, *nice!*"

No. This is not okay. None of this is okay. I'm not about to let Paisley get away with dancing on top of a fucking blackjack table, let alone get gawked at by a bunch of middle-aged men. This is where I draw the line.

I storm over to the table, ready to get her down by any means necessary. "Paisley," I call up to her, "what the hell are you doing?"

She pauses mid-dance, whipping her head toward me, long hair flying. "Dani, what the hell are *you* doing? Get your ass up here!"

I tell myself to breathe. Just breathe. This nightmare of a night is almost over. "How about you get your ass down *here*, and then we'll talk."

She swings her hips from side to side. "Either you're coming up, or the shirt's coming off."

My eyes widen. "Paisley—"

She doesn't even wait; she shrugs her top off right then and there, throwing it into the crowd.

"*Paisley!*" I screech, already scrambling up on top of the table amidst cheers from the people gathered. She is topless. In public. In a casino. In front of an audience. Oh, and did I mention *she's topless?*

She grabs my hands. "*Dance* with me, oh wise one."

"You're drunk," I say through gritted teeth. "We're going back to the hotel. *Now.*"

Someone in our little audience yells at us to make out,

naturally. Paisley leans in, and I can't believe I actually have to shove her away. She loses her balance, so I grab her shoulders to steady her. I scan the casino (partly because I want to see who shouted at us), and I spot a security guard heading right toward us. And he does *not* look happy.

"Paisley," I say, "we have to go."

"No." Her turn to shove me away. "*You* gotta go."

I pull a page right out of my mom's book. "I'm going to give you three seconds, and you'd better be on the floor when they're up."

She doesn't pay any mind to that. She just keeps dancing, throwing her arms above her head.

"One."

She dips down and back up, tossing her hair and rolling her hips again.

"*T—*"

"God," she groans, "dealing with you is ex*haus*ting. I need a drink." She goes to climb down from the table—very unsteadily, might I add. Once she's back on the ground, she starts toward the bar, but Jack, my savior, grabs her before she can escape.

"*Jack*ass!" she cries.

Jack, tired but relieved, locks eyes with me. "I've got— Hi, Cassie."

Cassidy is clinging to Jack's arm like a koala bear. Sure, I feel bad that he's got her *and* Paisley to deal with, but if he lets Paisley go, she's going to run off. And I seriously doubt that Cassidy is going to let go any time soon, given that she's holding on so tight.

"Where's Mason?" I ask Jack.

"He's with Elijah."

"Where's Elijah?"

Jack opens his mouth, then promptly closes it.

I toss my head back, letting out a loud, frustrated groan. "Elijah is too tired to deal with a drunk puppy with no impulse control. Did you really think he would be able to control Mason alone?"

"I—"

"Hey, homies!" Speak of the devil. Mason is grinning from ear to ear.

Elijah trudges over, visibly exhausted. "Can we go back to

the hotel now?" His eyes grow wide when he sees Paisley. "Um..."

"Problem?" Paisley asks from Jack's hold.

"Uh, yeah," Jack says, "big problem." He nods toward the security guard—a different security guard—heading for us.

We need to get out of here. That much is obvious. We're only drawing attention to ourselves the longer we stay here.

The only thing I can think to say is, "Run."

Elijah

we make a break for it, Breakfast Club-style, leaving the casino and the security guard in the dust. Paisley didn't have a chance to get her shirt back, so we have to duck into the first place we can find to buy her a shirt. Any shirt. And she's so drunk that she doesn't even care that it's four sizes too big.

I'm pretty sure all of us—maybe not Mason and Paisley—are ready to call it a night. All *I* want to do is curl up in Mason's arms and pass out for a solid twelve to thirteen hours. But, of course, I can't do that. Partly because Jack's staying in our room and partly because if I slept thirteen hours, I'd wake up well into the afternoon.

We all stop at the edge of the sidewalk. "Paisley," Dani says.

"Hm?"

"Where'd you park the van?"

Shit. Forgot that we kind of need the van to drive to the hotel.

"Up yours," Paisley slurs.

"That sounds about right."

At that, Paisley starts giggling.

Dani turns to Cassidy, who's still clinging onto Jack's arm. "Do you remember where you guys parked?"

Her forehead creases. "Um, I don't... No, I don't remember."

"She..." Jack looks down at her. I don't think he knows what the hell to do with her. "She's had a rough night."

Dani purses her lips. "Clearly." She sighs, rolling her head toward Mason. "What about you? Do you remember anything?"

Mason smiles. "I remember lots of things."

Dani's eyes shift to mine. She looks so absolutely done, and I don't blame her. I've been done for a while now. She turns back to my drunk boyfriend. "Does one of those things happen to be where Paisley parked the van?"

"Oh yeah," Mason says, "B36 in the lot right across the street."

If I had the energy, I'd facepalm.

"Great." Dani starts walking, and Jack and Cassidy are soon to follow.

Mason tries to dart away again because... I don't know, probably because he saw something shiny. I grab his arm and follow the others, towing him behind me. It takes a minute, but when I look back I see Paisley trying to catch up.

Good. We're all here. We haven't lost anyone else. Again.

"You know," Dani says over her shoulder, "I said it before, but I think it needs reiterating. If we're going to get through this trip alive, you guys have to behave."

Paisley, now walking beside me, scoffs. "Okay, *Mom*."

"We are behaving!" Mason protests.

"Maybe it's just me," Jack says, "but I wouldn't call abandoning the rest of us for a night in Vegas beha—" He freezes. I swear he stops breathing. Because Cassidy has wrapped her arms around his midsection. And since Jack has stopped walking, we all do, too. "Um..." He opens and closes his mouth. He doesn't know what to do with his arms, so they're up and awkwardly sticking out.

"I'm cold," Cassidy mumbles against his side.

"I..." He looks helplessly at me.

"I don't know what to tell you," I say. "I have Mason to deal wi— Mason!"

Why did I let go of him? He can't go a second without getting distracted and, in this case, running into the street. You'd think he'd tire himself out at some point.

I run after him, grab his arm, turn him toward me. "You stay with me, okay?" I tell him, trying to sound stern. "I don't want you dying in Vegas of all places."

His eyes are traversing my face, zoning in and out. "You're really pretty, Lijah."

I close my eyes. I'm so close to the end, I can feel it. I need a bed. Desperately. "Yeah," I say, "so you've said."

He shakes his head. "No. No. Like, *really* pretty."

Drunk Mason is so unpredictable, you never know what

he's gonna do. But the one thing you can always count on is him mentioning something about how pretty I am. My point? I am extremely, *extremely* used to this.

"Much appreciated," I say. "Can we get back on the sidewalk now, please?"

He doesn't move. He just stands there, staring at me, mouth slightly agape. He's still studying my face.

"Mason, work with me here." I'm basically pleading at this point. I just want to go to sleep. I just want to get back to my pot. "It's been a long day, and I can't drag your ass back to the hotel, so *please*. Work with me."

A car drives by then, way too close to Mason for my liking.

"*Shit!*" I yell as the car honks at us.

You know what? Fuck it. I grab Mason's hand and yank him as hard as I can toward the sidewalk, out of the street, storming ahead of the others and not looking back until I reach spot B36 in the lot right across the street.

I've never been so happy to see this fucking van in my life.

"I'll drive," Paisley says.

"*No*," Dani and Jack respond simultaneously.

Paisley tosses her hands up in protest. "Oh, come on! It's my van! And besides." She digs into her pocket and takes out her keys. "I have the—"

Dani snatches them out of her hand.

"*Hey!*" Paisley makes a grab for them, but Dani holds them up out of her way.

"Too slow," she says.

Jack takes Paisley's arm to hold her back, still weighed down by Cassidy.

Dani looks Paisley in the eye. "You have to sleep this off."

She sighs. "Okay. I will when we get to the hotel, but in order to *get* to the hotel, *someone* needs to drive. So hand 'em over."

Dani blinks. "You don't see a problem here?"

"Yeah. A pretty obvious one, too. You have my keys."

Another blink. And she must have given up because she turns to Jack and says, "Can you go put her down in the back?"

"Which one?" Jack asks.

Dani looks down at Cassidy. "Both, I guess."

Jack's eyes slowly close. "Okay, let's go." With one arm around Cassidy and the other gripping Paisley's wrist, he heads inside the bus to deposit them. I want to make a comment about it, but I doubt he'd appreciate me telling him that he looks like a tired single mother of two.

"I want shotgun," Mason says beside me.

Which prompts Paisley to somehow break away from Jack and step back outside the van. "Well, I *call* shotgun."

Mason's brow furrows. "Wait..."

"You can't just want something, Mason. You have to call it, or it doesn't count."

He deflates. "Dani," he whines.

Dani looks at Paisley, then at Mason, and shrugs. "You heard her."

Mason frowns, shoulders slumping.

We all pile into the van. Dani's driving. Paisley sits shotgun, as promised. Jack claims the corner, and Cassidy plops down next to him. As soon as she does, she leans her head on his shoulder, closing her eyes, and I'm pretty sure Jack has yet another existential crisis. He doesn't know how to handle this. Or any of this, for that matter. Cassidy's never gotten drunk before—none of us knew how clingy she would be.

As soon as I sit down, I let everything in me relax and lean my head back against the seat. Holy fuck, am I tired. I don't think I've felt this tired in my life. Every part of me is exhausted.

Mason doesn't even bother to take a seat. He just collapses onto the floor, even though he doesn't fit. His head is right by my foot, so I take the opportunity to poke him with it. "You still alive?" I ask him.

"No."

I sigh. "Okay." And I finally close my eyes.

CASSIDY MONTAG IS CONFLICTED. Her head is in the right place; her heart is not. She can tell herself what to feel, what to think, but she cannot force herself to follow through.

Her heart is angry—it has been for a while. Angry at the world for making things change so quickly, so drastically. Angry at herself for wanting things that she shouldn't want. But letting that anger slip out between the cracks demolishes the image she's built of herself. The image she's worked so hard to sustain because as long as she's been alive, she has wanted to be liked. By her family, by her friends, by her teachers, by everyone in between.

Perhaps more importantly, she wants more than anything to be loved. By one person. Someone she can give her whole heart to and be given one in return.

She's found bits of that in every guy she's dated since middle school. Bits of what she wants, pieces of what she needs, but never the full package. The closest she's ever come to it was taken away from her all too soon.

Her problem, whether she acknowledges it or not, is her fear of being herself. Every guy she's dated has dated a different Cassidy: Cassidy 1.0 versus Cassidy 2.0 versus... Well, you get it. She always, usually subconsciously, spends the time meticulously sculpting herself to be the version of Cassidy that most fits her boyfriend's mold. In this way, she makes herself perfect. She is the perfect girl, the perfect girlfriend, the perfect person.

Or, at least, she tries to be. Perfection, she has yet to realize, is unattainable, and even the most perfect version of herself is never enough. It's never enough because it's not her. The girl who spends hours in the bathroom before a date curling her hair and putting on makeup, the girl who holds her tongue, the girl who doesn't let herself get angry, is also the girl who ends up broken-hearted in the end.

There is only one person who has seen her through everything, who has seen her through all her flaws, all her anger, all her imperfections. And she hates that he knows. Hates even more that he seems to understand.

"Moving from Florida to Arizona, I didn't know what to expect. The transition happened so quickly, so suddenly, that I didn't really have the time to prepare myself. But even if I did have that time, I still never could have prepared myself for Will.

"Will was the first person I knew here. He was my introduction to life in Phoenix. When I first met him, I couldn't believe he was real. I had to convince myself he wasn't a jet lag-induced hallucination. I had never met someone so forward, so confident. He was... Well, he was perfect. He was too good to be true. Even to this day, I have no clue why he chose me.

"I remember the first time he texted me. I remember... because it was the day after we'd met, and he had texted me asking if he could come over to ask me out. He couldn't do it over text, he had to do it in person. He said... He said I deserved only the best. He... He didn't even know me at the time, but he said I deserved the best. Needless— Well, needless to say, I couldn't really say...

"No, I'm fine. I'm fine, I don't need a— a tissue, I'm fine.

"Will was suddenly in my life a lot. He— He was my life... there... for a while. He, um... He would pick me up for school every morning. He

helped me to navigate... to navigate...

"No, I just— I can't read... I can't— I can't...

*"I promised myself I wouldn't cry. I promised
Will— I just— I... This isn't...*

"I'm fine—*"*

Paisley

"wake up, puta."

I moan.

Dani tries again. "Shut up and get up."

"Eat shit."

"*Muere.*" She then does the unthinkable: she yanks my own pillow out from under me and begins to hit me with it. "Wake." *Hit.* "Up." *Hit.*

I roll over to block her attacks. She stops at this and drops the pillow.

I scowl at her; it doesn't last very long. With a groan, I mumble, "I'm never drinking again." My eyes wander, quickly finding my flask sitting on the nightstand. "Right after this."

The pillow is back up, hitting me in the head. "*No.*" She winces right after. And that's when I see it: she's all red. Her entire body. She's cherry as a tomato, she's burnt to a crisp.

I smirk. "Yeah, how's that sunburn doing?"

She drops the pillow and heads off to the bathroom. "You know, it's great, thank you."

"You look like shit."

"*Vete a la verga,*" she mutters. Little known fact about Dani: she tends to curse in Spanish when she's pissy. I've seen a lot of this, as I tend to piss her off more than the average person.

I emit another groan. "Don't even talk to me about Vegas."

"No. Not Vegas. *Verga.*"

I frown. "What does that mean?"

"It means I'm in *pain,* and you need to fuck off."

Yeah. I probably shouldn't be gloating. But how can I not? I was right. Dani was wrong. I warned her, and she didn't listen. She dug herself a grave, and I tried to take the shovel right out of her hands. But did she let me? No. And now she's lying six feet under in crimson agony.

I sigh. "Okay. I'm getting some aloe for your cranky ass." I actually get out from under the covers at this point. And *shit*, the sun's bright. I fumble for my aviators and a hair-tie and stumble out of bed.

I somehow—*somehow*—make it to the lobby, where I find Jack coming back inside, probably from hauling his suitcase out to the bus. He stops, looks me over, and stifles a laugh. I don't know why. Maybe it's the XXL "I SURVIVED MY TRIP TO LAS VEGAS" t-shirt. Or maybe it's the baby blue sweatpants with ugly, neon pink flames running up the ankles. Perhaps it's the fact that in my hungover confusion, I had slipped on Dani's wood and leather slide-on on my left foot and my bohemian thong sandal on my right. But it just might be the sunglasses plastered on my face and my ratty hair contained in a low pony to top it all off that's got him snickering. But either way, he's very close to hysterics. "*You* look like sh—"

"Ah." I hold up a finger. "Not a word, Dickinson. Not a *word*." I leave to go out to my van. It doesn't take long for me to find the aloe. I, with terrible skin, always keep some in the back in case of emergencies. I also keep a bottle of vodka back there for the same reason. I grab both and head back inside.

I pass Elijah, who takes the bottle right out of my hand before I've even unscrewed the cap. "Nope."

"Fuck you," I call over my shoulder.

"And fuck to you, too."

I finally stop, turning around. He's smiling. Not like he usually does, like he's just watched Hell freeze over and thoroughly enjoyed it, but like he's happy. Like he's actually *happy*. "What are you *on?*" Though I think I already know the answer.

"Pot."

I turn to see who had spoken. It was Mason, lying groggily on the lobby couch with a washcloth draped over his forehead.

"Yep, pretty much," Elijah chirps. "That and seven hours of sleep."

"Seven whole hours," I mutter, walking past them. "Fucking dream come true."

I head back up to the girls' room and open the door. Dani is standing in front of the bathroom mirror, towel tucked around her chest, trying to brush her hair out. With every motion, she grimaces.

"Here you go, you strawberry freak of nature." I hurl the aloe at her. Sorry. *Toss* the aloe.

It hits her (burnt) arm. "*Ow!*"

"Put that on, let it dry, rub some lotion on that shit. My lotion. Not your Bath and Body Works Flower's Ass-scented abomination."

Dani blinks. "I don't know how to respond to that." She bends down to pick up the fallen bottle.

"You don't have to. Is Cassidy up yet?"

"I mean, there's a lump on the other bed, so I assume not."

Indeed she is right. All the blankets are concentrated at the very center.

She groans from under the covers. "Up. I'm up."

Dani nods to the bed. "There's your answer."

I move to sit on the edge of Cassidy's bed. "You got sunglasses?"

"Yeah," says the unmoving bundle of sheets.

"Good. You're gonna need them. I'm gonna go down and get breakfast. Wanna come with?"

"No."

I scoff. "Believe me, you're gonna want something."

"I'm not hungry."

I roll my eyes. "Okay. How many times have you been hungover?"

"Um... once?"

"Not including right now?"

Silence.

"That's what I thought." I rip the covers up, exposing Cassidy in all her glory, clothes from yesterday and bird's nest for hair. I'd been able to at least change my jeans to sweatpants last night. But Cassidy? When she was down, she was *down*.

"Up and at 'em, bitch," I tell her. "Time to introduce you to hangover food."

She, like I did, winces at the sunlight. "What kinds of food?" she asks, hands on her face, muffling her voice.

"Breakfast foods," I say. "Apparently, you're supposed to eat fruits, but honestly? I go straight for pancakes and mozzarella sticks."

She peeks out from behind her hands. "Do they have mozzarella sticks at the breakfast buffet?"

"No. But I'll be damned if we don't stop for some on our drive to the dam." It hits me. "Aw, *damn*, I forgot about the dam! Ugh, *Dani!*"

Dani pokes her head out of the bathroom, hair in a towel, aloe all over her face. "What?"

"Do we *have* to go to Hoover Dam?"

"It's on the list. So yes, we do."

"You sure you didn't just add it on there to spite me?"

She gives me a look. "Just get dressed, Paisley."

"No. Breakfast first. Come on, Cassidy. Ass up. Out of bed."

She groans and pulls the covers up to her chin. "Ten more minutes," she mumbles.

"No. Up." I kick the mattress. "It's not gonna get any better, so you might as well suck it up and deal."

She groans yet again, louder than before, and rolls right off the bed. Okay. She faceplants onto the floor. *Okay.*

I kick her torso. "Up." She doesn't move. I kick her again. "*Up.*"

"I'm getting up, I'm getting up!"

I fold my arms. "Where are those sunglasses of yours?"

"In my backpack," she replies weakly.

I spread my arm. "Well, go get them!" Maybe I'm just cranky, but wow, is she getting on my nerves. It's almost like she's hungover or something.

She sighs rather dramatically and goes to get them out of her backpack.

"Better, right?" I say as she puts them on. "Okay. Let's go."

Cassidy

everything hurts. My head, my stomach, my muscles. It's like Pikes Peak all over again, except this time there's nothing to blame but my own bad decisions.

And alcohol. I guess I can blame the alcohol, too.

Before we left the hotel, we plugged in directions to the nearest fast food place so that Paisley could get her precious mozzarella sticks. None of us even argued the fact that it's nine in the morning—we just went along. It's easier that way. Plus, I've found that hungover me really craves fries, so it's kind of a win-win.

Paisley lets out a little cheer as Jack pulls into the drive-through. Strangely enough, he was the only one fit to drive this morning. Well, save Dani, who just didn't want to. Paisley and Mason are as hungover as I am, and Elijah got high pretty much as soon as he woke up. So that left Jack.

"Okay," he says, turning in his seat, "what does everyone want?"

"*Mozzar—*"

"I *know!*" He closes his eyes before saying softer, "Cassie, what do you want?"

"Fries," is all I say. Nothing else sounds even remotely good.

"Okay... Large?"

I nod.

The car in front of us pulls ahead, and Jack drives up to the menu, rolling down the window. A girl's voice crackles through the speaker. "*Thank you for choosing Sonic, what can I get you?*"

Jack leans out the window a bit. "Uh, can we get an order—"

"Two orders," comes Paisley's voice from the back.

"*Two* orders—"

"Oh," Mason says, "I could go for some mozzarella sticks."

Jack's jaw clenches. "*Three* orders of mozzarella sticks and a thing of fries?"

"*What size for you?*" the girl asks. She doesn't seem fazed by any of this. To be fair, it is Vegas.

"Medium for the sticks, large for the fries."

"*Okay, what else can I get you?*"

"Uh..." Jack turns to face the others.

"Water's fine," Dani says.

Jack turns back. "W—"

"*Cheeseburger!*" Mason shouts.

Jack bites his lip, annoyed. I bet he's regretting agreeing to drive right about now. I'm not regretting calling shotgun. I've got a front row seat to whatever this is. "A water and a ch—"

"Two cheeseburgers."

"T—"

"Three," Elijah chimes in.

Jack's grip on the steering wheel tightens. "*Three* cheeseburgers—"

"And a medium Coke?"

"—and a medium Coke."

"And a vanilla shake," Mason says.

"And a vanilla shake."

Still, the girl taking our order seems perfectly unfazed. "*What size for you?*"

"Medium."

"*All right, what else can I get you?*"

Jack takes a moment to think. "You know, a shake actually doesn't sound bad. Can we get a chocolate shake, too?"

Dani pipes up again from the back. "Wait, actually, can I get a breakfast burrito?" Naturally, she's the only one ordering actual breakfast food.

"And a breakfast burrito?" Jack relays to the speaker.

"*What else can I get you?*"

"I think that's it."

"*Okay.*" The girl pauses. "*I got three orders of mozzarella sticks, a large order of fries, a water, three cheeseburgers, a medium Coke, a medium vanilla shake, a medium chocolate shake, and a breakfast burrito.*"

"I hope to God that's right," Jack says.

"Actually," Mason cuts in, "can I get a chocolate shake instead?"

"You can just have mine."

"*Okay.*" The girl is back. "*Your total is $43.58 at the window.*"

"Holy *sh*—" Jack catches himself. "Uh, thank you." He pulls forward to the window, pays using the debit card that he's been reluctant to use until now. It takes a minute for the food to come out, and it takes a couple of bags and my help to get it into the van. Before we've even left the drive-through, Paisley grabs both bags and searches for her mozzarella sticks before handing the bags over to the others. I help distribute the drinks, and then we're on our way.

Once we're back on the road, I turn around to ask for my fries. They're warm, they're salty, and quite honestly, they taste like fucking heaven. I pull one out and offer it to Jack. "You want a fry?"

"Yeah, sure." He takes it without taking his eyes off the road, popping it into his mouth.

I study him. He's been a little off ever since... Well, since whatever happened last night. I don't really remember much. What I do remember is that he was surprisingly helpful. I vaguely remember the man from the bar and how Jack was the one who was there to help me, Jack was the one who sat with me while I was feeling shitty. So, if only to garner up the details so that I might be able to piece together what happened, I say, "Hey, so about last night..."

"You know what?" he says quickly. "Just don't worry about it."

Okay, yeah, he's definitely being weird. I rack my brain one more time, but I come up empty. What could have happened to make him act like this?

Through what I assume to be a mouthful of burger, Elijah says, "You looked like a koala, Cassidy."

Once again, Jack's hands tense on the steering wheel.

My eyes widen as it slowly dawns on me—the memory of clinging to him after he threw that punch, of not letting go, of wrapping my arms around him on the way back to the bus.

God, I *did* look like a koala. "Oh... God."

"You know," Paisley says, also with a mouthful of food, "I *do* remember that."

"No," I say, not because it's not true but because I don't want it to be. "No, no, *no*." I look over at Jack. "Did I..."

He's silent, eyes focused on the road ahead.

"Jack..."

He still doesn't say a word, fingers tapping against the steering wheel.

"No," Paisley says. I look back to see her sitting up from her spot on the floor. "I distinctly remember I was sitting right there" —she points to where I'm seated in the passenger seat— "and I looked back, and Cassidy was asleep on Jack's shoulder."

Oh no. This is bad. Not for the first time, my habit of falling asleep on people's shoulders has come around to bite me in the ass. "I didn't—" I look back over at Jack, whose eyes are wider than normal. What do I do? How do I fix this?

"Guys," Dani says, "leave him alone."

"Yeah, poor thing looks traumatized," Paisley says.

Apologize. That's the first step. "Jack, I'm sorry if I—"

"It's fine."

I close my mouth. That answer was way too swift for my liking. "But—"

"Nope. We're good."

"Jack, would you just—"

"You're distracting the driver."

"I'm just trying to—"

"Shut up."

Really? How am I supposed to clean up after my drunken self if he won't even let me get a full sentence out? "I'm hungover, and now you won't even talk to me about what happened? I don't even remember everything."

He sets his jaw. "Didn't want to be hungover, maybe you shouldn't have run off to Vegas with Paisley's vodka."

I let out a breath. Haven't we already covered that it was a bad idea? Didn't he already yell at me enough for making the stupid decision to combat my problems with vodka?

"Oh, come on, Jack," Paisley says. "You were *this close* to coming with us, too." She winces. "Oh, fuck, my head." And then she's climbing up over the divider to the front, climbing over the space between Jack and me.

"Paisley!" I protest, but she's quick to dart down and grab a thing of Advil before pushing herself back up and into the backseat.

My efforts to get Jack to talk to me are fruitless. He doesn't say another word the whole rest of the drive. To be fair, it's not a very long drive, but it's still annoying. It's like I've done this terrible thing. I mean, I know I screwed up, I know I got a little clingy, but isn't he being a little oversensitive about it?

Despite my lack of results, I try one more time once we've arrived and parked at the dam. This time he doesn't get to use driving as his excuse. "Jack, can we—"

"Whoa, look," he says, "we're here." With that, he scrambles to get out of the bus.

I sigh, following his lead, along with the others. But I'm not gonna give this up. "Jack, would you just *talk* to me?"

He turns on his heel and walks away. He literally just walks away from me. I'm left standing there, mouth agape, staring at his back as he retreats toward the dam.

Meanwhile, Paisley is complaining. Big surprise there. "I don't wanna go."

"You only did this to yourself," Dani says.

Paisley folds her arms over her Vegas shirt; I honestly can't take her seriously when she looks like this. "Fine," she says. "But I'm standing next to you the whole time."

Dani only lets out a sigh before turning to follow Jack.

"Hey, Dani, want some sunscreen?"

She only walks faster; I go to follow her. We have to walk for a bit, eventually crossing the walkway onto the dam. Jack and Dani have already found a spot to lean against the railing, looking out, so I do the same, sidling up next to Dani.

Okay, so I wasn't expecting it to be beautiful or anything, but I was expecting it to be a little less... disappointing.

"You know," Paisley says after a minute, "maybe I'm just pissy, but this sucks."

My thoughts exactly. I mean, sure, it's impressive. But all it is is concrete. One can only admire concrete for so long.

"I think it's pretty cool," Jack says, if only to piss off Paisley.

I look over at him. "You know what else is pretty cool? Talking to me."

He shoots me a weird look, brow furrowed, before pushing off the railing and heading down the walkway a bit farther.

I let my arms slide off the railing, too, turning to Elijah on my other side. "Did I really screw up that badly?"

He glances over, lips pursed. "Um... I don't know exactly what went on between you two, but for a second there, it looked like things were getting a little... you know..."

"What is that supposed to—"

Oh.

Oh.

Oh God.

Oh *shit.*

I think we might have kissed.

My stomach drops. No. We couldn't have kissed. At worst, we *almost* kissed.

Right?

I jog over and manage to catch up to him, grabbing him by the arm. He turns, sees it's me, and immediately calls for Dani.

"No," I tell him. Believe me, I don't like this any more than he does. "We need to talk about this. Did we almost..." I swallow. "Did we..." I can't even say it.

"I don't know what you're talking about," he says. But he's avoiding my eye. His jaw is clenched.

"Tell me, Jack."

He sighs, running a hand through his hair. "No. We didn't."

I let out a huge breath of relief. "Oh, thank God."

"*You* almost kissed me."

Shit. It was me? "Well... at least I had enough sense to pull away."

"No. You didn't." He turns and stalks off again.

And that's about when everything comes rushing back in blurry bits and pieces. Sitting on the curb with him, crying against his chest. Brushing the hair out of his face. Leaning in... and then Mason and Elijah. If they hadn't have shown up, would I have... No. No, I wouldn't have. Because even drunk me would know not to kiss Jack Dickinson of all people.

But then again, I didn't leave his side all night. I didn't want to. I think I even let him put me to bed.

"Wait, wait, wait, Jack, hold on," I call, jogging again to catch up to him.

He regretfully turns around. "No offense, but I *really* don't want to talk about this anymore."

"Okay," I say, "as long as you realize that that... whatever it was, meant *nothing*. I was drunk. I was confused. I wasn't thinking."

"Yeah, no shit." He stuffs his hands into his pockets.

"I don't want you or— or *any* of you thinking—"

"You know, you're making a really big deal out of nothing."

I don't know why, but that just makes me more angry. I don't know if it's the way he says it or the stupid look on his face when he does, but I feel this strong urge to keep pushing. To make my point *extremely* clear. "Exactly," I say. "It was nothing."

Confused, he glances toward the others still gathered over by the railing, watching on curiously. And he turns back to me. "What does that even *mean?*"

I scoff. "You know exactly what that means."

His brow furrows as he processes this, as he spreads his hands. "No, I don't!"

Okay, now he's just trying to piss me off. "You're such an asshole," I hiss, and without really thinking, I shove against his chest. "Fuck you." Satisfied, I turn, and I start back toward the others.

"Fuck you!" Jack calls after me, an air of confusion lingering in his voice.

Dani

"what just... happened?" I ask no one in particular. "That was the weirdest fight I've ever seen in my life."

Paisley snorts beside me. "You've obviously never seen the ones I have with my van when she won't get her lazy ass through the snow."

Sensing that she's about to elaborate, I hold up a hand. "I don't even want to know." Especially because I have no idea where she would've been recently that she'd encounter snow.

"Wise decision." And with that, she saunters off to go admire the view. Or, if I'm being honest, the lack of a view. She makes that evident when she proceeds to turn *away* from the railing rather than toward it. "Can we just go?" she groans.

I don't necessarily disagree with her. I'm wondering myself why Will wanted to come here so badly, and if he were able to come here, what he would think of it. But because he did want to come here (and maybe because I'm in the mood to irritate Paisley), I tell her, "No, we just got here."

"Why does Cassidy get to go back—"

"Because she's having a rough time." I glance over at Jack, who's leaning on the railing farther down the walkway, arms folded on top of it. I know someone should check up on him, so I take it upon myself.

"I'm not doing any better than her!" Paisley calls after me. "Hey, don't just walk away— You know what? Fine."

Ignoring her, I lean up against the railing beside Jack, looking him over. "Are you okay?" It's a stupid question, I know, because he's so obviously not.

"Fine," he says tightly. Curtly.

"You don't look fine."

He's silent, eyes cast out toward the water.

I sigh. "I'm sorry about Cassidy."

He dips his chin down before turning around and leaning against the railing with me. "It's okay," he says, hands in his pockets. "She's always been like this. Well, to me, at least."

"She'll come to her senses eventually." At least, I really hope she will. "You know it's just a mix of hormones, emotions, and, you know, the hangover."

Jack gives a tiny laugh, glancing down. "Yeah, well. I don't know. Last night, it just seemed... Never mind. It's nothing."

I raise my brow. "It doesn't sound like nothing. But hey, I understand if you don't want to talk about it."

He's silent. I'm ready to walk away. I'm ready to just leave it be, leave him be, but he speaks up as I'm leaving. "She just... talked to me. She's never done that before."

I turn back. He's still not looking at me, still taking interest in the ground beneath his feet. "Really?" I ask him. "We're still talking about Cassidy here, right?"

He smiles a little, meeting my eye. "Yeah."

Cassidy has always been one to tolerate Jack at best—when they're not yelling at each other, that is. On any other given day, it seems like they're simply putting up with each other because they have to.

"The power that alcohol possesses..." I muse mostly to myself, turning away again.

And as I'm walking back toward the others, I hear Jack mumble, "Yeah. Alcohol."

It didn't take us very long to give up on Hoover Dam and leave, especially since half of us are still hungover from last night. The walk back to the parking lot was quiet and tense, save for a few remarks from Mason and Paisley. When we reached the bus, we found Cassidy sitting against it on the ground. She didn't look up when she heard us coming, and Jack didn't look down.

The bus now is still quiet and tense. Cassidy and Jack have managed to suck some of the life out of us, sour our moods. But then again, maybe that was the dam's doing.

"What did I tell you?" Paisley says once we're back on

the road. And I can't tell her off, can't even shoot her a glare, because she was right. She seems very pleased about that, even more so because she finally got shotgun back. "I said that we'd be bored out of our minds, didn't I? But *nooo*."

To my and everyone else's surprise, Cassidy is the one who snaps at her. "Paisley, would you just shut. *Up?*"

Everyone—even Jack—turns to look at her, eyes wide. Because when Cassidy loses her temper, it's almost always at Jack. When that anger is directed toward someone else, let alone *Paisley*, you know she is really pissed off.

She folds her arms, slumping farther down in her seat. "We're here for *Will*, not for your sorry ass."

Jesus Christ. I don't think I've ever heard her talk to Paisley like this, who I'm pretty sure she's afraid of.

Paisley simply clicks her tongue in response. "Wow."

With a scowl, Cassidy turns to face the window.

Jack says over his shoulder, "It's okay, she's been like this all day."

And Cassidy's quick to turn back around. "*She* wouldn't be like this if you had just talked to me instead of acting like a child."

I don't have to see Jack's face to know that he's rolling his eyes. "We're still *on* that?"

"No offense, Cass," Paisley says, "but if anyone's acting like a whiny, stuck-up, hungover bitch—"

"Stay out of this, Paisley," Cassidy snaps with a glare. "And don't call me Cass."

"This was her argument, Cassie!" Jack protests from the driver's seat. "If anything, I butted in!"

Paisley groans. "No, don't bring me back into this!" She jabs her thumb at Jack. "And why is 'Cassie' okay, but 'Cass' isn't?"

Honestly, that's a question I've asked myself, too. For as long as I've known Cassidy, Jack has been calling her Cassie. And he's the only one who does it.

"Cassie's *not* okay." She pauses. "Except when— *No*."

Jack snorts. "Okay, *Cassidy*—"

"Shut up, *Jackson*."

Jack quickly glances over his shoulder, incredulous. "I can't win with you."

The tension in this bus right now is so thick you could cut it with a knife. Mason's asleep somehow, but I share a quick

look with Elijah, who doesn't look any more thrilled about this
than I am. We both know someone has to end this before it gets
out of hand like it did on the dam.

"Guys," I say cautiously, "can we take a step back? Relax?"

However, my efforts to put the fire out only seem to
stoke it.

"How can I relax when he's being a fucking asshole?"
Cassidy retorts, nodding toward Jack.

He scoffs. "I'm not doing *anything!* You keep bringing
shit up! You realize that, right? I get you're hungover, I get you're
pissy" —I get that she's menstruating— "but you've gotta stop
blowing up at me! You're part of the reason I didn't want to go
on this fucking trip anyway!"

That renders all of us speechless. Aside from the wind
rushing by the bus and the light sound of Mason's snoring, it's
completely silent.

And then, quietly: "That doesn't surprise me. You didn't
even speak at the funeral, of course you don't want to be here.
It's like you don't even care."

My eyes widen. "*Cassidy—*"

"Really?" Jack's voice is louder now. Much louder. "You
really *think* that just because I didn't have sex with Will that I
don't care? You aren't the only one who knew him, Cassie! You're
not the only one who fucking cares about him! You knew him a
year, and you still don't seem to have a grasp on that!"

Cassidy's demeanor has shifted drastically at his words.
She lets her arms drop, lets her face fall, lets a few tears slip
down her cheeks. "That's not what I—"

"You didn't *know* him, Cassie!" Jack shouts, grip visibly
tightening on the steering wheel. "You don't know what it fucking
feels like to lose him! You don't know how it feels to hold your
dying brother's head in your lap on the side of the freeway and
not be able to do a single fucking thing to stop it!" He sucks in
a deep, shaky breath.

My mind is reeling; my stomach is sinking. I can't even
bear to believe it. "Jack..." I say, voice soft, even to my own ears.
"You were in the car?"

Cassidy is bawling now; all the pain and all the guilt
reflected in her eyes is overflowing down her face and onto her
shirt. "I didn't *know—*"

"No," Jack shouts, voice bordering on hoarse, "you didn't know! You were so fucking caught up in how *you* felt and *your* grief that you weren't giving two shits about how the rest of us were holding up!"

I catch it just as Paisley does—the bus swerving in between lanes, drawing dangerously close to the car beside us before straightening out. "Jack, pull over," she says tightly.

But Cassidy pays no mind to that. "You should have *told* us—"

"Yeah, and how would you have reacted, huh? You're fucking psychotic, Cassie! One minute it's like you actually understand what I'm going through, what all of us are going through, and not two seconds later, you're accusing me of being a shit brother! *Why the hell do you think I would tell you anything?*"

"*Jack!*" Paisley grabs onto the steering wheel. In one swift movement, she's steadied the van, turned the wheel toward her and pulled the bus over onto the shoulder, put it in park.

Jack's hands are shaking, still gripping the steering wheel. His breathing is ragged and uneven; his face is blanched white, making his red eyes and the tears streaking down his face all the more obvious. This is the first time I've seen him cry since the accident, the first time I've seen him not okay.

Paisley darts out of the passenger seat, makes her way around the front of the bus to the other side, and yanks open the driver's side door. She doesn't even have to say anything. She just pulls Jack out of the seat and right into her arms. And I've never been so grateful for Paisley Joplin in my life because anyone can see that what Jack needs right now, more than anything, is a hug. He's still stiff in her hold, but his fingers are tightening on her shirt. His eyes are still wide and fearful. He looks like a lost, scared little kid.

Cassidy is watching out the window like I am, hunched over, hugging her waist. She's as pale as Jack. "Oh God, I didn't—"

I cut her off with, "Save it," before following Paisley's lead and climbing out.

When I head around to the other side, Paisley is telling Jack, "Congratulations, asshole. You've earned rights to shotgun."

Jack stays silent, not meeting Paisley's eye nor mine.

Paisley and I share a look of silent agreement, and she goes to get into the backseat. I stop on my way to the driver's seat to lay a gentle hand on Jack's arm. It takes him a minute, but he eventually climbs into the passenger seat.

When all the doors are closed, I look at him. Really look at him. I hate seeing him like this, hate that I can't do anything to make it better. I hate the fact that under slightly different circumstances, he wouldn't be sitting here beside me right now.

But I can't think about that. So I do the only thing I can do: I let out a tiny, minute sigh before putting the bus in drive and slowly merging back onto the highway.

𝕑 𝕑 𝕑

JACKSON DICKINSON FEELS HE IS A FAILURE. He couldn't even bring himself to speak at his own brother's funeral. He left so suddenly after his mother, tense but kind, told him that it was his turn to share his eulogy.

A crumpled piece of paper fell out of his hand as the door closed behind him.

"I'm sorry I wasn't fast enough. It should have been me."

Mason

the drive from Hoover Dam to Yosemite is about six and a half
hours total, if you take into account all the rest stops.

So yeah. It's a long drive. Well, for me it isn't. I end up
sleeping most of the way, as I still feel like shit from Vegas for
a good chunk of the day.

God, I don't even *remember* Vegas. Elijah was there. I
think Paisley had her top off? I might have almost been hit by a
car. I don't fucking know.

I do know that hungover Mason means tired Mason.
The only thing I wanted to do when I woke up was sleep, but we
had Hoover Dam and Yosemite on our itinerary. Thankfully, I
had time to rest during the drive into California. But that also
meant I missed a very important event.

I had woken up at some point during Jack and Cassidy's
screaming match. I think Jack was talking about how Cassidy
never knew Will or something along those lines.

I had snorted awake and muttered, "What?"

Elijah ran a hand across my forehead and simply said,
"Go back to sleep, Mace."

I'd mumbled a quick, "Okay," and done just that.

Which meant I was more than a little confused when I
woke up and no one was speaking to each other. It took Elijah
muttering a quick explanation for me to understand what had
happened.

All attempts at friendly conversation fail, from, "Look,
cows!" to "So, Nevada weather, huh?" No one even says a word
when we cross the border into California. I mean, it's *California*.

I quickly begin to get antsy, not just because of the

thickening silence hanging in the air but because all I've been doing today is sleep. Sleep and look at a damn dam. I need to do *something*.

"How much longer?" I whine.

Dani sighs. "For the millionth time," she grits from the steering wheel, "*we're almost there.*"

"I *know*, but how much—"

"The last sign I saw said three miles," Elijah informs me gently.

"Oh. Okay."

Paisley furrows her brow. "You're being awfully nice." She glances up at Jack, who's sitting passenger with his head against the window.

"Yeah, well." Elijah looks over at Cassidy. "Someone has to."

Cassidy has her arms folded on top of the divider, curled into the corner it makes with the spot she's chosen. She's buried her face down between her forearms; she's been this way for a while.

A few minutes later, the bus slows to a halt.

"We're here, guys," Dani says softly. She looks to her right. "Jack, you're sure you want to come?"

He nods, eyes to the dashboard. He can tell we're all staring right at him.

Cassidy, upon hearing his name, pokes her head up. "Jack—"

He steps out and slams the door without a word.

Cassidy jumps as he storms off, face falling even lower. She slowly rises, wiping her eyes discreetly on her sleeve. As she bends down to grab her sunglasses from the ground, Elijah tugs on my arm. I look over.

"C'mon, let's go," he mutters.

But I can't stop staring at Cassidy, how timid she looks, how sad.

"I'll catch up to you, Holliday."

Elijah can only sigh. "Okay." He (reluctantly, might I add) leaves me alone with Cassidy.

Paisley sees my exchange with Elijah and slowly closes her eyes. "Lock up when you're done," she says, tossing me the keys. "No joy rides." She glances at Cassidy. And then: "Godspeed, my friend. Godspeed." She gives me a single pat on the back as she heads out to follow the others.

I take a seat on the edge of the open van and look back

at Cassidy, who seems to be stalling by digging through her backpack.

"You okay, Cassidy?"

She glances up, surprised. "Yeah, of course," she says with a pained smile. Though it's generous to call it that. It's wavering and fluttering away with every glance downward.

"Yeah, well. I heard you had a pretty bad fight with Jack. 'Top Ten Anime Battles' worthy, from what Elijah was telling me."

"What the—" She furrows her brow. "Hold on, you didn't hear us?"

I shake my head.

It finally clicks. "You were asleep, weren't you?"

"Yup."

She kind of laughs. Kind of. "That's impressive."

"You should see Paisley," I tell her. "She slept through her house catching fire."

She stops, taken aback. "When did that happen?"

"Like, third grade. And seventh. And a few months ago. Her family's very reckless. Or, at least, her uncle is."

She purses her lips. "Noted." She goes to step out but hesitates, standing behind me on the edge of the van. "You know, it might be best if I just hang back." She casts her gaze down. "Again."

"Aw, man, what are you talking about? You have to see Yosemite."

She looks up. "What did you just say?"

I frown. "You have to see Yosemite?" I repeat.

"It's Yo-Se-Mitee."

"It is?" I'd been pronouncing it *Yosh-Mite*.

She shakes her head, smiling. It fades just as quickly as it did before.

I stand. "Come on, Cassidy," I press. "At least for a little while."

She shrugs. "Everyone's mad at me."

"Dani's always mad, Paisley's hungover, Elijah's high, and Jack just needs time to cool off. You're fine, homie." I nudge her shoulder but underestimate just how tiny she is compared to me, as I accidentally send her stumbling backwards a bit.

"It doesn't seem like I'm fine to them."

"You can stay by me while we wander."

She mulls this over, still nervous, still hesitant. "Well..."

She sighs. "Okay." She hops down, and we go to catch up with (and find) the group.

And *wow*, is Yosemite beautiful. I've been to California with my family before. I was born here, actually. We went to Yosemite when I was really little, but to be honest, all I really remember about Cali is Disneyland.

Now I'm just left to sit and wonder how I could forget something like this.

There's water everywhere; trees, too. It's lush and green and almost makes me hate Arizona for shielding me from such a natural wonder.

There's one thing I keep hearing Paisley complain about, and that's the switchbacks. I personally don't mind them, but there's something about going back and forth, back and forth, back and forth that's driving her insane.

Would she rather just hike straight up on an incline? Didn't think so.

At one point, Dani looks behind her, most likely to be sure that the whole group is here. Upon locking eyes with Cassidy, she hurries to catch up with Jack.

This only makes Cassidy feel worse. "What did I say?" she grumbles. "Everyone hates me."

I'm trying to come up with the right words to say. Trying but failing because all my concentration is being used on hopping over certain rocks and not falling into the lake adjacent to us.

Yeah. There's a lake, too. Several, actually, but the one I'm looking at has to be the most stunning. The water is made of diamonds; it perfectly reflects the sky.

Why is California hogging Yosemite all to itself? Let Arizona have a slice, you fucking pigs.

"Mason, what are you—"

I jump to another rock. "Come on, Cassidy, keep up."

"I'm not gonna— *Mason!*"

I slip on an edge, almost plummeting straight into the water. I look up once I regain my balance, plaster a grin of relief to my face.

Cassidy sighs with a small smile. "You know, it's really weird, but this is actually kind of cheering me up."

It's at this moment that Jack passes her, muttering, "Well, isn't that just fantastic."

And her face just *sinks*. It's heartbreaking to watch her guilt come flooding back.

I don't care what she did or didn't do. I don't care what happened during that fight that I somehow missed (slept through). I mean, come on. That's just cold.

You know what else is cold? Well, we're about to find out.

I run ahead at full speed, tackle Jack into some sort of hold, and run us straight into the lake.

Jack's hair flips up as he does; he's panting, cold, soaking wet, and his eyes are wild with shock. "*Dude!* What the *fuck?*"

"Holy shit." Cassidy's giggling from behind her hands.

"Survival of the fittest, bro," I say simply. "You know how it is."

"Dick." Jack splashes me. I splash him back. And suddenly we're in this all out war—

"Guys!" Dani shouts from ashore. "Knock it off."

Jack stops splashing. I stop splashing.

"Okay," I say, putting my hands into a surrender. "Okay. You're right. Let's just get out of the lake."

Dani sighs. "Thank you."

Jack steps out shortly before I do. But the second I'm out, I grab both him and Dani, one under each arm in a football hold, and run straight back for the lake.

"*MASON!*" Dani's head is suddenly underwater. Jack's head is suddenly underwater. Mine is, too, as we all fall in from my charge.

But the second we're above—

"*Mírame,* you asshole!" I can't tell if her stutter is from the anger or from the cold. "*Eres feliz ahora?* You fucking—"

Another splash interrupts her. It wasn't me this time.

She turns toward Jack and begins *hurling* water at him relentlessly, unyielding—

"Paisley, no, Paisley, no, *PAIS*—" Another splash and Elijah's in the water.

I turn to find Paisley smirking on the shore. She's shrugging her top off (probably should have thought of that) and turning to Cassidy. "You coming?"

Cassidy knits her brow. "No, I—"

"Wasn't a question." With a shove, Cassidy's soaked. With a jump, so is Paisley.

Sure. Maybe we're locked in combat, but at least we're talking.

The rest of the hike was miserable. We were cold, wet, and ready to get back to the bus by sundown.

Paisley drove us back because she was, shockingly enough, in the best mood out of the six of us with her dry clothes that we so envied.

According to Dani, it's only a two and a half hour drive from here to Sequoia National Park. However, given that Paisley, Cassidy, and I are still a little hungover, and the whole group is drenched and tired from the dam, the drive, and the hike in Yosemite, we decide it best to just get a hotel and hike in the morning.

It's a motel, much to Paisley's delight, because that means she can keep a closer eye on her beloved in the parking lot.

We have the same setup as the last few nights, girls in one room, boys in the other.

It's a relief once we get inside.

"I'm gonna shower," Jack tells us. "Because, you know. Someone pushed me into a lake."

I frown. "You got first shower last—"

Elijah's quick to slap a hand over my mouth. "That's fine, Jack."

What—

Oh.

Ohhhhh.

Jack looks confusedly between us. "Okay..."

The second the door's closed, Elijah's on top of me. Or, rather, his lips are on top of mine. "It's about damn time," he murmurs before kissing me again.

My arm comes to wind around him, up his back, pressing into his shoulder blades, pressing him into me. "Are you still high?" I ask his bottom lip.

He sinks deeply into another kiss. "Mhm," he hums, moving his hand under my shirt.

"Cool." It's like ecstasy, I swear to God. I know that Elijah knows a bit more about drugs than I do, but this. *This* has more addictive properties than his weed ever will. Kissing him this slowly while my heart beats this rapidly at the simplest movements...

Elijah Holliday has yet to realize that he has become a drug himself.

He's pulled me to the ground somehow, put me on top of him, positioned his fluttering eyes forever in the depths of my mind.

Then he stops. I'm pulled away by the antigravity this boy gives off; a simple thumb to my lip is enough to lift me so that he can lean up against the wall, sitting cross-legged with my body parallel to the door a few feet away. I roll over to look up at the ceiling, to rest my head in his lap.

And Elijah just sighs. "Today was a lot."

"Yeah."

"Jack and Cassidy need to learn to get along." He closes his eyes, leans his head against the wall. "We all do."

I nod. He's right. I know he's right. Will was the thing that brought us all together. Will still is that for us—he's the only thing that's gotten us this far in the first place. But if we're going to do this thing for him, we need to learn how to do it without him.

"They'll come around," I tell him softly.

He looks down, hand in my hair. "Did you know about Jack?"

"What about Jack?"

I almost expect him to roll his eyes at me. He doesn't. "That he was in the crash."

I should've known he was going to ask about that. I didn't find out with the rest of them; I found out afterward while we were headed toward the van going to the motel. Elijah debriefed me a bit more on what had happened. I was silent the rest of the drive here.

"No. I didn't." I've known Jack as long as I've known Will. Where there was one, there was the other, especially when we were younger. Will grew up with me as my best friend, but Jack grew up with us as our little brother.

Elijah's hands continue to hike through my hair. "How are you holding up?"

I suck in a breath. "Yeah, it's just... I didn't know there was the possibility of losing both of them in one go. That's all."

And saying it out loud. Saying it out loud is opening the flood-gate—both a weight off my chest and an excruciating amount of pain. I could have lost both of them. I'm not sure what I'd do if I had lost both of the Dickinson brothers.

Elijah hunches down to kiss my forehead. "I know." His finger is absentmindedly running down my chest, turning my grief into adrenaline, melting my suddenly frozen body. "I can't imagine if..." He swallows.

"Yeah," I say. "Me too."

The water in the bathroom stops.

We both sit up. With one nervous glance, we're scrambling back to our feet. Elijah slips onto one of the chairs, and I follow.

"No, not on my chair, you idiot!"

Fair point.

I hurry to the other one, making sure all my limbs are accounted for as I jump on.

Jack comes out in sweatpants and a t-shirt.

"Hey, homie," I greet as nonchalantly as possible.

This only seems to concern him. "I— Okay. Shower's up for grabs for whoever wants it."

I start to stand.

"Mine." Elijah's in the bathroom within seconds.

I sigh. Disappointed but not surprised.

Jack, meanwhile, is concerned with digging through his suitcase. The more I look at him, the more I find myself imagining that accident. How he must have felt, how he looked, the weight of his brother's body pulling his heart into his stomach—

"Hey, I know it's technically your night for the floor, but... uh, you can have the bed if you want."

Jack doesn't so much as look up when he shakes his head. "Nah, I'll pass."

"You sure?" I ask. "You look like you need it more than I do."

"I'm fine." He zips his suitcase and begins to set up his spot on the floor.

I stand and take him gently by the arm. "Jack."

He finally looks up. He has Will's eyes. I hate it, but he does. There are a few key differences, obviously: while Will's eyes were a subtle, alluring blue, Jack's have always been more striking. But they're the same nonetheless, and it kills me to look at him sometimes. It shouldn't, but it does.

"I didn't know," I tell him quietly. "I'm sorry."

His face almost pinches at this. "How would you?" he asks. "It's not like I told anyone."

"You should have."

He waves it away, pulling his arm back.

"You could have told me."

He stops at this. It's almost as if he's suddenly reminded of how close we truly are, that he wasn't the only one who lost a brother that day. "Yeah. Sorry."

"It's okay." I wait a beat. "You sure you don't want the bed?"

He hesitates. Strongly considers my offer. And he finally shakes his head, gathering his things from the floor and moving them to the nightstand.

"Jack?"

He looks back over at me.

I give him a lopsided smile. "I'm glad you're here."

And for the first time in a while, he smiles back.

⊘ ⊘ ⊘

"I CAN'T THANK YOU ENOUGH FOR DOING THIS, LAURA."

"Oh, honey, of course. Any time." And just like that, my mom had dismissed Mrs. Ocampo's anxiety with a single wave of her hand. She's always had that ability, that calming nature. It's what made her such a good mother, what made me so calm and Jack so fearless.

"Does Mason have any allergies? I'm making dinner, but I'll gladly fix him something if he can't have lasagna."

"Don't worry about that, he'll eat anything." Her eyes slid over to her son with a grimace. "Even glue."

My mom blinked. "All right then. Well, he's all settled to spend the night if need be."

"We should be home by then, but if not, I'll for sure let you know." She didn't sound so sure.

"Excellent. Well, you two go have fun!" I assume, looking back on it, that her husband was either in the car or already at the event.

Her eyes gleamed. "Yeah, about as much fun as you can have at a company dinner party."

They shared a quick mom laugh (you know the type).

And with that, the door shut, and she was off.

Her son looked at me, eyes huge and brown, hair fluffy and flying everywhere. It looked as though there was an attempt to tame it, an attempt that ultimately failed because no six-year-old can be still for long enough to have neat hair. Especially if that six-year-old is Mason Ocampo.

"Do you have any Legos?" His tone was serious. Immediate, but not frantic.

I remember nodding. "Yeah, me and Jack have some in

the basement."

"Good. I need to show you something."

"What? What is it?" What could he possibly need to show me that was so important? So urgent?

"Come on!"

We raced down to the basement, tripping over our sneakers to get there. I opened the closet and brought them out onto the wooden floor. The Legos were kept in a large, plastic box. I carefully pried the lid open and tossed it aside.

Mason stuck his hands inside and brought out a couple of pieces. He looked back up at me. "Okay. Ready?"

I nodded, anxiously awaiting his next move.

He put several pieces together and showed me proudly. "It's a *spaceship!*" He proceeded to fly the vessel around the room, making sound effects along with his running.

And it looked *just* like one.

"How did you do that?" I asked, amazed.

He vroomed back over and parked the spaceship (again with his mouth). "Okay. You take a piece like this..." He dug through the Legos again.

I watched intently all the while.

"And then you get this big piece here." He put a few more pieces together. "And then it's a spaceship."

I was in awe.

He flew his spaceship around the room again, leaving me with one of my very own.

"You have to show Jack!" I exclaimed.

Mason redirected his flight to run upstairs with me.

"*Jack!*" I called.

Jack was in his usual spot in the playroom next to a tiny stack of picture books we always kept in a corner. This was only the beginning of his addiction. It was shortly after this that Mom began to notice his habits and buy more books. Even though he was a year behind me, he learned to read faster than and before I did.

"JackJackJackJackJack—"

"What?" he whined.

I poked Mason, whose name I had heard only briefly, not enough to call him this.

Mason fumbled for his Legos and proudly showed Jack.

Jack frowned, confused.

"It's a *spaceship*," Mason told him.

"It doesn't *look* like a spaceship."

Mason pouted.

"It needs fire." Jack stood and waddled down to the basement. We followed after him as he made his way over to the Lego bin and dug through. He found the fire pieces after a minute and the other parts to stick them on. He showed us. "See?"

And wow. *Wow.* It looked like a spaceship before, but now it *really* looked like one. Mason and I were in awe.

We played liked this for a while, setting up our own colonies in separate corners of the basement—Mason in the living room, Jack in the guest bedroom, me by the kitchenette. We would trade different Lego pieces for Hot Wheels, Pokémon cards, and Beyblades. Whatever we could find, really.

It wasn't long after Jack decided to attack my territory, forcing Mason to try and intervene but only making things worse with his explosions, that Mom called us up for dinner.

The lasagna was good, the company was excellent, and I was happy because I was playing with a new friend and my little brother.

Mom's mood, however, quickly faded as she received a call on the landline. She migrated away from earshot and took the call. When she came back, she looked sympathetically at our guest. "Mason, sweetie, your mom and dad are running pretty late. I think—"

"Sleepover?" Before she could even finish the sentence. Before she could even imply that he would spend the night. His eyes were huge before the words so much as left her mouth.

And as soon as he said it, I repeated, "*Sleepover?*"

Jack, who barely knew what a sleepover was, sat there, eyes wide and fearful.

Mom hesitated. "Well..."

But we were already chanting. "*SLEEPOVER! SLEEPOVER! SLEEPOVER!*"

I'll say it: Jack didn't know what the hell was happening. Even at age five he knew what "fuck" meant, and he was feeling it loud and clear.

"We can sleep in the basement!" I suggested.

"We *can?*" Mason gasped.

Now Jack was on board. His face lit up with mine and Mason's as he looked at Mom.

She glanced over at Dad, who spread his hands helplessly. "Uh... sure?"

Dad sighed. "I can go set up some sleeping bags."

We cheered.

Cut to an hour after we were supposed to go to sleep, still chattering away like it was mid-afternoon and not almost ten.

"No, it's true!" Mason was insisting. "I have a pool *inside my house!*"

"No one has pools inside their house!" Jack told him. "The whole place would be wet!"

"Yeah, you're lying," I agreed.

"I'm not lying!"

"And you have a real life spaceship, too?" Jack caught onto sarcasm fairly early.

"No," Mason said. "It wouldn't *fit.*"

"Oh." Again with five-year-old sarcasm.

"Is that what your mommy's doing?" I asked Mason through the darkness. "Trying to make your house bigger?"

"Maybe," he said. "She never tells me."

We laid in silence.

"Maybe she's trying to buy a spaceship," Jack suggested.

Mason giggled brightly; it lit up the whole room.

"How much do spaceships cost, anyway?" I asked.

"Probably, like, a hundred dollars," answered Jack knowingly.

"A hundred *million* dollars," Mason corrected.

"A hundred ga*zillion* dollars," I added.

"That's not a real number," said Jack.

"Yes, it *is!*" I retorted. "I'm older than you, I know more things."

"My daddy says that to me a lot," Mason mused.

"Haha, Jack, you're dumb," I laughed.

"No, I'm *not!* I'm smarter than you, Mommy told me!"

"No, she didn't." Yeah, she did. He wasn't meant to hear. "Mason, who do you think is more smart?"

Mason paused. "Okay," he said finally. "I know how to be able to tell." Another beat. "Are you ready?"

Jack and I nodded.

"Okay." He drew in a deep breath. "Are you smart?"

We, again, both nodded.

"Then spell it."

I struggled to spell out, "S-M-A-R-T" as Jack spelled out, "I-T."

"Jack's more smarter."

"*Ha!*"

I folded my arms. "No fair. I'm older."

"Well, I'm *smarter*."

The fact of the matter was we were both kids ahead of the curve. Jack learned to read first, I learned to talk first. It was very in character for us even back then. I always tended to do the talking. He was usually the one to sit back, watch, observe, maybe make a comment or two on the side. Even though we both came off as impulsive in our own ways, him more so than me, we'd always been like this. He was more impulsive with actions; I was more impulsive with people. We would carry on like this for the rest of our childhoods, up until the day we parted.

Cassidy

the sun has barely poked its head above the horizon when I'm woken up. By what? I'm not really sure, seeing as it's completely silent, and Dani and Paisley are still asleep in the other bed. Part of me wants nothing more than to curl up and go back to sleep for a few more hours, but another part of me misses the feeling of being awake before the sun, like I always was during the school year. So I sit up. Except as soon as I sit up, everything comes rushing back to me. The argument from yesterday, the way I yelled at Jack, the way he screamed at me, the way he broke down when he...

He was in the car with Will. He was in the car with him, and I didn't know. He could have *died*, and all this time I was oblivious. The last time I saw Jack before the crash could have been the very last time.

And I never even apologized.

Never go to bed angry, isn't that what they say? And we did just that. I was pissed at him, and he had every right to be pissed at me.

Isn't that just for married couples, though?

I sigh. Trying to shake the thoughts out of my head, I push the sheets aside and climb out of bed. The air conditioning had been running all night, and neither Dani nor I knew how to turn it off, so I spent the night wrapped in blankets. Now, I take the comforter from my bed and wrap it around my shoulders, walking around Dani and Paisley's bed to open the curtains. And, of course, the first thing I see? Jack, sitting on top of the bus in the parking lot, facing the sunrise. I bite my cheek, staring at his motionless form for a minute. And I let out another sigh, letting the comforter drop to the floor. I need to fix this. Some way, somehow.

I put on the first t-shirt I can find, followed by Will's hoodie and the denim skirt lying on top of my suitcase. I pull on socks and sandals (I know, classy, right?) and grab the room key, trying to leave as quietly as possible. I look like a hot mess, I'm aware. I haven't even brushed my hair yet. But hey, can you blame me? It's barely five in the morning.

The parking lot is quiet. So quiet that I think my footsteps might be the loudest thing I've ever heard. I'm sure Jack can hear me coming, but if he does, he doesn't acknowledge it. He hasn't moved an inch by the time I grab the cold, slick rungs of the ladder and start climbing. He doesn't even bother to look up when I come up behind him.

"Jack?" I say softly.

He lets out the tiniest, nearly inaudible breath. He sits there a moment, unmoving. I start to wonder if he even heard me. And then: "We were on our way to school."

Even though he still hasn't looked at me, I take this as an invitation to sit down beside him. I bring my knees to my chest and wrap my arms around them, waiting for him to continue.

And he does. "Will was hurrying me along like usual. He was always the one who wanted to move fast in the morning. I think he was especially pushy because he wanted to get there early to meet you."

"You mean..." I trail off.

Jack sucks in a breath. "Things were pretty tense. We'd just gotten into a fight the night before. He took a while to apologize, though he didn't really need to. It wasn't him that started it. Well, not exactly." He finally looks over, and I meet his eye. "It was about you, actually."

"Me?" I ask warily. "What about me?" Though I think I know.

He glances down at his feet. "He said he loved you."

Shit.

"And you didn't say it back."

Shit.

"He came to me for advice, I guess, but I told him to just let it go. You'd come around when you were ready. Well, you know Will, he's very in tune with his feelings." He pauses. "*Was* in tune." He squeezes his eyes shut for a moment. "And he just assumed everyone else was, too."

Yeah. He did. That was one of those things about Will that I always aspired to be. In... control, I guess. Because I've always tried so hard to get control over my emotions. That's part of the reason I'm up here. Part of the reason I feel so terrible about what happened with Jack yesterday.

I swallow. Hard. "I was— I just... He just sprung it on me. Out of nowhere. I didn't realize that would be..."

"His last words to you," Jack finishes for me.

Yeah. Exactly. "And I said thanks." I cringe at the memory. "*Thanks.*"

He bites back a smile. "Well, at least you were polite about it."

I cast my eyes down, rest my chin on my knees. "It's not funny," I mumble.

"Don't be too hard on yourself," he says. "I get why you panicked."

I glance back up at him to see the slight gleam in his eyes fade.

"And I told him that," he continues, voice wavering. "It turned into a huge argument, even though the whole time I should have just minded my business. But I couldn't. It was just... I don't know. He needed a wake up call. And he got it the next morning. He told me he understood, he apologized to me... and I stayed silent. I didn't apologize to him for... uh." He sucks in a breath. "Claiming he didn't care." He rubs his palms on his jeans, nervously licking his lips.

I echo his advice: "Don't be too hard on yourself."

He smiles weakly at that, but it falters just as soon as he starts talking again. "And the fight started again after I didn't say anything. It just kept growing and growing and growing..." His breathing is getting shakier, his voice breaking. "And then he let out this huge moan... and it took me a minute to realize what was happening... He swerved the car—" His voice catches then, and he tries to cover it up by running a hand through his hair.

My heart jumps to my throat; I'm choking on it. "He had a seizure," I say hoarsely. It's not a question.

Jack nods, picking at his shoelace. "First one in a few months. And of fucking course it was while he was driving."

My hand clenches into a fist, fingernails digging into my palm. That doesn't help—I'm still shaking. "Oh God."

"And I couldn't do a single fucking thing to stop it," he grits, jaw clenched.

His features blur through my tears. Everything went numb when I heard what had happened; I almost blacked out. And I didn't have to watch him die. "Jack…"

"He slumped over… The car went left, ramming the driver's side right into—" His voice breaks again. He can barely breathe, let alone continue.

"Jack, I didn't—" Now my voice cracks. The breath I inhale is shaky. Rattling. "Why didn't you tell me?"

Except I know why he didn't tell me. Of course I know.

His gaze falls to his lap. "I didn't want to live through it twice," he murmurs.

Tears pool heavy in my eyes. This boy. This boy has been through a lifetime of grief, a lifetime of trauma. He holds a lifetime of guilt. And he's been carrying it all himself.

I look down at his hand beside me. I've never been the best at comforting, but as my tears fall and stain Will's hoodie, there's nothing I need more than to hold this broken boy's hand. So I do.

He freezes. Everything freezes. Everything except his hand, which he shifts to lace his fingers through mine.

"Why are you still being so nice to me?" I ask, looking back up at him. "I've been awful to you."

He finally looks up, and our eyes meet silently, unwavering, unblinking. He's saying everything at once, everything he can't say aloud, and I know I'm doing the same. And for just the briefest moment, his eyes quickly, almost subconsciously flit down to my lips and back up to my eyes.

And suddenly, I can't breathe. A wave has crashed over me, pushing my head underwater. A wave of guilt, of dawning, horrifying realization. Of everything that is and has ever gone unspoken between Jack and me. Between Will and me, too.

I'm reminded of the way I felt when Will first brought me to his house. When I first met his parents. When I first met Jack.

And I hate myself for it.

"No." I yank my hand away from Jack's. "No, I can't."

"I know," he's quick to say. "I'm sorry, I shouldn't've— I didn't mean—" He runs his hand through his hair. "*Fuck.*"

"I *can't*," I say, voice strained. "I love you."

Jack whips his head up.

My eyes widen. "*Will.* I love *Will.*" I look away in horror. "*Shit.*"

"Oh... my God." He breathes out.

I'm suddenly very aware of the hoodie I'm wearing. The hoodie that belongs to my dead boyfriend. The hoodie that's constricting me, tighter and tighter, making it harder and harder to breathe, to focus, to function. The hoodie that I shouldn't be—*can't* be—wearing. "Shit, shit, shit." I scramble to my feet, trying desperately to pull it over my head.

"What are you doing?" Jack asks.

"I can't—" I can't do this. "I don't—" I don't deserve it. I don't deserve Will. The harder I yank on it, the harder it is to take off. And before I know it, I'm stuck with it all twisted up. "*Fuck!*" I shout.

"Cassie," Jack says cautiously, "calm down."

I'm getting lightheaded. It still smells like Will. His smell is surrounding me, and it's intoxicating and poisonous at the same time.

"Hey, hey, hey." One of his hands grabs my arm, and the other tries to help me get the thing over my head. "Listen to me, I'm right here."

That's the problem, Jack.

With one last burst of energy, I tug the hoodie hard over my head, sending it flying somewhere off behind me. But I stumble in the process and find myself losing my footing, tilting off balance, my heel slipping off the edge of the roof.

"*Shit!*" Jack yells, wrapping his arms around me, catching me before I can fall. He steps back away from the edge, pulling me into him.

I'm frozen, half by the shock of what just happened and half by the feeling of staring into his eyes yet again. His very, very blue eyes. I've never realized just how blue his eyes are. Which, once again, dart down to my lips.

"I'm sorry," he says.

"Wha—" I start, but before I can finish he's brushing my hair back and kissing me.

He's kissing me. Jack Dickinson is kissing me. I'm kissing Jack Dickinson. Am I? Am I kissing back? The kiss deepens and— Yep. That was me. That was most definitely me.

I don't know how long it lasts. I don't even know who pulls away first. All I know is that I don't want it to end.

I swallow, eyes wide. "Fuck."

Jack

"fuck," i agree. This is not good. This is *so* not good. This is the least good thing to happen since Vegas.

Cassidy Montag is my brother's girlfriend. Cassidy Montag has always—*always*—been off limits. From the very first time my brother brought her home, her middle name has been, "Bad idea." Looking at her: bad idea. Spilling my soul out to this girl: bad idea. Kissing her again: bad fucking idea, Jack.

But here I am nonetheless, kissing her again, spilling my soul with every touch, staring right at her with my hands as they glide up her waist...

She's making me feel like Navajo Bridge all over again. But the adrenaline I felt then is nothing compared to what I'm feeling right now.

"We shouldn't be doing this," I tell her between kisses.

"No," she kisses, "we shouldn't."

"Then stop kissing me." I kiss her again.

"Only if you stop kissing me."

"In a minute," I mumble into her mouth.

We take more than a minute. It's like we can't stop. It's like if I let her go, she's going to disappear, she's going to go back to her usual self, the one that hates me beyond belief. And if she stops kissing me, I might do the same.

We keep going. This isn't good. This is a bad idea. But right now it feels like a worse idea to stop, even if—

She yelps, losing her footing and almost falling off the roof. Again.

I catch her (again) and somehow manage to hold her tighter still.

Her hands remain clinging to my arms. She looks up

at me. Her nostrils flare, and she kisses me again. "Stop doing that," she says.

I take her words in with yet another kiss. "Then stop falling." I trail my lips away slowly, taking some of her with me, before moving my gaze back up to meet her eyes. And holy shit, is she gorgeous. When she isn't yelling at me, when she isn't scowling or glaring, when she's completely and utterly still, she is *gorgeous.*

Cassidy sighs, wrapping her arms around my waist and laying her head on my chest. My movements should be tentative. Cautious. They're quite the opposite. My fingers come to run through her hair a little too naturally. They glide down her spine, causing her to shiver from my touch.

"This is not good," she mumbles.

I rest my chin on top of her head. "Nope."

"Not even a little," a new voice agrees.

Do you remember when Mason first came into my bedroom to kidnap me? Do you remember how scared shitless I was?

Put that feeling into present tense, into both of us, and imagine that within the context of being caught red-handed by Paisley Joplin of all people.

She stands on the ground, staring up at us with folded arms. "Sorry, was I interrupting?" She jabs a thumb at the van entrance. "Because I can come back later, you know, when your tongues aren't down each other's throats."

Cassidy's face flushes redder than ever.

I try to reason with her for Cassidy's sake. "Paisley—"

"*Paisley?*" she repeats with disbelief. "Are you fucking kidding me? You're kissing your dead brother's girlfriend, and you're gonna fucking *Paisley* me?"

Cassidy takes these words into careful consideration. "Let go of me," she hisses, not meeting my eyes.

I put my hands into a surrender. "Okay," I mutter. "Jesus."

She smooths out her skirt, looking back down. "Paisley, you're not gonna... You're not gonna tell the others, are you?"

My heart sinks. Of course. Of course she doesn't want anyone else to know. Why would she want anyone to know she's downgraded from *Will Dickinson* to his little brother? Granted, that may not be the reason. But it sure as hell feels like it.

I'm about to tell her off. I'm about to snap at her. But all I can seem to muster up is, "Wow."

She must realize what she's said because she begins to argue, "Well—"

But Paisley's loud groan cuts her off. She ends it with an annoyed sigh. "And now there's two to worry about," she mutters.

I furrow my brow. "What do you—"

"Don't worry about it."

I close my mouth.

"Just don't fuck in my van, and we'll be fine."

Cassidy's quick to jump in. "It's not—" She looks at me quickly, looks away even quicker. "Oh God." And she goes to climb down the ladder, to grab Will's fallen hoodie, to make her way back to her room.

"I mean it," Paisley says loudly as Cassidy walks by. "I want a Bible length between you two at all times!"

"Thank you." I drop my hands. "Thanks for that."

The motel room door closes behind Cassidy, and Paisley finally grows serious. "This is a bad idea," she tells me. "You know that, right?"

I avoid her eyes.

She sighs at my lack of response and goes inside the bus.

Paisley

are you fucking kidding me. First Mason and Elijah and now *this shit?*

I need a drink. Thankfully, that's what I was going to grab when I saw Jack and Cassidy—of all people—on top of *my bus* making out.

Wonderful.

*Wonder*ful.

Maybe it's just a phase. Maybe it's just one of those grief things. Some people drink (hi). Some get bangs. Other people do *that*.

I need to think. That's what I need to do. Except I'm rather bad at thinking when I've just caught Jack and Cassidy, who were *screaming* at each other not a day ago, making out *on my van*.

How long has this been going on? Is that why Cassidy clung to him in Vegas? Is that why their fight seemed so... messy?

Or did they just get a hold of Elijah's weed?

I don't know. I just don't know. I want to try and figure this out, but the problem is that my brain works best when it's bouncing off someone else's. But I can't *tell* anyone about this because I have to be a "good friend." Fuck me.

So yeah. It's a good thing I went outside to get some vodka. I'm gonna need it to deal with all of this.

I come back into the room that Cassidy just stormed into, locking eyes with Dani. "Well, I found Cassidy." I shut the door with my leg.

Cassidy doesn't look up. She's sitting on the bed, looking none too happy about the situation she's found herself in. *Put* herself in.

Dani, currently lying in the other bed, looks up at me. "She won't talk to me," she says. "Where did she go?"

"Oh, you won't believe this one, but she was making..." Cassidy whips her head up.

"...up some excuse about not being able to sleep when I found her."

Dani sits up a little. "Okay, but where was she?"

"Where?" I repeat. "She was on top of my van with Jack." Cassidy's eyes widen, wild and frantic.

Dani frowns inquisitively. "Jack?"

"Yeah," I say. "Jack Daniels? The liquor? I don't know how she found it. I guess I had a bottle in the back of my bus somewhere."

"Um, okay..." Dani looks uneasily to her right. "You were really drinking this early in the morning?"

Cassidy's eyes stay huge on the sheets beneath her.

I scoff. "Well, she sure as hell was doing something with it."

Dani pauses a really, *really* long time. "What was she *doing?*"

"Not a clue." I let my eyes slide over to Cassidy. "If you ask me, she's *lost her mind.*"

Cassidy stands wordlessly, grabs her clothes, and stalks into the bathroom.

Dani has no words either. Or, more accurately, very few. "What's going on, Paisley?"

"Nothing." Lie. "I just like giving her shit." Very true. "Are we leaving fairly soon or can I get a little more sleep in before we hit the road?"

"If by sleep you mean sleep, then yes. But if you mean *drink,* then no."

"Well, you saw right through me. I'm going back to bed."

Dani lies back down with a sigh. "Same here."

The drive is a living *hell.*

First off, you've got Jack and Cassidy sitting as far away from each other as physically possible. This, granted, we all saw coming, given yesterday's events. But add to that what *I* know, and it's just disgusting. There's no other word for it. It's gross.

Icky. Yucky. I would honestly rather they just make out in the backseat than have to see Jack glance periodically up from his book to see Cassidy quickly look away, even though she'd been staring at him for the past fifteen minutes (even though we've only been in the van for about two).

Mason and Elijah, meanwhile, are sitting as *close* to each other as physically possible without making it too obvious that this is their intention. So far, I have seen (a.) Elijah's ankle travel briefly up Mason's calf, (b.) Mason lean over Elijah's shoulder to "see what he's doing," and (c.) Elijah quickly fix Mason's hair because "he had crumbs or some shit in it."

All of this is being witnessed from my rearview mirror. I have no idea how they've kept this a secret. Because now that it's staring me in the face, it is *so* obvious. It's like they're not even trying to hide it. I mean, seriously, Jack and Cassidy are doing a better job than they are. And they made out on the roof of a fucking *bus*. My fucking bus.

Dani is none the wiser about any of this. It's frankly exhausting. I need something to keep my sanity.

We pass a sign for an exit that advertises a Starbucks as one of their restaurants.

"You guys want coffee? I want coffee." I swerve across several lanes to make the exit, leaving the others in muttered anger. "All right," I tell them. "This isn't Sonic part two. Tell me what you want, and if you so much as hesitate, you get *nothing*."

Dani frowns at me from the passenger seat. "Isn't that a bit harsh?"

"Yeah, I don't wanna hear shit, Ms. I-ordered-a-burrito-last-minute."

Jack, knowing full well what pain this caused him being the designated driver the last time we made the horrible decision to drive this group through a drive-through, strongly considers my argument.

Dani is on the verge of rolling her eyes. Deciding against the action, she says, "Well, in that case, I'll take a small black coffee."

"And no one is surprised. Jack?" I turn to face him. "What's your poison?"

"I don't know. Surprise me."

"You're gonna get a unicorn's ass if you don't decide right now."

"Fine. Americano."

"Great. Cassidy?"

"Um..." She doesn't look up from her phone. "Caramel frappuccino."

"Cool. Lijah?"

"Iced chai."

"Mason?"

"Same as Jack."

I stare. "An Americano?" I repeat.

"Yeah?"

I frown. "Why did I think you were going to get, like—"

"The unicorn's ass?" Dani finishes.

"Yeah, yeah, exactly." I almost smile. "Glad you were listening."

We pull up to the speaker.

"*Welcome to Starbucks, what can I get started for you?*"

"Hey, yeah, hi," I greet, "can we get a black c—"

"Actually, can I get that iced?"

I turn to Dani. *Slowly.* "You're on thin fucking ice." But I order it anyway, along with the other drinks, and we're back on the road.

Dani takes one sip of her drink and immediately spits it back out.

I eye her. "What's wrong?"

"It's *sweet*," she chokes.

Mason frowns. "Is it not supposed to be?"

"It's supposed to be *coffee*."

Many people describe a person's thoughtful expression or attitude as seeing their "gears turning." This is usually a descriptor utilized when someone is either processing an idea or coming up with a spectacular plan. When the gears turn in my head, it is typically not a good thing. It's more often than not because I've come up with a bad idea rather than a good one. Or, at least, that's what I'm told.

"Yeah, Mason," I say. "I mean, you expect one thing and get another. That shock can put you in a pretty pissy mood."

Jack and Cassidy are suddenly very uneasy. So are Mason and Elijah. Or, at least, Elijah is. Mason doesn't get the analogy I'm trying to make.

Dani also doesn't understand. "I mean, I'm not *that* mad.

It's not that big of a deal."

"No, no," I say. "It is a big deal. That open line of communication is *huge* when it comes to coffee, right?" This may qualify as a "dick move." But it is a much needed dick move if you ask me.

"Not really." Dani shrugs. "It's just coffee."

I completely ignore her. "I mean, the *relationship* between customer and barista is a sacred one. Trust is important."

"Uh..." Dani trails off.

Jack is sitting up now.

"I mean, Cassidy, what if you had gotten, I don't know. A caramel *macchiato* instead of a frappuccino?"

She's quick to respond, "I really wouldn't *mind*—"

"What if Dani had diabetes, huh? And she took a sip and *died?*"

"I wouldn't have *died,* Paisley."

"You should just march right in there. Demand a confession. Say, 'Tell me the truth: were you or were you not attempting murder?'"

Poor Dani throws her hands up. "Why would they be trying to kill me?"

I meet the eyes of every single one of those fuckers in the backseat. Jack, Elijah, Cassidy, Mason. All of them. "Beats me."

They each stare back with the same fear. Well, minus Mason, who still isn't exactly in on the joke.

"You know," Elijah grits, "maybe she's not *telling them* because there are other people to think about in the Starbucks, Paisley."

"Well, yeah, but it's *her* drink."

"I just don't see why you're making such a big deal out of nothing," Cassidy pipes up.

Jack swallows. "Maybe it wasn't nothing, Cassie," he says quietly.

And she finally, after this entire van ride, meets Jack's eye. "It's just coffee."

"Coffee's *pretty* important, though," I cut back in. "Especially to poor Dani, who now has to suffer without *any* caffeine to get her through the day. She is the *only one of us* without a drink. Isn't that sad?"

"I'm still going to *drink* it," she says. "It's not the end of the world."

"I wouldn't," I caution. "Not with your diabetes."

"I don't have diabetes!"

"Maybe you should just stay out of this, Paisley," Elijah says, fists flexing and clenching beside him. "It's Dani's business, not yours."

"She made it *all* of our business when she put that despicable drink on *our* card. We should just burn the Starbucks down."

Dani rolls her eyes. "Why are we still talking about this?"

"I'm wondering the same thing," Mason says with a frown.

Elijah slowly closes his eyes.

"Dani is to coffee as I am to vodka," I muse.

"*No,* I am *not.*"

"As Elijah is to weed," I continue. "Among other things."

His face just *pales.*

Jack furrows his brow. "What the hell is that supposed to mean, 'other things?'"

"You know, sketching."

"Right." Elijah's jaw twitches. "Sketching."

"*Ohhhh.*" And Mason finally gets it.

Cassidy, probably believing that Mason's understanding was that the conversation is about her, begins to visibly panic. She meets Jack's eye for the second time this morning. He only turns away.

"Well..." Mason tries. "Maybe..."

"Don't," Elijah says quickly, tiredly.

"Don't what?" I smile sweetly at them.

"*Qué demonios?*" Dani mutters to herself.

"Dominos?" Mason perks up at what he thinks he heard. "Pizza sounds good."

Elijah looks almost as bad as he did wandering the Vegas Strip. "Mason, no."

"We already got coffee, and look where that led us," I argue. "Imagine if we had coffee *and* pizza. I mean, those things just don't *mix.*"

Everyone stares at me silently.

"I never thought I'd say this," Dani says, "but Paisley? I think you need a drink."

I look her way, exhausted. "Yeah. You're damn right I need a drink."

※ ※ ※

IN CASE YOU WERE WONDERING, Paisley Joplin has always been "like that." She's a lot like Jack in that sense. Both have this "take no shit" attitude that always fascinated me. Even when I didn't really know her all that well, she just baffled me. I'd run home and tell my mom, "Guess what Paisley did today!" Just because that girl was so interesting to me.

I distinctly remember the turning point, when I went from questioning her from afar to getting a front row seat to her shenanigans. We were in fifth grade, and it was recess. All bad things happened during recess. All good things, too. It was a chaotic time, constantly.

Well, we'd gotten a group of us together to play Groundies. If you've never played before, I honestly feel terrible for you. For those of you who have, I'd skip this next paragraph.

Basically, one person is "it." The person who is it, obviously, is tasked with tagging the other players. The catch? The other players can't touch the ground. Or, they can, but if they do, the person who's it must shout, "*Groundies!*" at the top of their lungs, and then the poor soul who thought they could best them is suddenly it. They're also not allowed on the playset like the other players are. If the person who's it decides to go on the playset to tag the others, they have to close their eyes, which leads to a number of confused teachers looking up at the playset and seeing a swarm of children running away screaming from an apparent zombie.

Enough about the rules. At this point in time, I was it. Not my favorite position to be in, but hey, who am I to question the laws of Groundies?

For the record, I only partly knew half of these kids. I

could name almost everyone in the group, but my good friends only made up a small number. This number included Mason, who, after several long years of waiting, I was finally in the same class with.

I say that I could name *almost* everyone because many of them were fourth graders; I was in fifth grade at the time. Our recess was shared with the grade below us. This also meant that Jack was playing with us. Well, sort of. He was sort of playing.

And I was really getting into it. I had a few tricks up my sleeve that I'd been dying to use. The only difficult part was playing with Mason, who I'm fairly sure actually *wanted* to be it.

But I didn't tag him. I managed to tag the infamous Paisley Joplin, Groundies wizard. I didn't know how she did it. But somehow—*somehow*—she'd only ever been tagged by a handful of people. And now I was one of those few.

I grinned from ear to ear. I don't think I had ever smiled broader than I did that day, gloated more triumphantly than I did when I shouted, *"Paisley's it!"* to the rest of the group.

"No, I'm not!" she protested. "You didn't tag me!"

"Yes, I did!"

Mason, who was on the playset, watched intently from behind the railed bars. Jack watched, too, but for different reasons. While Mason looked nervous, Jack was biting back a little smile.

I shrugged at Paisley. "Okay, fine." I tagged her again.

She looked rather offended by this. "Quit being an *asshole!*"

I gasped. My eyes widened. She didn't. She didn't just say... *that.*

Mason frowned. "What does 'asshole' mean?"

Jack whispered in his ear, causing Mason's eyes to widen just as mine had.

I turned. "Ms. Hunter!" I called.

"No, don't!" Paisley grabbed my arm.

I pulled away from her. "You said a bad word!"

"So?"

She really didn't care. Even at ten years old.

I glared at her. She would be in *big* trouble if Ms. Hunter knew what she had said. It technically—*legally*—was my civic duty as a fifth grader to let her know what Paisley had said.

However.

I could use this to my advantage if I so chose. Though I liked to consider myself a generally good kid, I was not above such actions.

"Okay," I said. "If you say that you're it, I won't tell."

She mulled this over.

"Deal?" I stuck my hand out.

She scowled. And then the strangest thing happened. She said, "Fine," and she shook my hand.

I shook it back. My hardened glare slowly spread into a smile. "*Paisley's it!*" I ran off as she gave us the obligatory ten second head start.

And then it was game on.

It was chaos. I barely escaped. Mason jumped as Paisley's fingers poked through the chain-style flooring of the playset. Others screeched as her arms came up and through the bars out of seemingly nowhere. Many gasped at her ability to climb onto the playset—a bold risk in and of itself—and somehow sense where they were going to be next.

It was only a couple of minutes later that she managed to tag Jack.

"He's it!" Paisley, who didn't know Jack's name at the time, called.

"I'm not playing," he said shortly.

"You are now! *He's it!*"

"No, I'm not."

"Yes, you are."

"No, I'm—"

"Jack, come on," I called from my place on the slide.

Jack looked up at me. I clasped my hands under my chin, pleaded with him.

And finally, he rolled his eyes and climbed down from the playset to count to ten. Not two seconds after he did so, he called, "Groundies."

Mason, who had jumped to the ground, pouted. "Oh, come on!"

"I don't make the rules," Jack sang, climbing back up onto the playset.

Mason counted to ten. I'm not sure if you could guess, but Mason *sucked* at Groundies. He was fast, he was athletic, he played little league baseball with me after school. However, he didn't know how to channel these almost superhuman abilities into something good.

I'd also like to note that I, at this point in time, was taller than Mason. It is important to me that you know this. I was the tallest kid in my class until I wasn't.

"Wow, he's really bad at this," Paisley noted with a frown.

I watched him fumble over his own limbs, smack his head into a pole.

"Yeah." I cringed.

Mason tried to tag Jack. He leapt away, quickly dodging his attacks. Mason, in retaliation, climbed up on the playset and closed his eyes.

Uh oh.

Mason began to move in our direction.

Uh oh.

"This way!" I shouted to Paisley. We raced to the top of the tallest slide, which was situated on top of a sort of tower, with several short steps and two different platforms leading up to it.

But he was still coming.

There was only one thing I could think to do, one possible outcome that would favor me.

"Hey, hey, *hey!*" Paisley protested as I tried to push her down the slide.

"Every man for himself!"

"I'm more of a man than *you!*"

It turned into a shoving war, each trying to send the other down the slide.

And Mason was *right there.*

Paisley and I stopped, eyes wide.

She glanced over at me. "Bye." And with one swift motion, she slipped out of my hold, slid halfway down the slide until she reached one of the poles holding the structure up. From there, she jumped out and onto the bars that ran along the outside of the playset, climbing each wrung until she reached an opening that allowed her to step onto the platform next to Jack.

All without touching the ground.

My jaw dropped. I had no idea how she did that, but it was the most amazing thing I had ever seen.

In my state of shock, Mason had managed to tag me. He

wore a dopey grin as he did so, but I wasn't focused on that. No, I was focused on the girl standing next to my smug little brother.

I walked back down the steps past Mason and straight to Paisley. "Can you teach me how to do that?"

Paisley folded her arms, probably remembering how I had tried to push her down the slide. "No."

"Come on," I begged, "please?"

But beg and plead as I might, I received the same answer: "No."

"Why not?"

"I don't want to."

"I'll... I'll give you a dollar," I tried.

She narrowed her eyes. "Five."

Are you kidding? No kid had that much money! Or, at least, I didn't.

I looked up at the slide. "Mason, do you—"

Mason pulled a wad of cash out of his pocket and held it up. At my grin, he began to fold it into a paper airplane. I don't know why he always had some on him, or whether he ever really understood the concept of money and its worth. But hey, after he flew it down (he always made the *best* paper airplanes), I offered it to Paisley, who was debating taking me under her wing as her parkour apprentice.

She studied the plane. "Fine," she told me at last. "Deal."

Another handshake, and we sealed both the deal and a friendship that was to last me the rest of my life.

Elijah

i'm ~~speechless~~. Can trees take your breath away? Because right now, it seems, they can.

I haven't been able to relax, haven't been able to stop my shoulders from tensing since the bus ride here. But now... I mean, how could I possibly not be at peace walking through the most beautiful forest I've ever seen? I knew how giant sequoias were. I'd heard the statistics, seen the pictures. But the pictures don't do justice to how it feels to be standing beneath one, eyes following the trunk as its branches reach toward the sky. A little bit farther and they might break through the clouds. For one brief second, I can almost imagine it. I can almost imagine being big enough to tower over everything else. To see the world and everything in it for what it is: tiny.

And with one glance at Paisley wandering a few feet away, the spell is broken. I'm thrust back into reality.

I make my way over to her, check that we're far enough away from the others before saying quietly, "I know you were talking about Mason and me back there."

She stops, turns to face me. "Really?"

"I mean, you were making it pretty obvious." I gesture toward Mason, who's currently trying to climb over the fence farther down the sidewalk. "Even he understood what you were saying after a minute."

She shrugs. "I was just talking about coffee, man."

It's like she doesn't even realize what she almost did. What she could have shattered. One misstep, and she could've outed Mason. And even though I want Mason to come out more than anyone, I'm a strong believer in letting him do so on his own terms.

I shoot Paisley a look. "You know it isn't your place. It's his and his alone."

She shoots me the exact same look back. "I wasn't aware there was only one person in that relationship." She holds up her hands. "But hey. Not my place, right?" And with that, she stalks off.

I sigh, turning my gaze back to the trees surrounding me. It's as if they have this strange, magical ability to calm me. To suck all the stress from my muscles. With the wind whispering through the leaves, the sun painting dappled light on the ground, all I want to do is just stop and take a breath. Enjoy this the way that Will never could.

So I do. I sit down right there in the middle of the sidewalk and lie on my back. The fear that some passerby might step on me crosses my mind briefly before it too is sucked out, leaving only the calm in its place.

Not a minute later, Mason is kneeling beside me. He lies down without a word.

I haven't gotten the chance to talk to him yet, so I turn my head toward him, letting my finger trace up and down his arm. "I'm sorry about Paisley."

His voice is quiet when he says, "Me too."

Okay, now I'm positive that there's something about this forest, something in the air. Because I've never seen Mason so calm. So tranquil. He puts his arms behind his head, lets his eyes take in the scenery with a soft, easy smile, and God. He's as beautiful as the trees surrounding us.

I sit up, quickly digging through my backpack for my sketchbook and a pencil. And then I assume my usual position, sitting cross-legged, hunched over the blank page I've turned to. I study Mason a second longer before putting pencil to paper.

He looks over at that, sees what I'm doing, and starts to sit up.

I'm quick to say, "No, no, no, stay still."

He frowns, propping himself up on his elbow. "I wanna watch you draw," he whines.

I shake my head. "Just bear with me. Just for a second."

He sighs rather overdramatically and flops back down, resuming his position.

I work silently for a few minutes, my pencil pushing

itself across the page to capture Mason in this moment, serene and wonder-filled. There are few times when drawing comes this naturally to me, when I feel as though it's someone else holding the pencil. My perfectionist side rarely lets me get into the zone. More often than not, it takes me hours to do something that should take me thirty minutes due to constant second guessing.

But my perfectionist side can go screw itself because the only thing that matters is that it's him. It's Mason. The only thing that matters is that I capture him and the wonder on his face so that I can always remember it.

As soon as I'm done, I turn it around for him to see.

His eyes widen. "Is that me?"

"No, it's my other boyfriend."

He frowns, and I almost regret having said it. Almost.

I bite back a smile. "Of course it's you."

He sits up, gently taking my sketchbook to look at the drawing more closely.

I'm a surrealist. I like taking life and twisting it around. I like distorting reality into something that feels better—or worse. I only do cartoons on special occasions. Like now, for instance. Sequoia National Park Mason is cartoon Mason, eyes littered with stars.

Mason's smile grows bigger the longer he studies the sketch. "It's really good," he says, looking back up at me.

I take the sketchbook from him and close it, sticking it back in my bag. "Yeah. Thanks." I pull my backpack back on, look up at the sequoias, back down at Mason. "You look small for once. A goddamn miracle."

His eyes follow me as I stand. "I can't tell if that was a compliment or an insult."

I smile down at him. "Guess." And then I'm wandering away again, wandering down the sidewalk to take in more of this place. I come across a tunnel carved out of a fallen tree and duck through it, coming out on the other side to find Jack sitting alone on a bench not too far away. I'm not gonna lie—he's brooding. Batman over Gotham brooding. Which is why I approach him warily. I'm not sure if I should try to talk to him or just leave him alone.

Well, what the hell?

"You look like you're having the time of your life."

He looks up. "Oh yeah."

I nod, stuffing my hands into my pockets. To be honest, I don't know how to navigate Jack. I haven't spent enough time with him to know how to do so. Sure, I met him first, but Will was always the one I hung out with.

"Hey," I say, "I was gonna ask you. You haven't been sleeping, have you?" I woke up this morning to find him gone; I don't know how long he's been awake.

"I..." He hesitates. "Neither have you."

I shrug. "Well, at least I have a good reason."

His brow furrows. "What?"

I take that as an invitation to sit next to him, again pulling my sketchbook out of my backpack. I flip to the page with my most recent Will sketch. The cleanest, most cohesive of them all.

Jack freezes when he sees it. "That's... That's Will."

I nod.

"Can I..." He reaches for my book.

"Yeah, of course."

I study him as he studies it. It's almost like a flower blooming, petals opening slowly but surely as this look of springtime, this look of childlike wonder, spreads across his face. And it hits me all over again that what I've lost and am trying so desperately to hold onto is what he's lost times ten. And I feel something blooming inside me, too, because I was able to help him hold onto Will just a bit longer.

"It's a work in progress, obviously," I tell him. "I haven't even started—"

"It's beautiful." He looks over at me, and his face tells me I can't disagree with him. "How long have you been working on this?"

"A couple days."

He lets out a low whistle. "That's impressive, man." He glances at the next page, the page on which I scribbled my Mason sketch. "Is that Mason?"

Ah... shit. "Oh," I say nonchalantly. "Yeah. He asked me to draw him."

Jack nods. "Cool." And he hands me my sketchbook back.

That was easy. I swear, it's like fooling a baby. We could probably make out in front of him, and he'd be none the wiser.

But maybe that's just because he's distracted. His eyes

have suddenly been drawn to the opposite fence, where Cassidy happens to be walking along, taking pictures of the scenery on her phone. "Keep me updated on the Will portrait, okay?" he says quickly, absently.

"Will do, Jack."

He gets up to follow Cassidy, who looks over, sees him, and starts walking even faster, putting her head down. Jack is basically chasing her down at this point.

I shake my head at the two of them. They're still on bad terms after their fight in the van yesterday. I don't know how long their feud is going to last; I'm not sure how long they can go on loathing each other.

"I hate them."

I jump at Paisley's voice. Somehow she managed to sneak up behind me, standing with her arms folded on the back of the bench.

"Don't do that," I tell her.

"Can't help it."

I sigh, leaning back. "I'm still mad at you."

"No, you're not."

I scoff, ready to refute that, but she just walks off.

Yeah, okay, I guess she's right. What good is it to stay mad about something that could have happened but didn't?

With another sigh, I stand up to keep wandering.

Dani

it was a bit hard to convince the others to spend our first evening in LA doing laundry, especially after having been on the road most of the day. But given that we've been away from home for nearly five days already, we're all in desperate need of clean clothes.

So here we are, using up all our spare change on a laundromat in the heart of LA. Though not all of us have a lot of spare change, as it turns out.

"Does anyone have a few quarters I could borrow?" Mason asks the room.

"Nope," Elijah responds, not looking up from his phone. As soon as we walked in here, he delegated his load of laundry to Mason and hopped on top of one of the machines. He hasn't moved since. I honestly don't know why Mason's putting up with it.

Mason's brow furrows as he digs in his pockets. "Okay, uh... I only have a twenty. And some others." As he takes his hand out of his pocket, a hundred dollar bill falls out and flutters to the ground.

I purse my lips. "So you have a hundred but not a quarter?"

He just shrugs. "I don't like change."

I let out a loud sigh and empty my wallet of quarters, reaching over to deposit them in Mason's hand. He smiles and turns back to his machine.

I turn back to mine, too, but for some reason, my eye catches on something else: Cassidy pausing as she bends down to stuff her clothes into a machine across the room. From where I'm standing, it looks like her gaze has fallen on Jack, who's in the process of putting quarters into his own machine. This has been happening off and on for a while now. I'll catch one of them staring at the other, and as soon as the other notices, they'll look away. It's like they can't even bear to meet each other's eye, they're so mad.

Paisley seems to notice the moment, too, so she calls, "Hey, Cassidy, can you come here for a quick sec?"

This breaks whatever daze Cassidy's in, causing her to jolt and turn her head toward Paisley, hitting it on the door of the machine in the process. She winces and rubs her forehead as she straightens.

Jack looks over at the commotion and takes a step toward her. "Cassie, are you—"

"Fine," Cassidy says quickly, hurrying over to where Paisley's standing.

Jack simply drops his arms with a shake of his head and goes back to his laundry.

Cassidy hooks her thumbs through her belt loops. "What's up?" she asks Paisley.

"Can you look something up for me?"

"Oh, sure." Cassidy pulls out her phone. "Is your phone dead?"

Paisley smiles. "No."

Cassidy hesitates, frowning at her screen. "You couldn't have done it yourself?"

"Oh, I probably could've. Just didn't want to."

"Um... Okay." She holds up her phone as an indication that she's ready.

"Okay," Paisley says. "'How to stop staring at a guy's ass.'"

Cassidy presses her lips together, shoving her phone back in her pocket. And she goes back to her machine without another word.

"What is that supposed to mean?" I ask Paisley.

"Hm?" She turns to me. "Oh. Guy behind Jack."

I look over to where she's nodding. There's a man pulling his laundry out of a machine near Jack's, simply minding his business. I'm guessing he's old enough to be a grandfather. Which means she's just screwing with Cassidy. And me, I guess.

"Okay," I say. "Somehow I don't believe that."

"Figured you wouldn't." She claps me on the shoulder as she passes me to head over to Jack.

I can't even begin to understand Paisley right now.

Spending so much time with her recently has only made me realize how much of an enigma she is. An enigma I'd rather not solve, to be honest. She's foreign territory to me, and I imagine she views me the same way.

I press start on my load and step back. At this point, the only thing I can do is wait. Well, that and maybe check in with Mason, whose creased forehead tells me that he's struggling. "Do you need help?" I ask.

He looks up. "No, I—"

"Yes," Elijah says from his perch.

I fold my arms. "Shouldn't you be the one helping him? Since it is, you know, *your* laundry?"

He finally looks up from his phone, eyes big and defensive. He nods toward Mason. "He offered."

"I didn't—"

"I offered," he corrects. "He accepted."

Mason slowly closes his eyes. It's almost exactly the opposite of the usual turn of events, in which Elijah has to put up with Mason being the difficult one. For once, I feel bad for Mason and not Elijah.

"I'm just going to move past that." I turn to Mason. "Do you know how to do laundry?"

He opens his mouth to respond, then closes it and glances down. "No," he says quietly.

I sigh. Sometimes it's like dealing with children. Like dealing with my thirteen-year-old brother. "Well, first off, you're going to need detergent."

"Okay."

When he doesn't move, I fight the urge to sigh again. "Do you *have* the detergent I bought?"

Elijah reaches over to grab the bottle off Paisley's machine and hands it to Mason. Well, I guess he's good for something.

"Thanks, Lijah," I tell him, voice rich with sarcasm. "Big help." I turn back to Mason. "Okay, now you're going to want to put the detergent inside."

Mason nods, unscrewing the bottle. But his confidence falters as he hesitates. "Where?"

"Just—" You know what? Not worth it. I take the bottle from Mason and douse the clothes inside the machine with detergent. "Like that."

He nods again. "Okay."

"Can you guess what the next step is?"

"Uhh..."

Elijah, again, proves to be a *major* help. "Why do you think you need quarters, Mace?"

At that, Mason pulls the quarters I gave him out of his pocket and looks around as if trying to find someone to give them to. As if someone else is going to do his laundry for him. Oh my *God*.

I try to muster up some semblance of patience. "Mason, you put them in the machine."

"*Oh*, okay." He does just that, slipping his quarters into their slots.

"Okay, now start it."

He does, and I almost have to smile at the way his face lights up as he watches the machine come to life. His eyes follow the cycle as it spins around like he's never seen a washing machine before. Which, who knows, maybe he hasn't.

His wonder doesn't last very long, however. "Now what?" he asks me.

I gesture to the machine. "Now you wait."

He frowns. "Oh. Okay." He stands there for another moment, watching as the laundry whirs around. "How lo—"

"I'll give him something to do," Elijah says.

But who knows how long that'll keep him occupied? The only foolproof way, I've learned, to keep Mason engaged is through food. And sure enough, as soon as I say, "You can help me pick a restaurant," his face lights up once again.

§ § §

THE FIRST DAY OF FRESHMAN YEAR was a big deal, for obvious reasons. I was as nervous and as excited as any other kid wandering down those halls for the first time, and my last class of the day was no different. Except this class was a bit different than the rest, and here's why.

For one, AP World History was an upperclassman course. Freshmen weren't allowed to register for it, but I did anyway. I know, I know. Call me a rebel.

For another, there was a girl. A very pretty girl. A very pretty girl sitting alone at a table in the corner. She had her head down, and to be completely honest, she looked just as lost as I felt.

"Can I sit here?" I asked, gesturing to the seat beside her.

She looked up at me, startled. Her hair was so long back then—before she chopped it to her shoulders—that it fell in her face. She brushed it behind her ear as she said, "Oh. Sure."

I smiled. "Great." I sat down and turned to her as she leaned against the wall. There were still a few minutes left until class started, but she already had a notebook and pencil laid out perfectly on her desk. "I'm Will, by the way."

"Daniela."

"Daniela... Rocha?"

Her eyes widened. "You know who I am?"

I recognized her name, not her face. I remembered because I had heard it over the loudspeakers during the morning announcements multiple times during middle school. "You won the spelling bee last year, didn't you?" And the year before, I was pretty sure.

At that, her cheeks flushed a little. "To be honest, I'd rather not advertise that fact."

"Oh." My face fell. "I'm sorry."

"No, no," she was quick to respond, "it's fine. It's just embarrassing."

"Embarrassing? Why would it be embarrassing?"

"I don't know." She shifted in her seat. "People usually want to be remembered for winning a football game or getting first chair. Not spelling a couple of words right."

Okay, I would have to *strongly* disagree. Spelling is a feat of strength. Sometimes even I couldn't wrap my head around the English language. But I figured it wasn't worth arguing about, especially not with a girl I'd just met. "What was your winning word?"

"I—" She cut herself off with a surprised laugh. "I don't even remember."

I echoed her laugh, digging in my bag for a pencil as our teacher stood up from his desk. "That's a pretty big thing to forget."

She shrugged. "Well." It seemed as though she wanted to add more, but she didn't get the chance because the bell rang then, and the teacher began passing out our syllabus.

Class passed by very quickly. I knew from the moment the teacher opened his mouth that this would be the class I would look forward to all day, for multiple reasons. One of those being his animated teaching style; another being the girl sitting beside me.

"Well," I said when the bell rang again, "that was a lot."

"Are you surprised?" She tucked her syllabus neatly into her binder and closed it. "We're not even supposed to be in this class."

"I mean, yeah."

She stood up but hesitated for a moment, as if she didn't want to leave just yet. She shot me a small, almost timid smile. "So how many strings did you have to pull?"

"A *lot*," I laughed, sliding out of the desk.

She nodded. "Yeah. Me too."

And both of us, at the exact same time, said, "I just really like history."

I stared at her. She stared back. Of course that was why she was there. Not because some teacher said she was smart enough to take an AP class as a freshman. Not because her parents forced her into it. Because she wanted to be there, just like me.

"Well," I told her, "at least you had the spelling bee thing going for you, too. That's all I told them."

"But it was enough, huh?"

"Yeah. Guess it was." She was standing in front of me now, hugging her binder to her chest. I inched forward just a little so that I could nudge her arm. "Hey, I'm glad you're here, by the way. I don't think I could have handled being the only freshman."

She just lit up at that. I remember thinking how good it felt to make her light up. And I think that's about when I decided I would always try to make her light up. "Yeah," she said, smiling. "Me neither. If we go down, we go down together."

I grinned back. "Hell yeah, we do." The classroom was quickly emptying out around us, and I remembered then that I had a bus to catch. "Hey, I'll see you tomorrow, yeah?"

"Yeah."

I started backing toward the door. "Later, Dani."

"What?"

She stopped me in my tracks.

I don't know why I said it. Looking back, I still don't know what in our minimal conversation had brought me to call a girl I'd just met by a nickname. Maybe it just felt natural. It sure as hell felt natural every time after that, every time anyone called her that instead of her full name. It felt more than natural when I put her contact in my phone later that same week.

"Sorry," I said, "is that okay?"

She paused. She thought. And she smiled. "Yeah. I like it."

I smiled back. She liked the nickname I gave her. For some reason, it was very important to me that she did.

I left her there, standing, smiling. And I sat beside her the next day. And the day after that. And the day after that. And every day after that until the end of the year. Until I knew her just as well as, maybe even better than, I knew anyone else.

Mason

"oh my god, is that meryl streep?"

"*Where?*" Paisley stops in the middle of the street to look.

Jack grins. "It's too easy with you."

She only scowls.

Bucket List Item Number I-don't-know-which-one-we're-on: walk the entire Hollywood Walk of Fame. I've done it before, kind of, but never the whole thing. I guess I didn't realize that this was something that people intentionally set out to do. To me, this has always been the cool sidewalk outside the Hard Rock Cafe.

Los Angeles is an acquired taste. You either love it or you hate it. Paisley loves it. She's in her element. Not only is she a fairly decent movie buff, but she also belongs in California period. I've never really thought about it, but she totally fits in here.

Cassidy, meanwhile, does *not* like it.

"Why is it so dirty here?" she asks at one point on our walk, folding her arms.

"It's not dirty here," Paisley argues, kicking a rock off of Lin-Manuel Miranda's star. "Maybe you're just too prude."

Cassidy stares at her, dumbfounded. "I literally just saw a chair with a 'for sale' sign in the middle of the road."

Jack smirks. "Did you see the two rats going at it a few blocks back?"

I swivel my head. "Where?"

Elijah's quick to say, "Hey. No."

And that's all it takes for Cassidy to grumpily storm off.

Paisley looks up ahead, hands in her shorts pockets, squinting up against the sun. "You're ruining this for me."

Jack feigns offense. "Me? Ruin this? Never. Is that Mariah Carey?"

Paisley gasps and turns.

"That's getting old, Jack," Dani tells him.

"No, it's not," he laughs. Then: "James *Dean?* I think that's him!"

Paisley turns before glaring at Jack. "Shut up."

"He's dead, and yet you still turned."

She tries to protest, "I thought you meant—"

"No, you didn't."

She marches up to Jack to get a swing in, but Dani stops her with a firm, "No."

Paisley spreads her arms. "Come on—"

"Nope."

She drops her hands. "But he's—"

"Jack, knock it off."

"See?" She looks at Jack. "See what happens? You got *yelled* at."

He only rolls his eyes.

We go on like this for a while, admiring the street in silence. It's a bit difficult, as it's rather crowded. I don't think any of us took that into consideration. Some patches of the sidewalk are clearer than others, but we've ended up having to fight our way through some pretty tough crowds at some points. Paisley, thankfully, has always been pretty decent in crowds. She proved that much in Vegas. I think. I'm still having trouble remembering that night. But anyway, I can hold my own in a sea of people, probably because of my height, but Paisley can move *fast.* Several times, Dani has told her to slow down. And to stop shoving. And to not hit that guy, Paisley, we can't afford to use our money to bail you out of jail.

That guy wasn't the only one testing Paisley's temperament, however.

"Holy shit, I think that's Matt Damon," Jack calls out after a while.

Paisley looks over her shoulder. "Nope," she says, shaking her head. "Not falling for it."

"You already did."

"You know," Dani cuts in, "I always thought that Will looked like Matt Damon."

Her attempt at relieving tension only creates more. We fall silent at the mention of his name.

Paisley speaks up after a minute. "I could see that."

Another bout of silence passes. Well, mostly silent.

"Cassie thinks I look like a young DiCaprio," Jack tells us.

She whirls around at this. "I never said that."

Jack stifles laughter. "Okay."

Cassidy turns back to the street.

I look down at Jack with a frown. "Is she still mad at you, dude?"

"*Oh* yeah," Elijah answers for him.

Jack's hands sink farther into his pockets as we walk; his eyes stay dead ahead on Cassidy. "Is it that obvious?"

"Shouldn't you be the one mad at her?" I venture to ask.

He tilts his head just the slightest. "You'd *think*."

Cassidy only speeds up. She's becoming increasingly more frustrated with our conversation. Jack, meanwhile, is becoming increasingly more frustrated with Cassidy.

"Is this because of Vegas?" Elijah asks from beside me. "Or the van meltdown?"

"Little of both." Jack hesitates. "Maybe something else."

"Can you stop talking about me?" Cassidy yells over her shoulder.

"Why?" Jack shouts at her. "You got something to say?"

"Not to *you*, that's for sure."

"Oh, right. I forgot: you're not talking to me."

"Dick."

He spreads his hands. "You're still talking to me."

"No, I'm not."

I purse my lips. "Sounds like talking to me."

Cassidy stops at my comment, turns to face me. "Stay out of this, Mason."

"Cassidy, for God's sake," Elijah cuts in, finally fed up. "When are you going to let this go? We're in California, we're doing what Will wanted to do, why can't you just enjoy yourself for one *minute*?"

Maybe you've already gathered this, but Elijah doesn't do this sort of thing. If he's mad at someone, he'll let you know subtly. Internally. Like a "cold shoulder" type mad. He never blows up.

At first, I think that's what causes Cassidy's face to fall. But once she speaks, I realize it's for another reason entirely. "I thought you were on my side."

Elijah simply rolls his eyes. "I'm not on anyone's side. There shouldn't even *be* sides."

Jack does a terrible job of hiding a smug grin. Cassidy scowls at him. "You shut up." She spins around and keeps walking.

I emit a low whistle. "Damn."

"Yeah," Jack says quietly. He starts forward again, frustration renewed.

Dani sighs and follows suit. The rest of us eventually do the same.

Paisley wanted to go to the wax figure museum. Dani said, "*Hell no.*" Or something along those lines.

This led us to split up into two groups: Paisley and Jack at the wax museum; Dani, Cassidy, Elijah, and me at the Griffith Observatory. I've already been to both, so it didn't really matter to me which one I went to. Well, that's not entirely true, actually. Those wax figures always freaked me out. Part of the reason I opted to go with the Griffith group.

I find Elijah studying the pendulum. I can't blame him for it; that thing has always fascinated me. I remember when I was younger, and I would just watch it swing back and forth for hours and hours and hours on end. And that's exactly what he's doing. His eyes are following it, following the gold of the pendulum as it reflects back into his glasses, into the brilliant blue of his eyes...

He looks over to catch me staring at him. I turn and glance up at the mural painted on the ceiling, hand coming to nonchalantly scratch my neck.

I glance back only to see him tuck away a smile and push himself off the barrier using his palms. He comes up behind me to briefly, discreetly put his head on my shoulder. And he's gone just as fast as he came.

I bite back a smile of my own and follow after him. "You broke your own rule," I mutter.

He stares curiously into a display case. "I'm aware."

Another thing he never does. Must be in a good mood today. Probably because pot's legal in California.

I look over Elijah's head to find Dani and Cassidy a few feet away from us, over by the Tesla coil. They must be waiting for an employee to start it up.

I wander over to Cassidy and stand next to her. "Hey."

She frowns at my presence. "Hi?"

We wait a minute. In silence. A little awkward, but fine.

"Do you need something?" she asks me.

I look down at her. I said that before about talking with Jack, but with Cassidy I actually have to look *down*. I forget how short she is. Or how tall I am. "No," I say with a little laugh.

"Um... Okay."

The employee makes the announcement and turns the Tesla coil on. And wow, that doesn't get old. It crackles symphonically with each stroke of lightning, a miniature storm contained in the cage surrounding it.

"So..." I tread lightly. "About *Jack*."

She all but groans. "Really?"

"I have to ask."

"You really don't."

"I'm just worried is all."

"And why's that?"

"Because last I checked, *he* was mad at *you*. Did something else happen?"

She pales at my question. "No." And she walks away from the Tesla coil. Weird.

Anyway.

Dani is still looking up at the coil in wonder. She has this small smile on her face that makes her almost as entertaining to watch as the metal ball with lightning on it.

I move over to ask her, "Hey, where are we eating tonight?"

"I'm not sure," she says to the light show, "but I was thinking we could explore Grand Central Market. Maybe eat there."

"Oh. Cool." I continue to look up into the cage, half listening to the employee's speech about it, half frowning as I mutter to Dani, "Like the one in New York?"

Her amazement falters as she turns to look up at me. "Where do you think we are?"

I give her the look she typically gives me. "Dani. We're in Los Angeles. Keep up."

She sighs at this, looking back up at the Tesla coil with a shake of her head.

Paisley shrugs. "Honestly, I'm kind of wondering the same thing." She sniffles, rubs her nose as we stare at Beyoncé in front of us. Sorry, Beyoncé's *wax figure* in front of us.

"This is the creepiest fucking thing I've ever seen."

"Don't you read Stephen King?"

I turn to Paisley. Slowly. "*Exactly.*"

She shrugs again, looking back at the figure. "You just don't appreciate *art.*"

"This isn't art. This is a tourist trap."

She drops her hands. "Then why'd you come? You're ruining this for me, man. Again. What is it with you and ruining Los Angeles?"

I stare. "There's no way you're enjoying this."

"Uh, yeah, I am. I just met all the Kardashians for thirty bucks."

I think it's this comment that causes me to snap back to reality. Not that I wasn't snapped in before. But I'm still muttering, "Oh my God, we paid thirty dollars for this."

Paisley ignores me. "I've posed next to *Madonna.* How many people can say that?"

"I just threw thirty dollars down the drain. And for what?"

"To get away from Cassidy."

I stop. Blink. "I—" I turn to Paisley again, but she's already gone. I shake my head and catch up with her. "That's not why I came."

"Yeah, it is. No one in their right mind would come here without some ulterior motive. Hence why I'm here." She digs her phone out of her pocket to take a picture of who I'm assuming to be Michael Jackson. One of his songs is playing, so it isn't that far of a stretch.

"I'm not avoiding her."

She makes a face at Michael before focusing her phone's camera. "No," she agrees, "you're not. If you were avoiding her, you would make it a point not to talk about her."

"I'm not the one who brought her up."

"You could've easily shut me down, Dickinson. It's not like you haven't done it before." She moves on to the next exhibit.

I begrudgingly follow her. "If anything, she's avoiding me."

"Why, because you kissed her?" She hands me her phone and goes to pose next to... Yeah, I have no idea who that is.

I roll my eyes and raise her phone to snap a picture. "I didn't kiss her."

"Oh! Good technique! Make me laugh so the picture looks candid." She smiles brightly. "I didn't think you knew anything about photography."

"It was a mutual kissing," I correct. My voice must be louder than I intend because a few confused tourists throw a glance my way. I press my lips together as they walk by.

Paisley comes back over to pluck her phone out of my hand. "Did you kiss first?"

"I don't—" I give her a look. "I'm not gonna tell you that."

"You kissed first. So you kissed her. So she's avoiding you."

"But she kissed back."

"Do I look like an expert in women to you?"

"You *are* one."

"Oh. Yeah." She makes a face. And then she's off. "I may have a vagina, but that by no means makes me an expert in women."

"Can you maybe not say that in front of a group of kids?" The kids I'm referring to are ogling a figure of Katy Perry.

"What, vagina?" Then, louder: "*Vagina.*"

Thankfully, they seem too wrapped up in taking pictures with Katy Perry to care.

"I kissed her," I recap, ignoring her. "She kissed back. And now she wants nothing to do with me."

"Can you blame her? You're a dick."

Right. That's why I never go to Paisley for advice.

Wait, why am I going to Paisley for advice? What do I

even need advice on? It's not like that kiss meant anything.

All right. That's a lie.

"Thanks," I say. "That's just what I needed to hear."

"I figured." She gives me her phone again once the kids are gone and goes to pose.

I exhale, annoyed, raising the phone. "You know, we'd be fine if you hadn't have come out."

"Of course it's my fault." She sticks her finger in Katy's ear and smiles.

"We were fine. And you came out and made her feel bad about it."

"Come on, Jack, I didn't do anything." She finally has some reason in her voice, even if I don't want to agree with it. "And besides, she's been trying to get into your pants since she met you."

My eyes widen as she takes her phone back. I try my best to mask it with a frown, open my mouth to refute before she walks away.

"We all saw it," she goes on to say. "Just never told Will."

I shove my hands into my pockets, still trying to process whatever this conversation has turned into. "Have any of the others vocalized this opinion?"

"Not opinion. Fact. And no, they haven't. But I bet they'd agree with me if I asked them."

"No, Paisley. They wouldn't."

"Fine, then you ask them. But you'd probably end up admitting that you were sucking face with—"

"Okay."

This shuts her up, finally. Or maybe it's the next exhibit that does the trick.

"You're wrong," I tell Paisley flatly. "She doesn't want anything to do with me."

She snorts. "She certainly wanted everything to do with you—"

"*Don't.*"

"—in Vegas."

I stop. That's not at all what I thought she was gonna say. I thought she was going to bring up...

"Vegas?" I repeat.

"Yeah, Vegas."

"She was *drunk* in Ve..." My voice trails off as I take in the exhibit. "Is that *Jesus?*"

"Yeah, it's Jesus. You got something against Jesus?"

I study the scene before me. It looks like the Last Supper. "Why is Jesus in the Hollywood Wax Museum?"

"Because he's a celebrity. You don't think Jesus is a celebrity? Take my picture."

I take her phone again, almost too confused to remember what I was confused about prior to Jesus. "Cassie was drunk in Vegas."

"Exactly my point. You really think she would cling to you sober?" She throws up a peace sign next to the apostle Paul.

"No, but—" I open and close my mouth a few times, finally deciding on, "How the *hell* did Will put up with this?" This being Cassie. This being a girl spinning your head in circles. This being relationships in general. Why the fuck am I thinking about *relationships?*

"Well," answers Paisley with a frown and a tilt of her head, "for starters, he wasn't an asshole."

"Thanks."

"But then again," she's quick to add, taking her phone back, "neither was Cassidy." She hesitates. "At the time."

"So I just got the short end of the straw?"

"Guess so." She gives me a knowing look. And I hate that I know exactly what she's communicating through the subtle raise in her brow, the slight downturn of her chin.

Pray tell: how does one telepathically say, "fuck you"? I keep trying, but I just can't seem to express it enough.

"Face it, dickhead," she calls over her shoulder as I follow her to the next exhibit. "She let you put her to bed. And she didn't seem overly happy when you left. And I caught all of that *drunk.* What do you think this says about the situation?"

"I think it says that she would try and stick close to anyone who threw a punch for her," I argue through my teeth. Exactly. *Exactly.* I really did get the short end of the straw. Couldn't Dani have gone to find her? I should've been put on Paisley duty, anyway.

Except, I *was* on Paisley duty. Dani was supposed to find Cassidy. I just ended up finding her first. And now look where we are. Where *I* am.

Paisley was right about one thing: after we got back to the hotel room, Cassidy had a hard time letting me go back to my own room. It took her dozing off again for her grip to loosen, her hand to slip from my shirt. I was surprised to find that she actually looked... peaceful.

"Jack?"

Yeah, that's the word. Peaceful.

"Please don't leave me, Jack."

She wasn't making a point to rile me up. To get inside my head. She's always weaseling her way in, whether I want her there or not, and I hate her for it.

"Cassie, hey, let go."

No, I hate myself for it. I can't hate her. Hard as I try, I just can't bring myself to hate her.

But she wasn't letting go. She was doing the opposite, actually, as I set her down on the bed, trying to get her back fully on the mattress. Her arms were all but tightening around my neck.

"I gotta go back to my room."

She turned into me, lips finding my jaw to murmur against my skin. "Jack, please."

I found myself holding her closer, eyes fluttering closed, as hard as I tried not to sink into her, as much as I knew that I needed to let her go, as much as she needed to let me go—

And then she was moving, shifting, pressing kisses down my cheek, down my jaw, she kissed the corner of my mouth—

"Cassie, come on." I tried to make my voice harsh, but Jesus, I just couldn't. It broke. I was breaking. I was prying her arms off me and straightening, but her hands were clinging to my shirt, and I didn't want her to stop.

I put my palms over her knuckles and managed to tug her off. "Go to sleep, okay?" I told her. "You'll forget all about this in the morning."

"Hey." Paisley snaps her fingers in front of my face. "Jackass. Take my picture."

I shake my head, shake myself out of my thoughts to take her phone.

"So what are you gonna do about this?" Paisley asks me, putting her fist next to Betty White's face like she's throwing a punch.

245

I just shake my head again.

"Wrong. You're either gonna make a move, or you're gonna get over yourself." She steps down to take her phone back. "I'm not gonna go to China with a lovesick puppy."

"I'm not—" I frown. "Wait. *China?* What do you mean *China?*"

☒ ☒ ☒

PAISLEY IS NOT AT ALL worried about calling her parents. Why?
She doesn't intend to. Hell, her mom doesn't even know she's on
this trip. And just between you and me, she really wouldn't care.
Someone does, though, and that someone is her sister, Florence.

"You're going *where?*"

"Uh, China." Paisley glances over at Dani with a frown,
mouths, "China?" just to see Dani squirm. Instead, she just turns
away, glaring as she dials on her own phone.

"Why are you going to China?" Florence asks, redirecting
Paisley's attention once again.

"Dead friend's bucket list."

"Did you just—"

"*Paisley,*" Dani says through her teeth.

Paisley sweeps an offended arm over the handle of her
suitcase. The gang, at this point, is currently waiting in the
security line. Yup. That's right. They're already at the airport,
and they're just now notifying their parents that they're about
to leave the country. You know. Logic. Paisley's, actually.

"Hey," she had said, "in my experience, it's a lot easier
to ask forgiveness than permission."

They openly disagreed with her. But silently, she had
a point. Which is why every single one of them had put this off
until now.

Dani drums her fingers impatiently against her suitcase as she
listens to the dial tone. This is the third— Sorry, *fourth* time she's
attempting to get through to her parents. Both their cell phones

went straight to voicemail, which means her only option is to call the house. And now, it seems, no one is home.

She's about to give up and just try again once they've landed in Beijing, but someone picks up at the last minute.

"The fuck do you want?"

"Hey," she snaps immediately. "Language."

Jack gives her a weird look.

"Not you," she tells him.

"Not me?" her little brother says from the other end of the phone. "Cool."

"Santi—" She sighs, folding one arm over her torso. "Can you put Mom on the phone?"

"Why?"

"Because I need to talk to her."

"You really pulled me away from the PS4 to say that?" He scoffs. "She's not home. Bye."

Dani's eyes widen. "Wait, wait, wait, no."

Santiago pauses. Huffs into the phone. "What?"

"Is Dad there?"

"Yeah. Why?"

She slowly closes her eyes. She'd never admit this to anyone, but even though she loves her brother, she really does, this whole trip has been a nice break from him. A nice introduction to what it'll be like at college without him. Because Dani is intelligent. Santi, on the other hand, is not.

She musters up as much patience as she can to ask, "Can you put him on the phone?"

"Thought you said you needed Mom."

"I—" Another sigh. Another moment to calm herself. "Santi. Put Dad on the phone. Please."

"Yeah, give me a minute."

"I'm sorry, you're going *where*?"

Jack shifts. "I know how it sounds."

"Oh, do you? Because I don't think you do!"

He drops his hand. "Mom—"

"If you knew that it sounded *batshit crazy*—"

"It's not bat—" He glances once over at Dani, for fear

she might confiscate his phone if he were to curse again. He still isn't entirely aware that she had been talking to Santi instead of him. You know. The other little brother.

Jack sighs. "Look, we're already in California—"

"I thought you were going to California and then coming *home*, Jack."

"I thought so, too. This is kind of a last minute thing, and it'd be harder to—"

"If it's so last minute, then *why are you going?*"

"Because Will—"

"*Don't bring him into this!*"

Jack bites back his words. "Sorry," he says quietly.

It's not that Mom thinks it's a bad idea. She's just worried is all. She's been sitting home with Dad, awake almost every night of the trip, praying that she doesn't lose both of her sons.

"China?"

Elijah rolls his eyes. "Yes, *China*. We've been over this."

"No, no, you said *maybe* international. You said *maybe* Asia. *Maybe* Europe."

"Yeah, well." He shrugs. "It's not maybe anymore."

"Yeah, I *gathered that*."

He purses his lips at his mom's tone. "Just making sure."

Mason is the only one who isn't on the phone right now.

Dani, while (still) waiting for Santi to find their dad, takes notice. She puts her hand over the bottom of her phone. "Did you call your parents?" she asks Mason.

He frowns. "When?"

"Just now. Like you were supposed to."

"Oh." He passes his duffel bag to his other hand to fish for his phone. This is his basketball duffel bag, by the way. He was too lazy to try and find his suitcase. (Which I'm here to tell you was in his closet. Where it always is.)

"Hey, Mom."

Cassidy, on the other hand, is not so calm. She's chewing on her lip, hugging her waist.

"Let me talk to your father," her mom is saying.

"No, no, don't bring Dad into this. Don't—" She sighs. It's too late.

"Hey, kiddo."

"Hi, Dad," she says sheepishly. "Did she tell you what's going on?"

"She did, yeah. And I'm afraid I'm kind of on the same page as her."

She was worried about this. Which is why her voice is tiny, barely there, when she says, "But we already have tickets. We're at the airport."

"Oh, you're at the *airport*, oh, I— *Leslie!*"

She waits, eyes wide, for her mom to take the phone back. And once she does—

"You're *what?*"

She flinches at the volume of her mom's voice, pulls the phone away from her ear just for a second.

As soon as she does this, she catches Jack staring at her. She scowls at him and turns her back.

He just shakes his head. He's been doing this periodically just to make sure she's okay, even though she's so obviously not. But he doesn't say or do anything about her situation because (a.) he doesn't know how the hell to talk to her now, and (b.) he's trying to deal with his own issues.

Issues being our mother.

"I was hesitant when they mentioned bungee jumping. Even more so when they said you were leaving Arizona. I didn't even want you in California, Jack, and now you're leaving the *country?*"

At this point, it's useless trying to get a word in. He's in the midst of trying to say, "Should I even try to speak my case?" when she continues talking. Sorry. Yelling.

"Do you know how dangerous it is?"

"Can't be any worse than America."

"Now is *not* the time to get politi—"

"I'm not being *political*—"

"Your father and I are worried *sick*— You know what? Dan, talk to him."

Jack's eyes widen. "No, Dan, don't—" He sighs. "Hey, Dan."

"What did you just call me?"

"I said Dad."

"You said Dan."

"I didn't—"

"This really isn't helping your case."

Jack slowly closes his eyes.

"Santi, *lo juro por Dios*, if you don't put one of them on the phone—"

"They're unloading the car!"

"*Diles que es importante!*"

Santi only clicks his tongue. "Sorry. *No hablo Español.*"

"Oh, you do too *hablas Español.*"

"What? No, Florence, I'm not taking you to China. Do you know how long it would take to go and pick you up?"

"But—"

"Your sorry ass is staying home."

"Come *on!* You know how bad Mom can be!"

"Oh, cut the bullshit, you're her golden child. You're seriously trying to use my mommy issues against me?"

Florence falls quiet. "Sorry," she grumbles.

"Yeah, that's what I fucking thought." Then Paisley's grumbling, "Little shit."

They're at security now, which means they need to pause their conversations to let their phones go through the baggage scanner. Well, everyone except Mason, the only one who has the luxury of hanging up.

"Okay, cool. Love you, too." And that's it. That's the end of the conversation. Those who are able to pull themselves away from their disgruntled parents are in awe.

Jack's mouth dangles open. "How did you— No, Mom. I'm still here."

"Don't disrespect your mother like that," Dad warns.

Jack throws a hand up. "How was that disrespect?"

"We're trying to have a conversation with you, but obviously, your head is elsewhere, like always."

"Can you blame me? I'm in an airport security line for God's sake, these aren't exactly easy to— Ope, hang on. Gotta put you through the x-ray."

"*Jackson—*"

Jack all but throws his phone into his bin. His shoulders visibly relax.

Yeah. Dad's kind of a hardass. On him, at least. I, obviously, did no wrong. So Dad never had to get on me about anything.

"Harsh," Elijah says to Jack.

"You wanna take over?" he retorts. "Please?"

"Nah, I'm good. My mom doesn't yell at me."

Jack stares wistfully at him.

Elijah, instead of putting his mother into a plastic bin and shoving her through the bag scanner, decides to hang up on her and promise to call again once they hit the gate. Cassidy resorts to doing the same thing as Jack, as much as she first judged him for it. Paisley just flat out hangs up on her sister, no goodbyes or anything. As for Dani—

"*Santi.* Oh my *God.* Why are you being so difficult?"

"'Cause it's fun."

"Wha—"

"Dani?"

"Mom?" Her face lights up. "Santi, hand Mom the phone. Hand Mom the—"

There's a bit of commotion on the other end. I'm not sure what it is, and neither is Dani, and I doubt she even wants to know. But it only takes a second for her mom to take the phone from Santi and say, "Dani? *Cariño?*"

Dani lets out a breath of relief, telling her mom she has to go, she'll be back in a second, *please* don't hang up. And with that, her phone goes into a bin, too.

"*Jackson Bailey Dickinson, did you put me in a bin?*"

Elijah raises his eyebrows. "Your middle name is Bailey?"

Jack's eyes widen. "You heard that?" Then, into the phone: "Mom, people can *hear* you."

"*Good!*"

"Hey, I'm back."

"Cassie, you are *not* getting on that plane."

"But—"

"No. No arguing with me. This wasn't the deal."

"I told you, we already—"

"I don't *care* that you already have the tickets. That's what refunds are for."

Cassidy looks helplessly at Dani, who's sitting on a bench putting her shoes back on, phone between her ear and her shoulder. She meets Cassidy's eye and mouths, "Do you need me?"

Cassidy just nods.

Dani stands, walks over while talking to her mom, switches her phone for Cassidy's. Her smile is natural and bright as she says, "Hey, Mrs. Montag. It's Dani."

And Cassidy's mom relaxes instantly. "Oh. Hi."

Jack watches on, watches as Cassidy takes the easy out. He begins to wish he'd thought of that before Mom started shouting. Or crying. He can't really tell.

"Mom, I'm gonna be fine."

"I don't care if you're fine!"

Jack blinks. "Wow. Okay then. Thanks? I'll just be going—"

"We're not done with you yet," Dad jumps back in.

Jack stares deadpan as all of Cassidy's problems are solved before her very eyes. "Yay."

Cassidy takes her phone back from Dani a few minutes later, her shoulders relaxing at her mom's now calm, even tone.

"You're gonna call me when you land."

"Okay."

"Text me every day. I want to know where you are."

Cassidy nods. "I will."

"Dani's in charge. She's the only one I trust."

"I know."

Her mom sighs from the other end. "Stay safe, Cassie? Please?"

"I will, I promise."

"Don't wander off."

"I won't."

"There are some bad people out there, I don't want you—"

"Mom. I *know.*"

Another sigh. "Okay. I'll let you go now. Please, please, *please* be careful."

"I will."

"I love you."

"Love you, too."

And that's that. Cassidy heaves a sigh of relief as she tucks her phone into her pocket and grabs her suitcase. "Thank you," she tells Dani, who's back on the phone with her own mom.

"Don't mention it."

Jack looks between the two of them. And then, without a word, he holds his phone out to Dani.

She glances down at it, glances back up at him. And with a tiny huff, she takes it, handing her mom off to Jack this time.

"Whoa, I don't think— Hey. Uh, I'm Jack?"

"Her English isn't the best," Dani informs him. "Just tell her I'll be back in a second." She points at him. "And don't let her hang up."

Jack, slowly wondering if he should regret his decision, says to the confused Mrs. Rocha, "Dani'll be back in a second. She's just helping me with something."

"Oh. Okay."

Dani's time on the phone with Mom is a lot longer than with Cassidy's mom. She ends up taking the conversation away from security, all the way down the hallway as they walk to the gate, all the while assuring Mom that everything is under control, Jack'll be fine, she'll look after everybody.

And by the end of the conversation, Mom still isn't convinced.

Jack finds this out once he trades mothers. "Are we good here?"

"No, we are *not* good here."

"But Dani—"

"Dani is barely out of high school! And while I trust that girl, you know I do, I'm still having a hard time—"

"Trusting me?"

Silence. Just what he needs.

"No, honey, that's not what I'm saying."

Jack rings out a bitter laugh. "No, it's exactly what you're saying, Mom. Dad, too, but he was a little more up front about it."

"We're not saying any of that."

But they are. Even if Mom isn't being blunt like Dad is, that's exactly what she's worried about. She never really had to worry with me. I wasn't her problem child. Never was.

As soon as they arrive at the gate, Elijah settles into a seat to call his mom back.

"Okay," she says right off the bat, "I was thinking. I was gonna take you on a senior trip in the spring."

"Okay..." He kind of knows where this is headed. But he still wants to hear her say it.

"But if you're okay with this trip taking its place, then sure. You can go to China. You can go wherever the hell you want."

He blinks. "You're kidding me."

"Does it sound like I'm kidding you?"

"No, I just— This sounds too good to be true."

"Well, I mean, if I don't have to pay for it—"

"*There* it is."

"What?"

"That makes more sense."

"Hey, don't make me feel bad about it. I'm being a good mom here. I can always take it—"

"No," he's quick to say. "No. Don't take it back. You are a good mom. You're the best mom. And I love you."

"Aw, baby. Love you, too." She pauses. "No pot on the plane."

"That's illegal."

"I know. I wanted to make sure you did."

"I—" He sighs. "Okay."

"Okay. Text me when you're in Beijing."

"I will."

"Send me lots of pictures."

"You're getting *all* the pictures."

"I'd better. Have fun, sweetheart."

And with that, his mom blows him a kiss and hangs up. Dani hangs up, too, after her mom tells her she trusts her, she's old enough to make her own decisions.

"Mom, for the last time, I'm gonna be fine."

"I know you are. Because you're coming home right now."

He glances at the others, all caught up in their own conversations as they prepare to board the plane. He isn't exactly sure what he's fighting for. It's not like he wanted to come, anyway. It took Mason kidnapping him to get him this far. And now? Here he is, in the middle of LAX, trying to convince his hysterical mother that everything's going to be okay. She's not the only one he's trying to convince.

"Listen, Mom, I wanna do this, okay?" He finds himself glancing up at Cassidy. "I wanna see where this goes."

Mom sighs. "It's not that I don't want you to go, honey. I just... I can't do this right now. Okay? Let them go have their fun. Come home."

Something sinks inside of him. Guilt, maybe. But more importantly, an uprising.

"About that."

"Jack..."

"We're already at the gate."

The phone falls dangerously silent.

"In the" —he pulls the phone away to check the time— "two hours you've spent yelling at me, we've already made it past security, eaten lunch—which I didn't get to do, by the way—and now we're getting ready to board."

Both of our parents (Dad is grumbling somewhere behind Mom, he's basically given up) find a way to send their anger through the phone not with their words but with their very stances, the grip Mom has on her device, the breath Dad releases through his nostrils.

"Jack," Mom says lowly, "if you get on that plane, so help me *God*—"

"I'm getting on the plane."

Both start talking at once. His heart is pounding, and he's the last one on, but he's walking down the boarding bridge, dragging the suitcase behind him, and stepping aboard.

"Stop messing around, Jack!" Dad shouts.

"I am going to *fly out there myself* if you don't *come home this minute!*"

"Okay, guys— *Guys!*"

They're both stunned into silence.

Jack sighs. "Let's face it: this isn't exactly the worst thing I've done."

"Oh, I don't know, pal, jetting off to Asia's really taking the cake at the moment," Dad grits.

"*What could be worse than this?*" Mom screams.

As they continue to try and yell over each other, each reprimand more brutal than the last, Jack catches Cassidy trying to lift her suitcase overhead. He makes his way over and takes the bag out of her hands, lifts it above her head, and pushes it inside.

"Excuse me," he mutters, brushing past her.

"I didn't ask for help," she mumbles, grumpily plopping down in her seat.

He ignores her, taking his respective seat. Which happens to be right behind her.

"Where are you, Jack?" Mom demands.

"I told you, I'm on the plane." He holds the phone between his shoulder and cheek to shove his backpack under the seat in front of him. Cassidy's seat. I'm restating this not because it's important to you, but because it's important to her.

She twists in her seat to face him. "What are you doing?" she hisses.

He frowns, sitting back up. "I'm sitting."

"You have to sit *there?*"

While his parents continue to yell, he pulls the phone away to quip, "Actually, yes. I do. It's protocol, Cassie. Who am I to break the laws of the sky?"

Cassidy simply closes her mouth and turns back around in a huff.

I won't even try to sum up what's going on on the other side of that phone. Mom and Dad are shouting to no one.

Not ten seconds later, Cassidy turns again to say, "I know what you're doing."

"What am I doing?"

"You're trying to piss me off."

"Well, that sure does sound like me, doesn't it?"

She turns back, desperate to get him out of her head. "Well, I'm not gonna let it happen." And with that, she plugs in her headphones, takes out a book, and shuts him out.

This time, a whole minute passes before Cassidy yanks the earbuds out of her ears and whirls back around. "And another thing."

Jack gives her an offended shush, puts his finger first to his lips, then juts it to his phone.

She frowns, and she sits back to let him finish up before she goes on.

But she quickly gets tired of waiting, quickly decides that what she has to say is far more important than whatever my parents are yelling at him about. "I told you that what *happened* was nothing," she says. "And you keep bringing it up."

"Sir."

Jack looks up at the flight attendant who has suddenly appeared. "Yeah?"

"You need to put the phone away."

"Thank you." Then, to the phone: "Mom, Dad, gotta go."

"Don't you hang up on us, young man!"

"The flight attendant told me to! Do you want her to tell— Actually, hang on." He looks back up. "Do you mind?" He offers his phone to the woman, who shoots him a confused frown before heading back down the aisle. "Worth a shot," he mutters, bringing the phone back to his ear. "I'll call you when I land, I promise."

"JACK—"

He hangs up the phone. He takes a minute, takes a

breath, before pocketing his phone and leaning back down to fish through his backpack.

"And for the record," he says into the crack between Cassidy's seat, "it seems like *you're* the one bringing it up right now." He sits back up, book in hand.

She closes her mouth, opens it, pinches it shut again. She's at a loss for words. The best she can manage is, "Dick."

"All right." He flips to his page and settles in for the long flight. And Cassidy goes back to brooding. Sorry, I mean listening to music.

Except another two minutes later, she annoyedly presses pause. "Whatever you're doing isn't working. I'm ignoring you."

"Shh. I'm reading." He isn't reading. His eyes are on the page, but his head is somewhere else. With his parents. With the places he's going. With the places he's been. With the girl in front of him.

And, maybe most achingly of all, his head is still with me.

Acknowledgments

This book would not have been possible without the love and support of friends and family from both sides.

For starters, those who read the book before it was even published: Hope Chiappini, Jeremy Davidson, Lia Whitford, Ashton Moore; some even twice (looking at you, Teresa Greenhalgh). We'd also like to take time to thank those who had to listen to our incessant ramblings and inside jokes for the past year, including but not limited to our parents, our friends (Anna Hume and Alyssa Nelson, we're so sorry), basically anyone within earshot of us.

Our teachers, of course, deserve thanks. For all the late work turned in because of this book, to all the techniques learned from English teachers such as Jay Nelson, Heather Lurvey, Ashlee Tripp, Jami Hedrick, Jacob Yergert, and, of course, our creative writing teacher, Brooke West. This one's for your retirement fund.

Also on the basis of teachers, to Michael Agostinho. Yes, the AP World History teacher on page 232 was based off of you. And to Kendra Gish. Mama D was named after you, Mama Gish.

As a designer, I (N.G.) would like to thank Ashley Barr for teaching me the skills to build a cover, a website, and an eye for formatting the interior of this very book.

I (R.D.) feel it necessary to thank my first grade teacher, Leslie O'Breza, for igniting a passion for reading and writing in me at such a young age. I sincerely don't think I would be where I am today without your guidance.

I (R.D.) could not ask for a more supportive, loving family:

My mom, Suzy Warning, who saw my unbounded love for writing and nurtured it so that I thought it possible to pursue it.

My dad, Jeremy Davidson, who has spent countless hours helping me brainstorm, read, reread, and edit.

My sister, Abby, who somehow managed to put up with my insane ideas for years on end.

My aunt and uncle, Lacey Gaechter and Nat Warning, who have been nothing but encouraging.

And my nana, Irene Warning, who has been so incredibly supportive and invested in my projects, who has been looking forward to the day I publish my first book nearly as much as I have. Thank you all for believing in me, even when I didn't quite believe in myself.

And, of course, where would I be without my brilliant best friend and co-author? Nikki, thank you so much for embarking on this journey with me. Thank you for jumping on this little idea I had without a second's hesitation. 2020 was a particularly unusual year, throwing curveballs every which way, and you and this book were the only constants. When I was on the verge of a mental breakdown (and I was, quite often), this story was always there to fall into. And I wouldn't want to be telling this story with anyone else.

I (N.G.) have always known my family believes in me more than anyone.

My grandparents, William and Janis Jones, who have fostered my creativity more than I could ever ask for.

My little brother, who has managed to keep up with our conversations from such a young age.

My parents, my uncles, aunts, and cousins who are so numerous I couldn't possibly name them all. You know who you are--you watched me grow taller every year from a Microtel in Wellsville, New York.

And, though she was already mentioned, I'd like to thank my mom again, Teresa Greenhalgh. You've been my Lorelai Gilmore before I even knew who she was. Thank you for supporting me all these years, loving me and my work so unconditionally.

And Rachel. It's insane to me that we've gotten as far as we have in just a short year. I know that none of this would be possible without you, without such an unconditional love that I never expected to feel from one of my friends. You've now seen every inch of my brain, and you haven't judged me for any of it. Instead, you decided that you wanted to write a book with me.

I'm honored to call you a co-author, even more so to call you a friend. You are going to do such amazing things in your life, and I hope I get to witness every single one of them with my own two eyes.

Lastly, this book would be meaningless without you, dear reader. Thank you for opening this book and taking a chance on us. If you've made it this far, that means you saw potential in this. And potential is all we need. Thanks for letting us tell our story, thank you even more for listening.

About the Authors

Photo by Crystal Snow Photo Art

Rachel Davidson grew up in Parker, Colorado. She is currently a senior in high school. When she isn't writing or working on schoolwork, she can often be found reading, singing in her choir, playing cards with friends and family, or spending time with her dog, Harley (Davidson). Writing is her first love, and it has been her dream to publish for as long as she can remember. She intends to go to college to further pursue a career in writing and editing. *Glory Days* is her first novel.

Nikki Greenhalgh was born and raised in Parker, Colorado. She is a senior in high school with dreams of making her mark in the movie industry. Though she has surrounded herself by her words, she also has an untamed love for music. Recently, she has been implementing her graphic design work within her writing to further express herself and draw her readers in. *Glory Days* is her first novel.

CPSIA information can be obtained
at www.ICGtesting.com
Printed in the USA
BVHW030105240321
603261BV00004B/233